THE ZAMINDAR,
THE REBEL AND
THE REVOLUTIONARY

Jyotiska Ganguly is an aerospace engineer based in Los Angeles, USA. His educational journey began at St Xavier's, an American Jesuit boarding school in Patna, India and continued with a BE in mechanical engineering from NIT, Durgapur. He then completed his MS from the University of Texas, Arlington, with a full scholarship.

Currently, he works for a major American aerospace company where he specializes in designing subsystems for a wide array of aircraft, space and defence systems.

This is Jyotiska's first novel, based on ancestral lore.

The Zamindar, the Rebel and the Revolutionary

A Saga of Madaripur

JYOTISKA GANGULY

RUPA

Published by
Rupa Publications India Pvt. Ltd 2024
7/16, Ansari Road, Daryaganj
New Delhi 110002

Sales centres:
Bengaluru Chennai
Hyderabad Jaipur Kathmandu
Kolkata Mumbai Prayagraj

P-ISBN: 978-93-6156-151-1
E-ISBN: 978-93-6156-979-1

First impression 2024

10 9 8 7 6 5 4 3 2 1

The moral right of the author has been asserted.

Printed in India

To
my children
Abiral and Anurupa Ganguly

Contents

Characters

Generation 1: Keshav, zamindar of Madaripur

Generation 2: Mukund, zamindar of Madaripur; property manager of Darbhanga

Generation 3: Aneek, son of Mukund; freedom fighter in Calcutta after the Partition of Bengal

~

Afzal Mian: A highly loyal and principled Muslim farmer in Keshav's estate

Archana: Wife of Mukund

Aritro: Jimut's grandson; soldier in British Indian Army in the First World War; later in the Indian National Army

Bhabesh: A wealthy landowner, perpetually plotting against Keshav and Mukund

Bonka: An able, worthy, selfless Bagdi tribal; son of Naran

Bonka's two wives: Two dovetailed congenial wives

Claire: Girindra's Anglo-Indian granddaughter; marries Hubert

Cynthia Weatherilt: Wife of Robert Weatherilt; Hubert's mother

Damini: Aneek's fellow freedom fighter and lover

Flanagan: An Irish printer hired by Keshav; de facto overseer of Keshav and Mukund's estate

Girindra: Mukund's wealthy bragger neighbour

Gomosta: Keshav and Mukund's estate's cost accounts clerk

Hubert Weatherilt: Son of Robert and Cynthia Weatherilt; deputy director of the Indian Museum

Jimut: Keshav and Sheela's trusted head stagecoach driver; also head of 108 armed guards

Joggeshwar: Mukund's helpful cousin and neighbour

Kanak, Suhash and Mihir: Archana's two brothers and brother-in-law, respectively

Khushee: Keshav, Mukund and Aneek's cook

Koli: Girindra's daughter who marries a British man

Linda: Cynthia's sister

Madhuri: Mr Hall's adopted daughter; Aneek's wife

Mandira: Mukund's promiscuous second cousin

Moi: An erstwhile fisherman dismissed by Keshav, perpetually plotting against Keshav and Mukund

Mr Broad: British lawyer in eastern Bengal

Mr Hall: English physician, Mukund's guide and private teacher

Naran: A drug addict but honest Bagdi tribal; loyal to Keshav

Nobin: A wealthy spice trader, perpetually plotting against Keshav and Mukund

Nontu: Son of a Dom—Shanu—untouchable bathroom cleaner; killed by Nobin's men

Prachi: Sheela's widowed twin sister—married to Flanagan

Robert Weatherilt: Property manager to the maharaja of Darbhanga; Mukund's boss

Roy Babu: A tough zamindar and Archana's father

Shawn: Linda's estranged husband

Sheela: Wife of Keshav

Shitala and Shukla: Bonka's two daughters

Suhail: Farmer Afzal's drug addict grandnephew—reformed by an ageing Archana

HISTORICAL CHARACTERS

Indian Freedom Fighters:

Aurobindo Ghose, Bagha Jatin (Jatindranath Mukherjee), Barindra Kumar Ghosh, Basanta Kumar Biswas, Chittaranjan Das, M.K. Gandhi, Rash Behari Bose, Subhas Chandra Bose, Surendranath Banerjee,

Other Notable Historical Figures:

Ambika Charan Mazumdar: Founder of Rajendra College in Faridpur, eastern Bengal

Basanta Chatterjee: A traitor to India's fight for freedom; senior Calcutta police officer, loyal to the British Raj, who arrested numerous freedom fighters

Charles Tegart: Calcutta's British police chief in the 1900s

Lord Curzon, Lord Bentinck: Governor Generals of India

Lord Curzon: Governor General of India who planned Bengal's partition

Lord Hardinge II: Viceroy of India who moved India's capital from Calcutta to Delhi in 1912

Winston Churchill: British prime minister

~

Locations: Madaripur (near Dhaka), Khalia Village, Pabna, Dhaka, Bikrampur, Faridpur, Calcutta, Barisal and Darbhanga in British India, and Ireland, Cambridge and London

Part I

Chapter 1

The Landlord of Madaripur

IN AD 1879, KESHAV, A PROSPEROUS LANDOWNER, LIVED IN Madaripur, in eastern Bengal, British India. He was the descendant of a north Indian lineage that traced back to a royal endowment granted to his ancestors almost 1,100 years ago.

Roughly 34 generations earlier, in AD 860, two distant cousins who were Rajput kings ruled Kannauj (in Uttar Pradesh) and Rarh (south-western Bengal). Rarh's king was Adi Shoor, while the Kannauj kingdom's ruler was Mihir Bhoj, also known as Bhoj I. These two steadfast Hindu kings joined forces against the still-ruling but declining Pal dynasty. At that time, the Pal rulers reigned over much of northern Bengal, which was called Barendra Bhumi, but they lost Rarh to the Shoor dynasty. These regal Pratihara Rajput clans from the north initially brought five *upadhyays* from ancient Kannauj to the Rarh villages located along the mouth of the Ganga River. They secretly asked Keshav's earliest ancestors to emigrate from Kannauj to Rarh to eliminate drought by performing *yajnas*.

However, Raja Adi Shoor's primary and ulterior motive was to have the five upadhyays and their sons roam the villages of Rarh, steadily reconverting the rapidly expanding tantric Buddhists of eastern India back to Sanatan Dharma via countless religious and spiritual debates. The Rajput royals had trouble accepting these snake-, frog- and stone-worshippers as well as the animal-sacrificing sects of society. Over the next 500 years, these emigrants' success in the reconversion effort was phenomenal. They came to be known, from Raja Ballal Sen's times (AD 1175 onwards), as the Kulin Brahmins of Bengal. But that is a story for another day.

Unusually tall, long-faced and slender, Keshav loved to wear a white turban that resembled the cushion rings used for the tabla. At 6 feet 4 inches, he had biceps and triceps moulded like a boxer's and looked like a fair Rajput king of the Himalayan Mountains. At the same time, he had immense compassion for the needy and helpless. When away from home, he always carried a long sword, even though he was accompanied by armed guards. Like his ancestors, he was deeply spiritual, well versed in Sanskrit and Persian and an ardent devotee of Lord Krishna. Yet his large stature, huge moustache and penetrating gaze intimidated most of his fellow Kulin Brahmins living in the area, who were too dogmatic for his liking.

From his early youth, his peers dared not impose their rigid superstitions and rituals upon him. Keshav's perennial, ready-to-confront attitude helped him get away with the many exceptions in his life as a 19th-century Kulin Brahmin. His peers called him the 'new axe-wielding, justice-extracting Parashurama'. When faced with vain, condescending, and judgemental peers, he behaved like a ruthless despot and did not flinch at taking up arms. He had a total of 108 highly skilled armed guards to protect his family and landed properties including two mansions, agricultural farms, a huge flower garden, fisheries, barns, orchards, lakes, temples, granaries, stables and eight palanquins. Because of his highly weaponized existence and mini army of heavily armed guards, no one dared to mess with him on the socio-cultural front either. For example, he hired several 'untouchable' lower-caste people to work in various areas of his estate as beekeepers, gardeners and farmers. In sharp contrast, Keshav's peers limited the role of the lowest caste of Dom only to cleaning latrines and working in cremation grounds. However his peers were too scared of Keshav to demand or suggest that the community ostracize him and his family.

From his childhood, no one could match his swordsmanship or his aim with a 'Brown Bess' British-made musket, which he had inherited from his father. This musket, the standard weapon used by the British during the Indian Rebellion of 1857, was often flaunted by Keshav to deter his caste-conscious peers. With opulent gifts, lavish feasts and tax cuts, he pampered all his tax-paying subjects, including his farmers, fishermen and orchard caretakers, during festivals such as Janmashtami, Holi, Ram Navami and Ratha Yatra. He treated his Muslim and Hindu subjects with equal ardour, and they reciprocated with matching devotion.

During his childhood, and also later, Keshav and his father witnessed the huge increase in taxation and economic hardship that the British had levied on every farmer, labourer and artisan in the subcontinent. This was a result of the British effort to recoup the cost of suppressing the rebellion. The British government seized control of India from the East India Company, making India a formal colony of the British Empire. The economy was brazenly restructured to serve British interests openly. The mutiny took off when sepoys working for the British were issued new Enfield rifles with cartridges that had to be bitten open. These cartridges were lubricated with grease containing a mix of pigs' and cows' lard—an impure practice for both Muslim and Hindu sepoys. Moreover, before the rebellion, sepoys were becoming increasingly reluctant to fight and die in battles solely being fought to advance various British interests in Europe and elsewhere.

During the mutiny, rebellious sepoys were shackled and imprisoned, but their outraged comrades shot British officers and marched on to Delhi. The resultant two-year conflict was brutal on both sides, ultimately ending in defeat for the Indian troops. Keshav bitterly recalled the sight of the bodies of dead Indian sepoys at street corners in nearby Dhaka, a grim reminder to future draftees against rebellion. During the worst phase of the rebellion, the British officers accused Keshav of supporting the sepoy uprising with funds and refurbished muskets. During this period, he would ride his favourite horse for miles, cross the Padma River by boat in the darkest hours of the moonless nights and reach Sonargaon on the outskirts of Dhaka. He had found a disused mint there, which had been set up by the Pathan rulers who had ruled eastern Bengal prior to the arrival of the British. Therein he survived for three days and nights on dates, cashews and pistachios. Drowned by grief when the sepoys lost, Keshav fasted for three days and shaved his head in mourning.

Keshav's vast farmland, though prone to cycles of drought, rain and floods, was a picturesque inheritance that produced rice, jute, fruit and fish. He was the youngest of six children; four of his elder siblings had died before puberty. His surviving elder brother had moved away to become the head priest of the Raja Ram Mandir in Khalia village, also in Madaripur district. Keshav's resolute personality might have stemmed from the steely characters of his ancient forefathers like Bhrigu, Bhargav, Jamdagni, Chavan and Parashurama. He consistently defied and triumphed over the growing dogmatism of some of his own kin—the Kulin Brahmins of Bengal and their oppressive practices such as untouchability, the repression of female children, prohibiting widow remarriage, etc.

By now, Keshav was in his middle age. His wife Sheela had lost three children during childbirth and one child who died at the age of two from malaria. So, their only surviving son, Mukund, was precious to them. A distant unmarried uncle of Keshav was the zamindar's *naib*, overseeing various daily operations of Keshav's estate. But this elderly uncle was so addicted to drugs like ganja that Keshav increasingly relied on a 30-year-old bachelor Irishman named Chris Flanagan.

Until her teenage years Sheela was raised by her Brahmin, Maithili-speaking maternal grandmother. So she fully understood

Maithili and loved its nuances. Her grandmother hailed from northern Uttar Pradesh's Kannauj. Thanks to this kind elder, Sheela became highly compassionate towards the poor.

Following her grandmother's example, every day at dawn, Sheela collected bel and tulsi leaves from her private garden to offer at the red stone temple inside her home, worshipping both Shyam (Lord Krishna) and Shyama (Mother Goddess Kali) with equal ardour.

In addition, Sheela observed *nirjala* every *chaturthi, ekadashi, trayodashi, amavasya* and *purnima*. This meant that during these different lunar phases, she did not eat any solids or drink water for 24-hour periods. Moreover, she fasted on Maha Shivratri, Janmashtami, Ratha Yatra, Lord Ram's victorious return to Ayodhya during Deepavali, Ram Navami and Govardhan Puja.

Sheela also worshipped the sun during the Chhath Puja, an ancient Vedic practice that venerates the sun god Surya and his sister, Chhathi Maiya, for granting life, energy and healing on Earth. From the age of 13, spurred by her Didima, Sheela performed the puja twice a year, in the months of Chaitra (March–April) and Kartik (October–November). During Chhath Puja, the slender, vegetarian Sheela slept on the floor and after sunset, ate kheer, gur and roti in solitude. She broke her Chhath fast only after immersing half her body in the river and offering slices of coconut, sugarcane, bananas, pitha, hara chana and *thekua* to the sun god. She meticulously prepared the cookie-like thekua from wheat flour, jaggery, ghee, cardamom, cashews and raisins.

On her birthday, Keshav liked to please her to the hilt. However, one year, she surprised him by requesting British-made cosmetics, which he reluctantly agreed to. Later, realizing that the items were indeed made in England, he felt disappointed. Sheela, sensing his discomfort, orchestrated an exchange with the Rani of Paikpara, a noblewoman in North Calcutta, who gladly traded the foreign goods for armbands and anklets that had a historical connection to an ancient Rajput queen. Despite her ability to have her way in most household matters, Sheela understood and respected her husband's patriotism, avoiding sensitive topics to maintain harmony in their marriage.

Keshav avoided associations with other landlords who mingled closely with powerful British administrators. Many of these native aristocrats indulged in various amusements, from vacationing to hunting and engaging in lecherous pursuits. Some collaborated with the British-run mills and companies, reaping benefits and titles. Despite his affluence, Keshav refrained from such collaborations, which led to high tax assessments for him.

Mukund, Keshav's son, was raised in a simple lifestyle; he was influenced by his parents and Jimut, the faithful guard. Keshav, having lived through the Sepoy Mutiny of 1857, dreamt of an India free from subjugation and held a deep admiration for valiant Sikh chieftains in his heart. His anti-British sentiments often led to conflicts with his wife, particularly when she expressed a desire to buy British-made items. When Sheela proposed remodelling their mansion after a British villa, Keshav resisted, leading to a three-day silent protest from her.

Mukund, destined to witness significant changes globally, grew up in the comfort of his father's opulent mansion, which boasted multiple rooms, crystal chandeliers, a fanning room, scented baths and plush carpets, all reflecting the family's affluence.

Keshav had a complex relationship with his sharecroppers, and while he drank the intoxicating bhang with them during festivals, he also tried to regulate their views and behaviours, especially concerning their daughters' marriages. However, his attempts were met with resistance, as the peasants considered their daughters to be liabilities. Keshav's disdain for native landlords who mistreated their servants was well known. He was powerful and did not hesitate to seize any opportunity to punish philandering, alcoholic husbands in his estate or his area. However he only intervened when a long-suffering wife approached him for help. On at least a handful of occasions, Keshav had 10 of his best guards disguise themselves as masked out-of-town bandits and loot the errant landlords who had a long-standing record of spousal torture or mistreatment of their workers. In one instance, during the dead of night along a notoriously spooky stretch of the Arial Khan River's shore, Keshav's men horrified a habitually brutish zamindar who was petrified of ghosts.

Keshav's fiery reputation stemmed from incidents like wrestling a peer to the ground and nearly splitting him in two with his sword. He held strong reservations against British officials who believed India couldn't function independently. While he rarely disciplined his employees, when he did, he handled it personally. One such incident involved caning a fisherman, Moi, who had a gambling problem. Keshav's strict action led Moi to quit his vice and find employment elsewhere. But Moi never let go of the grudge he held against Keshav.

Tall and burly, Bhabesh was a wealthy landlord who lived in a large brick house five miles away from Keshav's estate. The wooden home of Nobin, a wealthy spice trader, was located within walking distance from Bhabesh's. Moi, along with Nobin and Bhabesh, formed a criminal alliance, engaging in muggings and other illicit activities. Bhabesh, having seized scenic resorts in the Sundarbans, exploited them for profit, and the trio found ways to swindle unsuspecting tourists and customers. This criminal enterprise brought them financial gains but also made them audacious, leading to confrontations with others in the area. Bhabesh was also known for seducing poor needy women, even sodomizing needy pre-teen boys whenever he could.

Bhabesh, Moi and Nobin harboured intense animosity towards

Keshav due to his staunch opposition to their illicit methods of amassing wealth. Though wiry and short, Nobin, known for his violent tendencies, once allegedly broke a farmer's skull for booing at him. Despite sporadic attempts at charitable gestures to improve their public image, their massive egos and compulsive buying habits overshadowed any positive action. They routinely attended auctions related to bankruptcy, taking advantage of others' misfortunes to acquire valuable items at minimal prices.

In one instance, a Muslim farmer, who worked for Keshav, sought to open a snack and stationery store, with Keshav's support. However, Nobin, already operating a profitable shop nearby, felt threatened by this new competition and complained to Bhabesh. To eliminate the threat, Bhabesh hired goons who brutally attacked the Muslim farmer. In response, Keshav's 10 best guards, led by their chief, Jimut, teamed up with Flanagan. They fought valiantly with swords and lathis and defeated the attackers. Thereafter, determined to support the new entrepreneur, Keshav provided armed guards to protect the farmer's kiosk. The villagers rallied behind the venture, stocking the store with more goods than originally planned. The strategy backfired on Nobin and Bhabesh, as the new stall owned by the Muslim farmer quickly surpassed Nobin's sales of snacks, lanterns, notebooks, paper, pens and pencils.

Chapter 2

Arrival of the Irishman

FORTY-FIVE-YEAR-OLD KESHAV GRADUALLY GREW FOND OF Chris Flanagan, his estate's de facto naib and most valuable employee. Sheela was 33, and three years older than Flanagan, but the fine-looking dark-haired man appeared much younger than his age. Sheela and Mukund would often eavesdrop on Keshav's exchanges with Flanagan, sometimes from behind the mansion's curtains and other times out in the open. Through many an afternoon, the lad and his lively mother keenly watched the zamindar's transfixed gaze whenever the flamboyant Irishman entered their living room. Seven summers ago, he even volunteered to coach Mukund in mathematics, geography and civics. To everyone's delight, especially the youth's, Keshav had accepted the offer.

Almost eight years earlier, Keshav had first hired the blue-eyed man to set up, operate and maintain a new printer for his estate. Within a year of his arrival in Madaripur, the long-faced Irishman had managed to win over his new boss. On one occasion, when Flanagan released the zamindar's caged pigeons and prized mynahs without informing him, Sheela could not believe her husband's lack of anger. The efficient and charming printer's continuing immunity from reprimand often surprised everyone else in the mansion as well. His frequent work-related interactions with various employees of the estate, along with semi-literate Sheela and Mukund helped him learn Bengali at an impressive speed. Before long, he also became an ardent fan of Bengali cuisine. After arriving in the subcontinent, Flanagan briefly worked as an English translator for a wealthy landlord in rural Punjab's wheat belt, where he developed a fancy for lassi and sarson ka saag. Hence, whenever Sheela invited him for a Sunday lunch, she made sure to cook a spicy concoction of mustard greens. Flanagan even bought Mukund his first bicycle and taught Mukund the easiest way to push a dinghy into the river, weave a stout rope in the best possible way and master the safest response when charged by a pack of wild dogs. Mukund would watch in quiet awe how quickly the Irishman repaired his mother's Remington sewing machine or typed letters using his father's Sholes and Glidden typewriter.

When 12-year-old Mukund was caught smoking, he received 10 lashes of the whip from his father, who then informed Flanagan about the incident and requested strict disciplinary action if the offence recurred. A year later, when Mukund was caught smoking again, Flanagan took decisive action, jabbing Mukund's cheek and ribs hard enough to make him briefly pass out. Neither Sheela nor Keshav questioned the Irishman's seemingly harsh measure, and Mukund never smoked again.

Almost every week, Keshav and Flanagan attended open-air jatra performances by a roving mobile theatre group in rural locations. Their favourite shows were those based on famous historical characters like Mir Kasim, the long-deposed Nawab of Bengal defeated by the British in the Battle of Buxar. To avoid receiving special treatment, both ensured they weren't treated like royalty during the performances. Keshav even taught Flanagan how to wear a dhoti and fold it properly for the dew-laden evening shows. They would throw coins in appreciation towards the actors on stage during their poignant soliloquies or duels with villains.

In Keshav and his family's frequent company, Flanagan's command over Vedic traditions and the Bengali language grew significantly. One day, he and Keshav travelled to a newly built outdoor coffee shop in Faridpur overlooking a man-made waterfall. To the Irishman's sheer surprise, Keshav asked Flanagan to lay the foundation of a Hindu temple for the farmers near one of his fruit orchards. The farmers loved Flanagan so much that they did not raise an eyebrow about a white Christian breaking the earth for a Hindu temple.

In return for such adoration, a grateful Flanagan provided advanced English tutorials to Keshav, focusing on the intricate governmental terminologies and jargon used in various offices of the British Raj. Their discussions often extended to scientific advancements and the peculiar rules of foreign exchange brokerages in London. Flanagan also shared stories of Ireland's struggle for freedom from foreign domination, recounting events like Robert Emmet's attempt to seize Dublin Castle in 1803 and the Irish Catholics earning their first seat in Parliament two decades later. The tales of the 1845 Irish Potato Famine, which caused over a million deaths due to crop failure and England's policies, brought tears to their eyes, as this devastating event permanently changed Ireland's demographic, political and cultural landscapes.

To quench the carnal desires of his youth and flesh, Flanagan occasionally visited a comely Hindu widow who seemed to endear him deeply. However, she never dared to suggest remarriage to a white man, fearing for both her own physical safety and that of her lover. She had lost her husband a few months after marriage, at the tender age of 15, some years ago. The lovers masterfully met at different places, donning disguises to keep their meetings a secret. Only Keshav knew of their affair, but he never told anyone, including Sheela.

The Irishman's maternal ancestors hailed from Scotland, and the tales from the Highlands enriched the landlord's living room conversations. Flanagan recounted survival stories from the Battle of Dunbar, where Sir David Leslie led a covenanter army supporting the royalists during the English Civil War. Victorious Oliver Cromwell strategically outmanoeuvred the Scots, leading to their defeat at Dunbar. Mukund learnt that during the post-battle chaos, a direct ancestor of Flanagan had managed to escape being sold into slavery.

Flanagan would often dress like a Scottish Highlander, wearing a redshank cloak and a sporran—a decorated pouch worn in front. Mukund once borrowed Flanagan's kilt and sporran for a play. Like the Indian dhoti, the kilt was a basic garment made of tartan cloth, offering free movement in the Highlands' climate and terrain. The sporran served as the Highlander's pocket, a necessity since the kilt didn't have any.

Flanagan's heart would race every time the zamindar's wife made an appearance. He had not seen a more beautiful woman anywhere in the world. The tall, long-limbed Sheela's hair tendrils curled gently around her flushed, fair cheeks. Completely unaware of the passion she stirred in him, she, too, sharply drew in her breath every time they met. He did well to conceal his desperate awareness of her supple mind and body's proximity. Flanagan was enamoured by her smooth glowing skin, her quick witty retorts, her alluring rosebud mouth, her unhurried yet self-assured gait and the elegant swing of her sari's frontal pleats.

The bachelor's eyes quietly adored her immaculate features and dimpled cheeks; the extra-long, fulsome streak of sindoor flooding the parting in her hair, accentuating the large round bindi in the middle of her forehead; the wide-bordered, elegant saris she wore; and her ears embellished with shapely gold leaves. Most of all, he thrived on the ethereal kindness in her eyes. He loved the way she let her cook's little daughter curl up in her lap as if the child were her own flesh and blood. Every time she played her sarangi, his heart skipped a beat, captivated by the melodies she created on the metal strings of the instrument.

At times, Flanagan would arrive at the printing room at dawn to work on urgent printing tasks. Sheela made it a point to personally deliver hot tea, buttered toast and a well-made omelette, with a large spoonful of home-made guava jelly on the side—just the way he liked it. Then of course, the maids brought him the day's variety of native breakfast, from malpua to suji and more.

Sheela, in turn, could not help but admire his genuine curiosity for Indian classical music and his innately confident way of carrying both Western and Eastern attire. Deep inside, she did not mind that some of his garment-related experiments bordered on the immodest. She almost swooned once when he angrily yanked the shirt off his hairy, brawny chest before crawling under the malfunctioning printer. Sometimes, she secretly yearned to escape her life and live a vastly different one on a faraway planet. Occasionally, she found herself alone with the young Irishman in the printing room, late in the evening, helping him after the workers had gone home. Yet she never had to defend herself from his advances because he made none. There were no overt innuendoes from the impossibly appealing white man.

Sheela had become familiar with the strong, stiff, scented starch he had his dhobi put in his clothes. Without ever touching him, she could easily recognize the aroma of the starch mingled with his body odour.

Under Flanagan's guidance, Sheela had learnt how to serve a plethora of fancy sandwiches arranged on sparkling silver platters. By reading European cookbooks, she had mastered the art of making snack rolls using pickled cucumber, watercress, dill, slices of tomato and chicken breast. In hopes of winning his appreciation, she added home-made kasundi to her specially cooked dishes for the Irishman, instilling an Indian flavour in them. After all, no one but Flanagan could restore and repair the beautiful palanquin she occasionally used to visit a nearby temple. However, it was only her husband who spoke to Flanagan in the event of delays in payments for his services, offering every lame excuse under the sun.

One afternoon, Sheela walked into the printing room and asked Flanagan to demonstrate the workings of a new-generation daguerreotype that Keshav had purchased. Two days earlier, Flanagan had captured an image of her clad in a sari using the amalgam of mercury and silver. Peering into the picture, she playfully demanded how the new contraption her husband had funded worked. She stood inches from him as he began to explain.

Sheela interrupted, 'Mr Flanagan, thank you for showing me the new daguerreotype. But why do you have my picture sealed inside a glass cover?' Her broken English and Flanagan's rapidly improving Bengali overlapped well to ensure a meaningful conversation.

Flanagan's chest thudded wildly at their proximity. 'The image can easily be rubbed off with the fingers, and it will oxidize in the air. That is why, from the outset, I mount daguerreotypes in sealed cases or frames with a glass cover.'

Even the tinkle of her gold bangles made mesmerizing music, making it increasingly difficult for him to rein in his thoughts. The romantic tension, the kind that sometimes simmers when a beautiful woman and an equally charming man are alone in the same room, was palpable. His fingers toyed nervously with a fountain pen clipped to one of the four pockets of his khaki bush shirt.

Flanagan looked for divine interruption but received none. For a moment, he looked lost—like a debutant stage actor who had suddenly forgotten his closing lines. Wishful scenarios haunted his thoughts: why did this married woman, unlike some of the other landlord families he knew, not hide her bottomless beauty behind her sari's veil? Why was she so brash and bold?

Sheela urged, 'Go on, Mr Flanagan. Why did you stop?'

While his hands fumbled through a row of bottles filled with printing-related chemicals, Flanagan strove to refocus his distracted mind. After the scorching heartbreaks of his teenage years back in Ireland, he expected nothing from the fairer sex—not even platonic love or solace. Yet how could he ignore her magnetic presence, so perfectly balanced between her quiet, unassuming inner strength and sheer femininity?

He avoided looking into her grey almond-shaped eyes. 'In the past, I have used vapour from a pool of heated mercury to develop the picture plate, which consists of a copper plate with a thin coating of silver rolled in contact. The silver is sensitized in advance to light with iodine vapour.'

Sheela, keen to match the conversation's intellectual tone, asked, 'What happens to this vapour?'

Flanagan struggled to keep his facts straight. 'It forms silver iodide crystals on the silver surface of the plate. Recently, I have reduced the exposure time by using bromine to form silver bromide crystals.'

He pretended to look out of the only window in the printing room at an uprooted tree within the compound. Outside, one of Keshav's farmers happened to be smoothing out a fresh load of straw he had laid out on top of a mini barn's roof with a pitchfork. Sheela had requested the roof to be redone. The rain's pattering had ceased, though not long ago, a violent storm split the roof into two halves like a twig breaking in the middle. In the distance, one of the river's levees, long teetering on the brink, threatened to break at any moment. Whenever the white public works engineers needed to selectively blast the embankment, they sought Flanagan's help. He guided them in selecting the optimum breaching spot to minimize the impact on the golden rice fields overlooking the river.

Sheela's velvety voice continued in a random mix of Bengali and English. 'Why are these lenses much bigger than what my husband had before?' The long-legged woman straightened up for a moment, and the top of her head nearly reached the tall Irishman's earlobes.

Flanagan said, 'By replacing the Chevalier lenses with much larger, faster lenses designed by Joseph Petzval, we have been able to significantly reduce the exposure time.'

Sheela's fingernails gently scratched the base of a microscope dear to both her husband and the Irishman. 'Enough scientific talk for one day... Tell me about something else.'

Social worker that she was, Sheela often probed into his personal life. She had decided to save him from himself—from his make-believe mental blocks about getting married. Sheela tried a new approach, saying, 'Well, you are now 30 years old!'

Flanagan sensed trouble brewing. 'What are you getting at?' He yearned for fresh air to soothe his aching heart. For a moment, he briefly contemplated hiding in the cobweb-covered attic for reprieve from the interrogation.

Flanagan huffed uncharacteristically and hurried to the nearby printer supply room, 'I will be back with some fresh chemicals for the new photo machine.'

Sheela stared hard at him.

A few minutes passed. Sheela headed to the spice room next to the kitchen and returned with a bag of raw spices still in the form of pods. The room was soon filled with the sound of her crushing them with a mortar and pestle.

When Flanagan returned, she immediately resumed her premeditated line of questioning, undeterred, 'Tell me what is stopping you from marrying a nice girl from Great Britain? Nowadays, you'll find so many of them in Calcutta, Dhaka, Patna and Ranchi. Today you must tell me what is it that makes you shy away from marriage.'

After remaining silent for a long time, Flanagan offered a partial explanation. 'How can I please anyone else—a lifetime's mate—if

I am not pleased with myself? How can I?'

Sheela responded, 'So you do not consider yourself qualified enough for marriage because you lack a college degree from Dublin, Glasgow or Cambridge? That is so ridiculous! I have not seen another man who can act as a doctor's perfect aide on one day, an engineer's perfect ally the next, and then be a printer and farming expert on other days.'

'Are you making fun of me?'

'No. But you must have some other reason not to tie the knot.' In her eyes, the most enchanting aspect of the Irishman was not just his looks but his sense of duty and compassion. Flanagan donated a quarter of his monthly income to welfare causes, driven entirely by an inner calling. His earnings came from the printing business and the fixed monthly salary he received from her husband. He mostly directed his endowments to fight against deadly diseases in Madaripur and Faridpur. In these areas, relentless rain, heat and humidity, typhoid, polio and infection-induced infant mortality assiduously played musical chairs to wreak havoc.

Flanagan decided to disclose the second reason in his three-pronged hesitation about marriage. 'Until 16, I lived in a small town near Cork. Between the ages of 15 and 16, I learnt a lot about printing and presses. At that time, I also had a girlfriend.'

Sheela was all ears now. 'Go on, don't stop.'

Though he neither talked nor walked like a sage, his presence seemed to unconsciously fill her home with a peaceable, blissful spirit she quietly cherished.

Flanagan continued, 'We were roughly of the same age. We eventually vowed to marry each other. But when her father introduced her to a rich haberdasher's Oxford-educated son, she changed her mind. That day, I promised myself that I would never marry.'

Sheela asked, 'Is it her sketch among the pictures on your hallway wall?'

Flanagan nodded. 'Yes... The girl with honeysuckle flowers and a white rose in her hair.'

Sheela said, 'Tell me about her.'

'Like me, she was fully Irish but our destiny together was not meant to be. She loved handmade English lace on her clothes, fancy French Chantilly gowns, mauve satin and candied apples. On her 16th birthday, her innkeeper father arranged for her a multilayered custard cake as tall as me.'

'If my guess is right, it has taken you many years to heal her loss.'

'She taught me there is no market for grief. It is best not to publicize one's pensive feelings.'

'Perhaps it means valuing relationships more than one's ego. But tell me, how did your parents react to all of this... Your girlfriend's change of heart and her leaving you?'

Flanagan sighed. 'My parents never met my girlfriend. When I was three years old, they died in a road accident. My much older brother raised me until I was 16. Though poor and prone to drinking, my widower brother tried his best to take care of me. Every night, he taught me to read and write. In my childhood, he often spoke about India, which caught my interest. The day my girlfriend moved to London, I was heartbroken and left home. Four months later, I found myself working as a translator on a rich landlord's estate in Punjab.'

'Bad promises, such as the one you made to yourself, are meant to be broken.'

Flanagan couldn't quite agree. 'If you will excuse me, I must meet your husband in a few minutes.'

'There must be yet another reason,' Sheela insisted.

Flanagan felt a wave of nervousness. How could he reveal that he longed to marry someone just like her? He knew the odds of finding someone like her were next to none. Trembling, he prepared to leave the room.

Sheela asked, 'If I may, where are you going?'

Flanagan said, 'To the estate's warehouse where the farming tools are stored.'

Sheela moved aside to let him pass. 'Why?'

'The contractor repairing the warehouse roof seems to have used spurious cement. And as you know, in this mansion I am not just your printer…I am your naib—jack of all trades.'

'I prefer it when you describe yourself as the man for all seasons,' replied Sheela with a smile.

Flanagan grinned self-effacingly. 'Not really. The Queen of Britain should make you her speechwriter.' With a deep and unhurried bow, the Irishman made his way towards the door.

Sheela teased him with harmless intent. 'Why do you care about him so much…far more than you worry about my stuff?'

Flanagan's smile widened. 'I care about both you and your husband. From the time I was 22, Keshav has taught me so much. I cherish my new life in India and owe it all to him.'

Chapter 3

The Unconventional Mr Hall

THE ONLY OTHER BRITISH PERSON KESHAV KNEW VERY WELL was Mr Hall, a warm-hearted Englishman and the grandson of an East India Company administrator. Mr Hall's grandfather had played a significant role in Keshav's daily life, monitoring the company's profits from opium and indigo dye plantations while serving in the Dhaka Collectorate. Mr Hall himself was an insurance underwriter by day, providing policies to the growing upper-middle-class babus, native traders and British companies in India. His education and early training had been in medicine at Cambridge, so he occasionally filled in as a physician when required.

Mr Hall and Keshav became acquainted when the former intervened during a fire incident at Keshav's grazing yards. One of Keshav's horse aides had accidentally started a fire near the big brick-and-wood stable. Mr Hall, passing by, took swift action by rescuing the horses and preventing further damage.

Known for his thin, plain-looking suits customized for the hot tropics, Mr Hall's residence overlooked a rivulet that swelled into a foaming river during the monsoons—an area that had once been ruled by cudgel-carrying bandits. Despite Mr Hall's attempts to become an inventor, inspired by the American electric arc light pioneer Charles Brush, his ambitions ended in failure after a horse kicked him hard in the loins while working a treadmill to generate electricity.

Naran, the long-standing farmer on Keshav's land, had twice come to Mr Hall's aid in perilous situations. On the second occasion, Naran fortuitously rescued the Englishman from a bear's clutches by breaking the feisty beast's backbone with his lathi. Earlier, Naran's pet dog had saved Mr Hall from a bull. The little dog, hiding under a wandering fakir's robe, leapt into the air and clawed at the bull's face, preventing a potentially fatal encounter between Hall and the bull's horns.

Once back in the safety of his bungalow, Mr Hall felt immense relief at narrowly escaping death. Naran, displaying no signs of the recent danger, stood quietly on the porch as Mr Hall treated his minor bruises from the bear's attack with ointments from the well-stocked mini-medicine cabinet he maintained in his capacity as a medical expert, out of concern for the members of Keshav's family and staff.

Closing and locking the door of the mahogany repository, Mr Hall shuffled closer to Naran. 'Your loyalty to Keshav, his estate and his family is well known, isn't it?'

Naran's breath stank of a decaying tooth. Furrowing his eyebrows, the man stepped back, but the Englishman, ignoring the foul stench, drew closer to the self-conscious tribal again.

Naran's dark eyes lit up like a springtime sunrise. 'I am a poor farmer. What should be equally well known is how much Dadathakur (Keshav) and his forefathers have done for us and other tribals.' Naran had rarely spoken to a white man before. Growing tentative, he quailed, 'Sahib...shall I go on?'

The race-blind Englishman, still feeling the numbness in his feet due to the bear attack, assured the farmer in broken vernacular, 'Yes, of course.'

Seeking confidentiality, Naran drew closer. 'Due to my ganja addiction, I nearly died several times. Dadathakur brought me back to life. His ancestors have protected my forefathers in many ways. His eight-year-old son Mukund is also very dear to me. He, too, is now like my underage, beloved master.'

~

The marks on Naran's back and shoulders, reminders of the brutal lashes he had once endured from the landowner Bhabesh's long whip, still looked fresh. Since Naran worked for Keshav, it was none of Bhabesh's business to bully the farmer. This punishment was inflicted after Bhabesh accused Naran of driving his bullock cart erratically on the main village road and staring at the landlord's gaudy, palanquin-riding wife for a second too long. Earlier, Bhabesh had once fabricated a petty theft accusation and smacked the farmer with his palm shoes. Afraid of angering Keshav, he then tried to appease Naran by offering him a dairy cow, which the latter had refused.

Bhabesh's cruelty and greed knew no bounds. He was shameless enough not to compensate one of his deceased farmer's widows after her husband's tragic death. Nobin, Bhabesh's wealthy crony, had tricked the poor farmer into eating wild poisonous mushrooms, leading to his death. In the preceding months, Nobin had hoped he would be able to coax the dead farmer's attractive but penurious wife to be his mistress. In the quest for descendants, lust, or both, the unscrupulous Nobin was said to have impregnated his own widowed and childless daughter-in-law after his son died of jaundice.

When Bhabesh turned down the murdered farmer's wife's plea for financial help, she took her own life rather than live as a concubine of a man she loathed.

~

Mr Hall, with his thick hair slicked back, asked Naran, 'Now tell me... How can I repay my debt?'

The tribal stepped back, ignoring the reward money of Rs 20 Mr Hall offered him. 'You owe me nothing, sahib, nothing. It was all destined.'

Mr Hall's long, bushy sidelocks twitched involuntarily. He led his unexpected saviour to the music room, his face brimming with sheer joy. 'Amazing coincidences! For the second time, you have saved my life.'

As soft, unfamiliar music began, Naran replied, 'Oh, it was my duty to help a passer-by. Please do not push me towards the path of destruction by luring me into the ways of the rich.'

Though deeply admiring Naran's simple, truthful and contented life with minimal needs, Mr Hall stood resolved to respond to his kindness. 'Yes, go on. You must speak your mind. Whatever you wish and I can afford will be done.'

Naran thought long and hard. Sheela's recent enquiry about finding an alternative tutor for Mukund's Western education flashed through his mind. 'My master's wife would be very happy if you could provide private tuition to young Mukund.'

'Has your master's wife expressed such a clear-cut wish?'

Naran nodded. 'Oh yes. As recently as last week, she was upset with Dadathakur for not finding someone quickly enough.'

Mr Hall wiped away a large teardrop of gratitude welling up in his eyes. 'Well then…your wish is my command. I will go to Keshav's mansion tomorrow and offer my services. For you, that is the least I can do. But there is one thing—I will not accept any money from your master or his wife.'

Naran leapt with joy. 'But she will gladly stuff you with the best snacks the world has known!'

Far less enamoured by Indian food than Flanagan, Mr Hall tried to sound upbeat, 'We shall see.'

The tribal hurried out to break the good news to Sheela.

True to his word, Mr Hall began tutoring Mukund the following week.

In the evenings, Mr Hall supplemented Flanagan's efforts to improve the lad's English grammar, literature and penmanship. Mr Hall learnt valuable health practices from Keshav's Ayurvedic methods and incorporated Chinese techniques like acupuncture and massage therapy to manage his myopia and arthritis. Drinking four glasses of water on an empty stomach each morning and consuming cantaloupes became part of his daily routine for preserving good eyesight.

Mr Hall never accepted lunch or dinner invitations from Sheela, preferring a quick exit after tutoring. Instead of tuition fees, Sheela donated funds to a potter's charity supported by Mr Hall. Sheela treated both tutors equally and showed uncommon consideration by positioning chairs, serving tea, and occasionally dissolving her usual imperial bearing. Rumours among the mansion's servants speculated that Mr Hall harboured a crush on Sheela, akin to Mr Flanagan.

In a rare feat, Mr Hall and his young student moved Sheela's bulky dresser into the inner chambers. Despite suffering a cut, Mr Hall persevered until the task was complete. On another occasion, when a band of bandits swept past the village, Mr Hall arrived at the scene just as Sheela returned home in a palanquin. Though unarmed and clueless, Mr Hall stood by her side, and the bandits, wary of consequences involving white men, spared them and fled. The relieved palanquin carriers praised Mr Hall's miraculous intervention, spreading the story throughout Madaripur.

Sheela's respect for Mr Hall's teaching prowess was evident during an event when he accidentally damaged her expensive Persian carpet. Instead of fussing over the mishap, she instantly blamed her son, putting the Englishman at ease. She coerced Mr Hall into accepting a lavish lunch she had cooked herself, showcasing her understanding and consideration for him. Even when the Englishman participated in Mukund's plan to catch grasshoppers or toads and tied them with kite strings, Sheela didn't intervene, affirming her regard for Mr Hall's role in her son's education.

Mr Hall was a married man, and his wife, though diligent in maintaining their home, left the task of teaching their sons exclusively to him. Despite his shyness, Mr Hall actively participated in Bengali plays organized by Sheela, portraying a variety of characters, such as a Dutch businessman or a saucy French colonial tax collector. His involvement in the annual play was appreciated, and Sheela honoured him with expensive plaques and gilded medals.

During his recovery from an appendix operation and pleurisy, Sheela nursed Mr Hall back to full vigour, displaying her care and concern for his well-being. Despite her disdain for men who smoked, Mr Hall was exempt from her scorn due to the perceived virtue of the education he imparted to her son.

Mr Hall preferred private prayers and avoided ostentatious displays of faith. His life took a tragic turn when he lost his younger son to dengue, leading to an irreparable rift with his elder son, who believed their negligence caused the death. Shortly thereafter, the elder son disappeared. Nobody found out his whereabouts and it was rumoured that the boy had been kidnapped. Sheela, deeply moved by the underwriter's grief, shed silent tears for days.

Over time, Mr Hall found solace in solitude, sleeping alone in the smallest room of his bungalow while his mostly estranged wife slept in the master bedroom. Despite his shattered family life, he developed new interests, including mediating debates between his insurance assistants and participating in impromptu debates about Hindu deities. The grief-stricken man also discovered a passion for dancing with potters during full moon nights in a nearby village. Donning a mud-smeared sherwani, he danced with abandon, panting heavily yet resuming each time he crashed to the ground. The festivities took place in a village benefiting from Mr Hall's self-initiated loan programme.

During one such celebration, Keshav caught a fisherman named Moi for selling stale fish and using counterfeit measuring weights. As punishment, Moi had to compensate each affected potter with a week's worth of groceries, and cook and feed khichuri to the entire village.

Mr Hall effortlessly carried stacks of clay pots on his head, shedding his customary bashful nature during these colourful occasions. The tribal people adored him, chanting 'Raja Hall' in appreciation. The festive night transformed him, and his uninhibited dancing helped him to temporarily escape the sorrows that had befallen him. The purity of the tribals' hearts and their adoration provided a momentary respite from his grief.

Mukund eagerly joined the insurance underwriter during the potters' revelries, drawn not just by the tutor's generosity but also by the presence of tribal girls. He had no qualms about potentially encountering lice from their long hair while dancing with them. The potters danced through rain-soaked celebrations, relishing various local foods. Mr Hall aimed to improve the potters' financial status, introducing them to alternative, more profitable occupations, and providing microloans to those willing to retrain.

Teaming up with a Calcutta-born Sikh and the local deputy magistrate, Mr Hall fought against manufacturers who produced counterfeit medicines, causing fatalities across rural eastern Bengal. Mukund watched these efforts while enjoying the festivities. During these monthly binges, Mr Hall acted as a peacemaker when Mukund and his cousin, Joggeshwar, scuffled over proximity to the dancing girls. Mr Hall's wife, understanding his need for respite, didn't mind his periodic exuberance. Despite his exhaustion, he kept a watchful eye on Mukund and Joggeshwar throughout the night, afraid of potential dangers in the wild.

Intrigued, Mukund occasionally followed Mr Hall home, observing the insurance underwriter's contemplative moments under a railway bridge or amid nature. Mr Hall's heartache over his sons was palpable, evident in his distracted actions and sorrowful demeanour. He also fought against the lecherous Bhabesh, who abused his power by harming prostitutes and widows and coercing farmers. Bhabesh used lethal snakes, huge scorpions, crocodiles and large man-eating wolves held captive in underground dungeons to terrorize farmers into giving up their savings, even resorting to kidnapping and other brutal tactics. Despite Keshav's efforts, Bhabesh's inhumane practices persisted, causing immense suffering among the locals. Mr Hall's life was fraught with personal turmoil and battles against injustice as he strove to uplift the marginalized and curb the cruelty perpetuated by powerful individuals like Bhabesh.

The day Bhabesh's bulldog forced Mr Hall to climb a tree, Mukund used his guile to drive the aggressive canine away. In another incident, Mr Hall, leaving the mansion after a tutoring session, saw a monkey snatch Sheela's necklace. Quick on his feet, he threw his muffler at the monkey, prompting it to drop the ornament. Mukund, though amused at the situation, concealed his laughter, recalling his own encounters with mischievous monkeys.

While Mr Hall's wife cooked daily with the help of her maidservant, he preferred canned sardines and seafood soups over Indian cuisine. His grief over his younger son's death and the kidnapping of the other cast a profound shadow on his spirit, driving him to late-night bouts of drinking.

Mrs Hall often blamed herself for the family's misery and deeply regretted her overreaction to her husband's platonic affection for their washerwoman. This began when she saw her husband innocuously kissing the washerwoman's forehead and patting her head in a fatherly way, misinterpreting it as evidence of a long-standing romance.

Despite his wife's unfounded accusation of adultery, Mr Hall remained calm. Teaching Mukund and attending to his life insurance and medicine needs seemed to rekindle his sense of purpose. He had a handful of English friends in the area and found solace in helping farmers during crises, such as redirecting floodwaters during the monsoon.

With time, the collaboration between Flanagan and Mr Hall in tutoring Mukund proved highly successful, leading to his remarkable proficiency in English, literature, civics, world history and geography. Eventually, life found a way to iron out the marital ridges between Mr Hall and his wife, though their son's disappearance remained unresolved.

Chapter 4

The Noble Tribal

ONE AUGUST AFTERNOON IN 1879, 14-YEAR-OLD MUKUND AND his mother were returning home in an ornate carriage drawn by two horses, skilfully guided by Jimut, their coachman. They cantered through a landscape adorned with wooden and steel-truss bridges spanning rivulets and canals. Acacia, banyan, jackfruit, betel nut and jujube trees lined the bumpy road, occasionally giving way to single-lane dirt paths.

Sheela sat inside the covered, curtained passenger compartment, while Mukund perched on the seat next to the coachman. On Sheela's command Jimut had taken an abrupt detour to pursue and apprehend two new bandits in the area who were reportedly napping in an abandoned granary after a night of plundering. These robbers had recently moved from the jungles of Bikrampur. While nine security guards usually escorted the zamindar's wife, on this particular day, it was only Mukund and Jimut accompanying her. However, Jimut had a Martini-Henry rifle and its bullets hidden under the seats inside the horse carriage, in case of any emergency.

Despite being on the steepest highland in the area, the road was treacherous during the monsoon season, with floodwaters often cutting off the link to nearby trading hubs. Mukund merrily tossed peanuts at the mongoose, rabbits and gibbons bounding alongside the carriage, glancing at the occasional pushcart or abandoned palanquin in the roadside clearings. Sometimes, commercial bullock carts dropped tools and wares on their way to Faridpur, contributing to the eclectic collection of discarded items along the road.

The journey brought a mix of fragrances, from the stench of decaying leaves to the enchanting scents of wild blooms and aromatic trees. On one occasion, Mukund stopped the carriage to buy sweets for his mother, seizing the opportunity to pick up an antiquated muzzle of a rifled musket from the roadside. His curiosity about the now-defunct East India Company had been piqued, fuelled by tales from his tutor Mr Hall, about the company's opium sales in China and its profits from Indian commodities.

Mukund harboured a secret desire to visit the Red Fort in Delhi, imagining the balcony window from which Mughal emperors had once watched the common people and landed gentry. However, he kept these thoughts to himself, knowing that his father was deeply immersed in dreams of India's emancipation and might not share his enthusiasm for such tourist attractions.

As the journey continued, the horses neighed and snorted, occasionally showing signs of skittishness. Sheela remained vigilant, particularly around low-hanging bridges where she kept an eye out for swamp crocodiles. The scenery unfolded with busy potters painting clay idols of Goddess Durga, water buffaloes wallowing and farmers working in the waterlogged paddy fields, portraying a serene coexistence of nature and human bustle.

The carriage encountered diverse wildlife, from lemurs to mongooses, and passed female labourers heading to the village market with gunny bags balanced on their heads. Despite the rich flora and fauna, there was no recent sign of elephant herds or leopards straying from the Chittagong hills.

The carriage jolted over a pothole, snapping Sheela's attention back to the present from her daydreams of the wedding they had gone to attend in Tungipara. Mud splattered on to the spokes of the wheels as the afternoon sun beat down on the monsoon-drenched fields. Sheela gazed at the distant horizon, where the Padma and the Arial Khan rivers converged.

Mukund, with his keen eyes and tall stature, observed the small fishing boats with round bottoms, each designed for specific fishing techniques. He enthusiastically identified various types of dinghies used in his father's fisheries, appreciating the nuances of their designs and functions. As the stagecoach continued its journey, Mukund also spotted a rhesus monkey, jumping from one tree to the next. The air grew thick with the late afternoon heat, and the surroundings filled with the sounds of howling dogs, chirping birds and the occasional regal carriages passing through the rustic glen. Sheela, adorned in a beautiful blue Jamdani sari and exquisite jewellery, added to the picturesque scene.

Mukund was still perched on the seat next to the coachman. Sheela peered into her leaf-shaped looking glass before sliding the carriage's curtain and calling out, 'Will you stop bugging Jimut?'

Mukund replied, 'Yes, Mother. I will be inside very soon.'

Just then, Mukund noticed two men prancing inside well-decorated cardboard horses, entertaining a circle of youngsters in the emerald-green meadow alongside the main road. Leaving the animal show behind, the carriage cantered past a dense forest. A bullock cart laboured along the trail, pulled by two sprightly bulls. Periodically clicking their horns, the two synergic beasts chewed endlessly as they carried a medley of wares and a load of fresh merchandise destined for the general stores in the area.

After passing a thicket of babla trees, Sheela's eyes fell on a dark-skinned tribal man who was attempting to catch a fish from a nearby pond.

Seeing him, Sheela called out joyfully, 'Is that you, Naran?'

Jimut swiftly brought the horse carriage to a stop.

Naran turned around and stood up, reverently bowing to his master's wife. He wore only a loincloth and ran towards Sheela with his hands folded, the veins bulging out of his sinewy arms and legs.

One of her erstwhile guards, he was now an addiction-maligned man. She enquired, 'How is your son Bonka?'

Naran replied, 'Ma, Bonka is well. He is nearby—playing near the pond and helping me fish.'

A leather thong hung from the tribal's wrist. He lifted a delaminated bamboo pole out of the carriage's way. With his thick lathi, he swiped away a row of knocked-down coconuts.

Naran belonged to the lowly Bagdi caste, but he was not greedy like some of the rich folk he knew in the village. Years ago, Naran's father had saved 10 fellow miners during a collapse in one of the Raniganj coal mines. On another occasion, Naran's kettledrums had alerted villagers and helped trap a dangerous elephant in the neighbouring village. In recent years, Naran's extreme laziness and ganja addiction had forced Keshav to discharge him from duty, though he refused to remove him from the payroll.

Just then, a large brown bear burst out of the forest and charged towards the stagecoach. Whipping around, Naran morphed into a gladiator in a battle for survival. With a swift, calculated movement, he plunged his pointed lathi into the bear's chest. The wounded bear veered away from the stagecoach, redirecting its fury towards Naran. Undeterred, the tribal began circling the bear, suddenly whipping out a long steel knife from his waistband and hurling it at the bear's heart with lightning speed. The bear staggered but tried to regain its footing. Naran, seizing the moment, dived at the groaning beast, retrieved his bloodied knife and stabbed repeatedly at the bear's eyes and nose. The brutal assault worked instantly—the bear collapsed into the tall grass and never got up. By this time, Jimut had loaded his Martini-Henry rifle, but seeing the bear fall, he did not shoot. Instead, for added security, he used his lance to pin the bear to the ground. Sheela's screams finally subsided.

For a few minutes no one spoke. Naran caught his breath while Sheela, who was breathing heavily, reached inside her purse.

Intending to reward the faithful servant, she pulled out her coin pouch from the large purse.

Sheela placed her hand affectionately on Naran's scraggy hair and blessed him copiously. Naran prostrated before her with sheer reverence. She then tried to place three gold coins in his hand.

But Naran, still gripping his lathi, politely refused to accept the reward. Still shaken by the bear's sudden attack, Sheela tried again.

The sharp-featured tribal farmer declined once more by simply lowering his head and stepping back. Stoically, he brushed a tendril of windswept hair from his eye.

Sheela's gratitude deepened. 'Come closer; your fishing can wait. Let me take a closer look at the coalmine hero's son. It seems saving people's lives runs in your family's blood.'

As Naran stepped forward, Sheela gently caressed his fish-bitten wrist with maternal ardour. Naran watched in respectful wonder as she took her long kerchief and bandaged his slightly bloodied hand. Jimut appreciated the tender moment with a contented smile.

Sheela asked, 'Where have you been?'

Casting a submissive gaze typical of the humble, Naran replied, 'Ma, I returned from Manikganj yesterday. I had gone there to pay the last instalment of the dowry I owed to my younger sister's in-laws.'

Though she appreciated Naran's sense of duty towards his siblings, Sheela hissed with disdain, 'Your sister's in-laws are shameless. Despite being far more affluent than you, they still try to squeeze out everything they can from you.'

At her words, Naran lowered his head further, burying it into his hairless, V-shaped chest. Like a child seeking comfort, he sat down on the dusty ground near Sheela's carriage.

Just then, the tribal's young thin-faced son, Bonka, appeared. With the agility of a monkey, he scampered up a tall, leaning tree and plucked a tender coconut. After climbing down, he deftly split it into two halves and offered it to Sheela. Silent yet profusely radiating appreciation, she eagerly accepted the refreshing fruit from the boy's hands.

At the time of the advent of the East Indian Railways in 1854, British entrepreneurs were rapidly expanding coal mines in the resurging coalfields of southern Bihar and western Bengal. In 1878, Naran's father lost his life during a mine accident when a greedy foreman pushed him and fellow miners to extract more coal from a given channel than the safety limits allowed. The crew ended up damaging some of the pillars that had held the colliery's roof. Within minutes, the entire structure came crashing down, killing four men immediately. Naran's father managed to dig an escape route for the survivors but, trying to be the last one out, he perished when a localized fire caused another crash near the makeshift exit. Trapped and with no air, Naran's father suffocated before help could arrive.

Sensing the root of Naran's hesitation, Sheela probed, 'Why do you not come with me today and meet my husband?'

Known for being absent from work due to his drug addiction, Naran replied nervously, 'He can smell it on me. If I go today, master will immediately know I have been consuming ganja. It will upset him a lot.'

Sheela smiled. His desire to stay clean in her husband's eyes intrigued her. 'Why is it so important to you that my husband perceives you as a good person?'

Nearby, little Bonka munched on peanuts, too young to fully fathom the weight of the conversation.

Naran answered, 'I regard him as my father. My master's young age doesn't matter to me.'

Sheela chastised him gently, 'If you feel so warmly about my husband, why do you not heed his warnings and quit your opium and ganja addictions forever?'

Naran grew restless. 'I will, I will. I swear this is the last time you will see me intoxicated. I swear by my deceased mother...'

Touching her *chandrahaar* with self-assurance, Sheela asked, 'Do you promise to visit the doctor my husband asks you to meet?'

An embodiment of servitude, Naran mumbled, 'Yes...'

'Good. We will head home now. Jimut, let's go full speed.'

Jimut, Naran and Mukund joined forces to drag the dead bear's carcass from the edge of the forest-lined road, and the stagecoach resumed its journey towards Madaripur. Sheela's misty eyes remained glued to the road, watching until Naran was no longer in sight.

In the next few weeks that followed, Keshav arranged for Naran to be taken to a noted British physician at a newly built hospital in Dhaka for drug rehabilitation.

Chapter 5

A Promise Fulfilled

A YEAR PASSED. IT WAS NOW 1880.

While Naran's drug dependence had declined, the local hospital in Faridpur diagnosed him with liver disease. Despite such acute illness, he came to his master Keshav's aid by appearing as a key witness to clear Jimut, who had been falsely accused of murdering a well-known brass utensil peddler by Bhabesh's overseer. The overseer had alleged that Jimut was the killer after the peddler's body was discovered by a fisherman at the edge of a cremation ground. The British magistrate was about to convict Jimut based on hearsay when Naran's testimony provided an irrefutable alibi for Jimut, saving the sentinel's life. A few days later, after combing through the deathly bat- and owl-infested corn fields at night, Naran also proved that it was the washerman who had slaughtered the peddler after he had refused to give his daughter's hand in marriage to him.

Just weeks before his death, Sheela visited the ailing Naran in his modest straw-and-bamboo cottage. Although her palanquin and carriage often traversed these dirt roads and she regularly stopped to talk to the peasants, this was her first visit to the tribal's home.

Naran pointed to his six-year-old son, Bonka, who was joyfully cartwheeling in the veranda. 'Do you see Bonka? He does not know that I am nearing the end.'

Sheela glanced at the scrawny boy lost in his world of merriment. 'Yes, Bonka is a good lad. From what I have heard from your neighbour and my servants, he listens to his mother and sister, unlike my incorrigible boy.'

The landlady looked around, noting the flawed, amateurish paintings on the hut's mud-plastered walls. The first depicted Jesus with his disciples, the second offered a bird's-eye view of Mecca, while the third showed the Demigoddess Manasha seated upon her mythical conveyance.

Admiring the tribal's secular devotion, Sheela asked, 'Who painted these?'

Naran offered a faint smile. 'Various friends... I have added them to my wall collection over time.'

Sheela enquired further, 'Friends including Mr Hall, I presume?'

'Yes.'

In the adjoining bare-bones kitchen, Naran's wife was preparing shidol fish stuffed with pumpkin leaves—a dish dear to her ailing husband.

Naran looked at Sheela and spoke slowly and with difficulty, 'Ma, I may be leaving the world soon, so, I want to ask something from you. You will take care of my son, Bonka, will you not?'

Her eyes fixed on this selfless soul, Sheela stood up, grateful for the chance to repay a small fraction of the entire village's debt. She assured the sickly farmer, 'I will always take care of Bonka as if he were my own son.'

Feebly staring at the straw-bound ceiling, Naran mumbled, 'But I am just a lowly tribal—'

Sheela interrupted almost angrily, 'Not at all. Your life is as valuable as mine. My family and I will always care for Bonka. We would have done so even if you had not asked for our help.'

Naran's eyes lit up like the final splendour of a setting sun. 'May God always be kind to you.'

Sheela tried to lift his spirits. 'Why speak of death already? You still have so much to do besides saving our lives. I must leave now—Afzal's youngest son is very sick and has asked for me. I will come again...the day after tomorrow. Meanwhile, you take care. If you do not, I will surely wring your ears the next time.'

Naran smiled weakly, touched by her kindness. The tribal felt too exhausted to rise from his bed, watching Sheela's figure until he could no longer see her.

Two weeks later, Naran passed away on the night of Muharram. He breathed his last while listening to a group of travelling fakirs, his eyes closed peacefully to the strains of *jarigan* filling the air. Scores of Hindu and Muslim farmers and craftsmen who lived nearby rushed to pay their respects to Naran—a beloved figure who had helped many time and again, even during the most recent cholera outbreak.

A few days after Naran's death, as Sheela was returning home from the weekly market in her stagecoach, she bumped into Naran's frail wife. She had been walking home after buying medicines for her son from Mr Hall's pharmacy. The Englishman routinely subsidized his tribal customers' purchases from his earnings. The two women stood beneath a massive sal tree, its branches splitting the cobalt blue sky into pieces.

After exchanging greetings, Naran's wife broke into tears. 'Now Bonka is very ill.'

Sheela's concern was immediate. 'What illness? Is he at home and in bed?'

Naran's wife nodded. 'Yes. The kobiraj says he has a severe lung disease.'

Sheela responded with urgency, 'We must waste no time. Take me to your home and to the little boy.'

As Jimut helped them climb into the stagecoach, Sheela continued, 'From now on, Bonka will stay at my home more often than at yours. I promised your husband I'd take care of him, didn't I?'

Naran's wife managed a faint, self-pitying smile. 'Yes.' A small pockmark marred her otherwise comely face. She stared at a black moth pressed against the stagecoach's curtains. Once a strict spouse, she now appeared utterly defeated and crestfallen.

~

True to her words, Sheela ensured that young Bonka stayed in the estate's guest quarters at least three days a week. Over time, Bonka became an integral part of their lives, his warm presence permeating the estate whenever he visited.

Following his father's wish, Bonka learnt the basics of English and maths in a Madaripur grade school. Under Jimut's guidance, he honed skills in swordsmanship and marksmanship. At 21, Bonka tied the knot with a 16-year-old from his Bagdi tribe. On Keshav's and Mr Hall's recommendations, his wife assumed the role of the head housekeeper in a government-owned dak bungalow.

With the passage of time, many tales, including his Herculean efforts in single-handedly cooking fish curry for 400 wedding guests, became cherished anecdotes in Keshav's family. Inspired by Bonka's resilience, Mukund developed an enduring sensitivity towards those existing on society's fringes. Encouraged by Keshav, Bonka joined the Royal Indian Mail Service, before serving in various new occupations as the 20th century approached.

Through life's unpredictable vicissitudes, Bonka remained a loyal guardian, protecting Mukund and his family from the storms of fate with unwavering dedication.

Chapter 6

Beyond Faith and Race

BY 1889, 24-YEAR-OLD MUKUND HAD BLOSSOMED INTO A MAN bearing a striking resemblance to his father. He adeptly managed the responsibilities of overseeing his father's estate and the remnants of the family printing business with a maturity beyond his years. Flanagan, now 40, continued to reside nearby, overseeing the estate's printing operations and providing invaluable support to the family. The often-reclusive Keshav made occasional appearances to check on his cherished enterprise.

Meanwhile, Mr and Mrs Hall still grappled with the loss of their sons. Amid this, a scandal further rocked their world when Mr Hall and Flanagan inadvertently caught Mrs Hall having sex in a neighbour's house with a Welsh civil engineer, who was their long-time bridge-playing companion. Cornered by Flanagan, the Welshman admitted that his affair with Mrs Hall had been going on for many years, back to when her boys were tiny tots.

Despite this revelation, Mr Hall chose to forgive his wife's transgressions, and they remained together. However, the ongoing tragedies took a toll on Mrs Hall's mental well-being. Clad in a kitchen overall, Mrs Hall roamed the meadows and desolate trails, calling out to her missing sons.

The weight of Mr Hall's grief affected Sheela, who fell ill, prompting the worried Keshav to take action. He sent Mukund to convince his long-widowed aunt, Prachi, Sheela's only sister, to come and live with them. The plan was to entrust the care of Sheela and the management of the vast household to the much younger Prachi.

Standing on the ground floor veranda, Keshav introduced the young widow to the Irishman, 'Flanagan, this is Prachi, Sheela's younger sister.'

Catching a glimpse of Flanagan, Prachi lowered her gaze. The Irishman had just returned from church after praying for Sheela's quick recovery, his attire more formal than usual. The tip of his white handkerchief peeked from the pocket of his double-breasted jacket. Prachi's eyes momentarily locked on his handsome face and imposing sinewy frame. His dense, unruly hair curled slightly over his shapely forehead, and his charming presence filled the sprawling hallway. The sudden intensity of his presence made her head spin— the floor seemed to shift beneath her and her knees felt unsteady.

Flanagan did not fare much better. As the widow turned, her long hair elegantly billowed around her face, causing the Irishman to draw in his breath sharply. Though he had heard of Prachi and knew about her widowed status, he was taken aback by the striking resemblance between the sisters. The same indomitable beauty seemed to embrace the newly arrived widow like a delicate veil. He was mesmerized by her trim, petite waist, her curvy hips and slender limbs.

Nervously, Flanagan's fingers fumbled with an old bronze navigation instrument inside his jacket pocket. His attempt to conceal his joyous surprise at seeing this gorgeous woman was futile; he was stunned to see the Brahmin widow with long, dark hair. As he quickly tipped his derby hat in her direction, Prachi offered a wan smile. His kind eyes and calming voice seemed to ease a deep-seated longing within her.

Noticing the Irishman's astonishment, Keshav quickly explained, 'This is my idea.'

Confused, Flanagan asked, 'What is your idea?'

Keshav replied, 'To flout the warped tradition that requires our widows to shave their heads.'

'I see nothing wrong with your idea—unless a widow desires such austerity herself. I am equally impressed by your influence over the ultra-orthodox pandits four villages away!'

'Not just that. Driven solely by my stubborn insistence, unlike other widows, Prachi not only no longer abides by the short hair tradition, but I also ensure she does not subsist solely on a malnourished diet of rice and potatoes.'

Flanagan was even more impressed. 'Good for her. I appreciate this aspect even more.'

Prachi softly interjected, 'But I prefer to wear the white sari expected of me. There is nothing more profound and regal than white. Moreover, it is so soothing during the hot, long summers we endure every year.'

Flanagan took in a jerky breath and responded, 'Indeed.'

Keshav continued, 'Prachi was married at the age of 10 and her husband died when she was 12. At my request, she no longer lives with her in-laws but with a well-off and widowed aunt of mine.'

No one except the zamindar and his wife knew that Prachi had never consummated her marriage with her now deceased husband. At the onset, her in-laws had scheduled their obedient son and 10-year-old daughter-in-law's conjugal consummation on the latter's 14th birthday. The times were such that there were many such virgin widows in Bengal and the rest of India.

For a moment, Prachi gazed pensively out of the window. Filled with paternal affection, Keshav stepped towards her and gently touched her long dark hair. 'Looking at this beautiful woman, who would believe she was a little tomboy when I married her sister?'

Flanagan nodded. Could she be the one to break his long-standing vow of bachelorhood? All pretences of indifference to the fairer sex vanished in an instant. He stepped into a narrow shaft of sunlight that illuminated the veranda floor.

Keshav added, 'My sister-in-law has a weak heart. Mr Hall

estimates it functions at 85 per cent of its maximum capacity. That is why, at times, she is out of breath. But other than that, she is quite the catch.'

Blushing profusely, Prachi gazed at her beloved brother-in-law with deep reverence. 'Will you stop praising me? This man must be getting terribly bored.'

Keshav looked hard and long at his printer. 'I do not think so. Flanagan, my sister-in-law will be staying with us in the mansion for a few months until Sheela recovers. When around, you will make her feel at home... Will you not?'

Flanagan replied, 'Yes, of course.'

Less than six months later, at the urging of Keshav and Sheela, the youthful-looking Flanagan decided to marry Prachi.

Mukund, working behind the scenes, also encouraged Flanagan to break his bachelorhood vows and marry his aunt. The Irishman, perhaps subconsciously waiting for a Sheela lookalike to enter his life, seized the opportunity when Prachi emerged as a potential partner. Despite a simple wedding in a small temple, it raised many eyebrows among Keshav's Brahmin peers and relatives, who vehemently disapproved of the widow's remarriage to a Westerner. Many of these dissenting Brahmins began to incite Bhabesh to create as much trouble for Keshav as possible.

Amid the familial celebrations, Bhabesh began to hatch dangerous plans. Under his instructions, Nobin set out to disrupt the post-marriage festivities at Flanagan's mansion. A week after the wedding, late at night when everyone was away watching a play, Bhabesh and Nobin's goons pelted Flanagan's mansion with stones, shattering windowpanes and awnings. Horses from the stables were stolen, and further damage was inflicted on the zamindar's property.

Not satisfied with the level of retribution, Bhabesh devised more sinister plans to bring further tribulations upon Keshav for arranging the remarriage of his widowed sister-in-law to a beef-eating white man.

In one such plot, Keshav, returning home in his four-horse stagecoach after a village council meeting, was targeted by Moi, who was paid handsomely by the colluders to kill him. Riding a dapple grey horse, Flanagan intervened just in time, using a lathi to strike Moi and preventing Keshav's stagecoach from falling into a ravine. Moi, his face bloodied, abandoned his plan and fled, leaving behind a large stray dog as an inadvertent witness to the attempted murder.

Returning his sword to the scabbard, Keshav leapt out of the coach and embraced the Irishman repeatedly. Nudging aside a fallen branch with the toe of his *naira*, he remarked, 'Flanagan, you should never again risk your life for me. It is far more precious than mine.'

Flanagan asked, 'But why?'

Both men inwardly laboured to maintain composure as their hearts pounded and blood pressure surged.

Keshav replied, 'By marriage, you are now a very close relative. I see you as my beloved sister-in-law's newly wedded husband. I cannot bear the thought of her becoming a widow for the second time.'

Flanagan shook his head. 'Do not ever say your life is less valuable than others'. You have many important duties left on this earth.'

'Like what?'

'For example...helping your young son become a worthy man.'

Despite the near-fatal accident, Keshav managed a smile. 'Goodness! In the course of this challenging life, I thought you were going to help me with my increasingly difficult burdens...'

'Yes, I will.' Flanagan suddenly pulled out his pocket watch and glanced at it. 'But right now, I am late for a meeting. Let us talk later.' The Irishman turned towards the stagecoach driver and instructed, 'Jimut, take your master home. There should be no more trouble...at least not today.'

Having just received a new lease of life, a highly relieved Keshav sank back into his seat.

Later that afternoon, Flanagan took Keshav aside to a quiet corner of the backyard. Neither spoke about the close call earlier. The Irishman took out a smoking pipe and clamped it between his teeth. In the distance, they could faintly hear the clatter of brass plates as the maids washed up after lunch.

Gratitude was written all over Keshav's face.

Flanagan broke the silence. 'I do not want my marriage to Prachi to cause you any kind of trouble.'

Keshav was perplexed. 'What do you mean?'

'Should my wife and I move away...somewhere else?'

Keshav refused outright. 'Of course not! How could you even suggest that? I am prepared to face the consequences of my carefully considered decision to support your marriage. Are you not happy here, with Prachi?'

'I am more than happy to have her as my wife, and I am grateful to you for making it happen. But after years of working on your estate, I have become a wealthy man. To keep you out of trouble, my wife and I could move away...even go back to Ireland.'

Keshav looked pensively at a sheepherder guiding his flock through an unpaved glen just outside the backyard fence. 'Impossible. Why must you do that? Are you afraid of malevolent critics?'

Flanagan quickly responded, 'Oh no!'

Keshav, sounding like a child unexpectedly tricked by a trusted playmate, asked, 'Then what is the problem? It seems you are only focused on one thing now—the sweet dreams of Prachi... You no longer care about others, like me, my wife and Mukund...'

Flanagan defended himself, 'Oh no…certainly not. Your entire family is like mine.'

'Then there are no ifs and buts. You are family. In the end, those who seek my death or wish to punish me will have to face the Almighty's judgement of what is right and wrong.'

'Indeed. But can I at least pay for the broken windows, the stolen horse and the earlier damages caused by the hoodlums? After all, they too were the result of your bold decision.'

'Of course not.'

He looked up at the garden gazebo's wooden high ceiling. A feather was caught in a dense, hard-to-reach cobweb. Pigeons in the sky filled the air with the beating of their wings and frantic cries.

Life went on. The mansion's guards did what they could to find the identity of the assailants. It was rumoured that the orthodox Brahmins in the area remained furious for a long time about Flanagan's marriage to Prachi—a union transcending both race and faith.

Chapter 7

The Curse of Untouchability

SHANU, A DOM, LIVED ON THE OUTSKIRTS OF MUKUND'S village. Having lost his wife during childbirth, his existence was built entirely around his two sons, eight-year-old Nontu and seven-year-old Montu. With no one to look after them, the struggling father took his boys with him wherever he worked, even to places like cremation grounds and public toilets. Shanu ensured his children stayed out of the premises of his upper-caste employers. The boys, full of youthful energy, spent their days climbing trees, sucking neem twigs, or floating in ponds using inflated buffalo skins.

From time to time, Shanu worked as a day labourer in the sprawling compound of Nobin, a wealthy spice trader. Belonging to the Kayastha caste, this was the same Nobin who had had a few run-ins with Keshav when his men trespassed on the zamindar's fishery.

One tragic day, too young to be aware of the chasms of caste or religion, Nontu and Montu entered one of Nobin's orchards, drawn by the sight of a colourful kite stuck in the shrubs. The siblings ventured into the grove to retrieve it, accidentally trampling a few marigold plants in the process. Earlier, their only other unwitting infraction occurred when Nobin's overseer had asked them to help their father during a clean-up—the little boys had missed picking up some of the fallen leaves off the ground.

These two trifling incidents sealed the way to the ensuing tragedy. One of Nobin's servants caught Nontu and unleashed a brutal assault on the boy. They beat him mercilessly while mucus and blood flowed copiously from his nose. Calling Nontu an imp and a devil, they kneed him in the groin. The abuse continued until he passed out, eventually succumbing to his injuries from a brain concussion. Their helpless father was summoned and informed of his son's 'gross misbehaviour' and warned never to show his face again on the spice trader's estate.

Few higher-caste villagers attended Nontu's final rites. Nobin quickly sent Moi to the local faujdar's office to file a false report. As per Moi's account, Nontu had entered the trader's premises long after incurring the injuries inflicted by an unidentified child abductor. Those were times when some of the untouchables were so poor that they could not afford to buy wood to ensure a proper cremation of their relatives. They usually buried their deceased young ones along the silt strips of nearby rivers or streams. Some tried to cremate despite all financial odds.

Keshav, hearing of the tragedy, asked Mukund to pay for Nontu's cremation on the far side of the Arial Khan River. Filled with quiet rage, Mukund watched the funeral pyre burn, standing not far from a devastated Shanu. Nontu's distant and emaciated grand-aunt wailed and wailed into the night sky. Mukund's most loyal peasant, Afzal Mian, also stood close to them, ready to assist the outcaste at the first call for help. As the cremation neared conclusion, Mukund sensed the Dom desperately clinging to a shred of dignity. His eyes streaming with endless yet silent tears, Shanu stared at Mukund with sheer gratitude.

Inspired by Mukund, some of his farmers, who normally kept their distance from untouchables, quietly hovered around Shanu—a gesture that would be viewed as unthinkable under normal circumstances. Only a few of the zamindar's Hindu peers and a handful of farmers, displeased with Keshav for allowing his widowed Brahmin sister-in-law to marry the white Flanagan, were not in attendance.

Mukund knew he needed to do something to fight the

long-standing societal atrocities even if he failed. He felt a burning need to set a precedent for justice for the cruelties levied on the lower castes. The next day, Mukund travelled by train to Faridpur, and met with the British legal officials, recounting the brutal death of Nontu. The Brits took long notes in elegant hardcover notebooks and promised an inquiry, which never materialized.

Mukund also offered to help the still-disoriented Dom by writing and filing a formal complaint. However, like a lamb thoroughly battered by life, Shanu declined, seemingly afraid of losing his high-caste clients if he took that step. The entrenched bigotry that Mukund had witnessed since childhood now confronted him with brutal clarity. This time, intolerance loomed too close to home— Nontu's innocent suffering drove Mukund to take decisive action.

Mukund and Flanagan rushed to meet Mr Broad, a British lawyer born in Madras and known for taking up the cases of the downtrodden, regardless of their race. Mr Broad had completed his undergraduate and law degree in Calcutta before choosing to work in the Faridpur District Court rather than in the empire's prestigious high courts. In 1861, he became the first secretary of the Faridpur Bar Association.

Mr Broad leaned back on his divan and lit a cigar. 'You look all puffy and red-eyed. Have you not slept lately?'

The room was lined with law books, covering nearly every wall of the sprawling chamber.

Dabbing his sweaty face with a handkerchief, Mukund fervently said, 'It is great that we are sweating to break the last shackle from our motherland's waist. But unless we desist from segregating among our own, our "untouchables" will someday pull us back.'

Flanagan, his wide forehead creased with concern, added, 'Yes. Every nation that consistently mistreats its minions or so-called drudges eventually pays a terrible price. Look at the once-powerful Rome and Egypt—'

Mukund commented, 'Sometimes I wonder if we are a nation yet...the way we put each other down...people from various provinces of British India. I agree with Flanagan. It does not matter. Sometimes, the collective payback of a group of people bound together by some reason takes two, twenty, two hundred or even two thousand years. But it comes for sure.'

Mr Broad offered a cautious reply, 'Let me see what I can do. Meanwhile, do not get the Dom's hopes up too high.'

Flanagan, puzzled, asked, 'Why do you say that?'

Mr Broad replied with a resigned tone, 'In the unlikeliest of places, personal interest, the lure of bribes and extortion are becoming part and parcel of administration.'

Mr Broad knew all too well the gross inequities that plagued the system. Despite his caution, Mukund's wrath over the brutal death fuelled his decision to act.

But his recent premonitions ended up being more than accurate. On Shanu's behalf, Mr Broad filed a case in the Faridpur District Court. He and Mukund collaborated to draft the Dom's legal deposition. Despite the brutal killing and Flanagan's best efforts to present evidence, the case was doomed. Not a single witness showed up during the hearing; none of the five bona fide witnesses corroborated the Dom's complaint and affirmed the circumstances that had led to the wrongful death of eight-year-old Nontu.

True to Mr Broad's apprehensions, the case was dropped. Taking turns, on 10 occasions, Flanagan and Mukund visited the law offices and requested the file to be reopened. Each time, a clerk keen to please his supervisor told them to return the following day.

On one such occasion, grossly enraged by such delaying tactics, Mukund grabbed a heavy wooden gavel from a nearby desk and hurled it at the Bengali babu. The gavel missed the targeted skinny, self-glorified typist-cum-record-keeper by a whisker. Just then, passing through the hallway, a British lawyer saw the infraction.

Before anyone could say or do anything, Mukund bolted from the room and fled home.

Mukund knew that at worst, there might be an arrest warrant issued in his name for disorderly conduct in a public place. Preventive measures had to be taken. For the next three days, Keshav had his son stay completely out of the public eye. At his commandeering insistence, his grown son hid himself in an underground jute granary, surviving on a small packet of dried fruits and a clay pot of drinking water. Luckily, no charges were pressed.

Chapter 8

Of Secrets and Tradition

At the age of 20, Mukund experienced a full introduction to the carnal aspect of manhood. It came from Mandira, a breathtaking and rarely seen relative. Mandira, a 24-year-old widow and Mukund's second cousin, had been married off at the age of nine and widowed at 15. Despite always wearing a white sari, she looked ravishing. At Keshav's insistence, she kept her hair short instead of maintaining a completely shaven head expected of most widows at the time. Known to be a fine cook, Mandira's chance encounter with Mukund came about when she was visiting Keshav's estate and the rest of the household had gone to attend a play three villages away. Slightly ailing and deeply depressed, the sex-starved widow had decided to stay home. For better or worse, Sheela had asked Mukund to be her sentinel and caretaker just in case her ailment worsened.

After they were all alone, Mandira made the first and only move. Unlike the courtesan who had failed to seduce Mukund years ago, his kinswoman did not disrobe at all. Instead, she simply sat up in the bed and asked for a drink of water in her inimitably husky voice. The zamindar's son quickly obliged. While returning the tall brass cup, Mandira tugged at his arm ever so slightly. Her gorgeous, sad yet eloquent eyes held a silent plea. For a moment, her lips quivered with sheer sensuality. Sensing the unspoken invitation, Mukund could not resist. He slammed the door shut and plunged into the bed, undressing her with fervent urgency.

The grateful widow closed her eyes and let him unravel and explore to his heart's content. Mukund, having long struggled with intense desire since his previous near-temptation, found his genetically built-in inhibition about sexual intercourse before marriage crumbling like a pack of cards. Being a footballer who ran five miles every day, he repeatedly drowned in her blissfully receiving receptors with the prowess of a grown, Herculean man. The tall and sinewy youth came again and again. The girl and her utterly oblivious parents left for their home in nearby Munshiganj the next day at dawn.

No one ever came to know about Mukund and his second cousin's wondrous misadventure. He made it a point to never meet her again and she also did not try to reach him in any way before or after his marriage. Upon learning of her parents' death, he discreetly sent her an adequate upkeep allowance until her demise many decades later.

~

Despite the substantially late start in marital life, Flanagan fell into the groove like a seasoned man. In 1889, to please his much younger wife, he was said to have travelled far to Medinipur district to procure blue shrimp and chital freshly caught from the Subarnarekha River. Prachi also loved to go sightseeing or backpacking in the evenings, perched in Flanagan's horse or decorated bullock carts. Sometimes they creaked their way into enchanting woods and distant hamlets, often returning well after midnight. Despite being an expert horse rider, Flanagan seemed to have caught on to his wife's passion for the leisurely charm of the bullock cart. While everyone in the zamindar's family remained apprehensive about Prachi's adventurous spirit, her equally audacious and exploratory husband never refused her.

As a diehard numismatist, Flanagan owned coins from various dynasties including the Gupta, the Mughal, the Dutch and the Portuguese. His proficiency in reading and writing Bengali also surpassed that of many around him.

On nights he returned late, Prachi would cry off all her make-up and eat nothing but curd and rice. When inoculating the farmers all over the village with cholera and rabies vaccines, he rode from dawn to late night, never feeling tired. In this regard, Mr Hall could not have asked for a more dedicated volunteer. Upon returning home after such hectic sessions, Flanagan would fall asleep as soon as he hit the sack, sometimes in Prachi's arms, with her mouth by his ear and his face nestled against her breasts.

Prachi admired the way her husband, at times, laboured through the night over stacks of paper, getting new printing typesets ready; the way he had looked out for his asthma-afflicted friend, Ballantyne, in Calcutta, the one who now lived in a spacious flat over a Mughlai eatery. Her chest heaved with pride the day he took one of the major London-based publishers to court for cheating one of his friends—an Irish writer—of thousands of pounds in royalties. She loved it when he let her clip his fingernails or taught her romantic sentences in English and Irish. To please him, she learnt how to bone a duck and mix an Indian version of pina colada. Sometimes she would make barley soup customized to his liking and accompany him to the church on select Sundays. In turn, Flanagan always listened with curiosity when she chanted sonorous mantras from the *Samaveda*. When Prachi needed a specific shade of auburn lipstick to match her Banarasi silk sari just days before a wedding invitation, he journeyed to a general store in Sonargaon to procure it.

Prachi strove hard to match her husband's horse-riding skills. Now and then refusing help from her maidservants, she clambered into the saddle and rode into the nearby woods. Unexpectedly recalled to living life to the fullest, the erstwhile virgin widow's every synapse tingled at Flanagan's magic touch. One day, the perpetually sari-clad and ritualist Prachi surprised everyone at a family gathering by showing up in a navy blue kimono. Sheela and everyone else were thoroughly amused rather than offended when they learnt that the Irishman had gifted Prachi the dress on her previous birthday. On days when Flanagan indulged in mud-wrestling fever with competitors nearly half his age, she no longer groaned and objected. Instead, as soon as he returned home from the *akharas*, she would bathe him and scrub him clean.

~

Mr Hall and Flanagan laboured diligently in Mukund's printing business until the latter bagged several new customers, including privately owned European companies. When the medicine man suffered from dengue, Sheela worked round the clock to cure his dangerous malady; she prepared scores of herbal potions, fresh squash, papaya juice and honey mixed with sugarcane molasses and had Jimut deliver them to Mr Hall's modest bungalow.

Mukund's clients included some of the nearby British administrative offices as well. Even when dealing with Westerners, he never wore anything but a white dhoti and a khadi kurta. Whenever activists fighting for the nation's independence needed to print any protest letters or flyers, they came to him.

Several Muslims worked in Mukund's predominantly Hindu estate. His inner turmoil knew no bounds due to the persistent prejudice and discrimination he saw prevalent among the common people in his estate in Madaripur and beyond. Poor Muslim farmers and fishermen were often treated shabbily by people like Bhabesh, whose estate was located not far from Mukund's. Mukund discovered that the intolerance was not confined to Faridpur but extended to adjoining areas, including Dhaka and Barisal. Besides the rich glossing over the rights of the poor, most Brahmins, including many Kulins, still chose to steer clear of the low castes. Keshav, however, was a notable exception.

Keshav had recently hired a Chinese chef to work one day a week. Trained in Calcutta's Chinatown as a teenager and later employed by British officials, this chef was known to be the best in all Madaripur. Every Sunday morning, he showed up at the porch in a white linen suit and black bow tie. After changing into his working attire, he would work his magic in the mansion's renovated kitchen. The semi-retired master chef never allowed the slightest trace of turmeric powder or crushed coriander to stain his spotless clothes while preparing Indian-Chinese dishes like Manchurian duck and Szechuan fish. Before departing, the zamindar and he engaged in a round of *mahjong*.

~

One unusually cold winter evening, Keshav stood in the garden with Mukund near an old mango tree that had been planted by Keshav's ancestors nearly 200 years ago. Sheela used its leaves during every worship ceremony, including the daily offerings to Lord Narayan at her home altar. Two lively squirrels lived in the ancient tree, trained by Sheela to never enter her spick-and-span home. Neither did they damage anyone's farms or barns. Twice a day, they patiently waited for their mistress to come out with a heaped bowl of sumptuous food.

In the fading light of dusk, one of the estate's gardeners hurried to repair a damaged section of the lawn before the last rays of light disappeared. The zamindar seemed to be in fine disposition, buoyed by the recent bountiful harvest of rice, jute and even the non-irrigated crops of wheat and pulses. All his godowns were in surplus. A servant was hauling coal from a wheelbarrow into the metal chute of a basement brazier meant to keep the huge living room warm on rare cold days. The brazier, constructed by Keshav in his youthful exuberance, was seldom used due to the generally temperate climate. Decorative rocks near the mansion's main steps and in the foyer's waterfall had been loosened by recent untimely rain.

The dark leaves of the mango tree blended with the deepening night. As with every evening, the sound of Sheela blowing the sacred conch charged the quiet surroundings. Without fail, she serenaded her four-armed Narayan deity with flowers, fruits, portions of freshly cooked food served in small golden bowls and a *chamor*—a hand-held fan made from horsetail. During these moments of worship, she always wore a white sari with a broad red border.

Keshav turned to Mukund. 'Son, it is time for you to take full charge of the daily affairs of this estate.'

'Father, I am not quite ready to manage such a large property. I haven't even swum in all your ponds and walked through all your fruit orchards,' replied Mukund.

Keshav smiled gently. 'Sometimes if your head is screwed on right, you do not need to do all that.'

A reluctant Mukund said, 'I can manage, however, especially with Flanagan's help. But...'

Highly pleased, Keshav looked up expectantly, 'But what?'

'I have one condition.'

'Go ahead, speak your mind.'

'Can I reinstate a 400-year-old practice in our family Joggeshwar told me about?'

Keshav was curious. 'We have given up on so many old customs. Which one do you have in mind?'

'Can we ask Afzal, the oldest among our Muslim farmers, to pluck the first basket of flowers to be offered to Lord Vishnu every time we perform a Satyanarayan puja or a Durga puja at home?'

Keshav pulled his son to his chest and caressed his hair. 'Yes, it's a good idea. Afzal is a wonderful human being; he can do us the honour.'

Despite Mukund's efforts to stay calm, his limbs trembled with unbounded joy. 'Do you mean you agree with my proposal?'

Keshav nodded. 'Yes. It is time to bring back the vision of inclusiveness our ancestors once dreamt of.'

Mukund hugged his father even tighter. 'So in tomorrow's meeting with our orchard overseers, fishery foremen and other staff, can you announce your decision about Afzal?'

Keshav replied warmly, 'I certainly will. Do not worry; I will also inform the men overseeing the horse corral. But first, I will tell your mother tonight over dinner.'

'I already spoke to her yesterday, and she readily approved.'

Not surprised, Keshav grinned. 'Good,' he said. 'I can see that you are more ready to take on the challenges of this estate than you realize. I pray to the Almighty that your heart may always feel just as it does now.'

Chapter 9

A Narrow Escape

RIDING HIS HORSE, MUKUND WAS RETURNING FROM HIS mentor Flanagan's home. He often took this shortcut—a winding trail through the dense forest that had become second nature to him. As he rode past a thickly wooded creek, Bhabesh's men, hiding in the shadows, sprang into action and successfully kidnapped the youth. The five-man gang had been waiting patiently, their ambush carefully planned. They killed his horse after it tumbled into a moss-covered boulder—a deadly trap laid out by the attackers. Earlier, they had concealed the rock beneath a carefully transplanted patch of overgrown grass, ensuring the horse's fall.

Mukund hit the ground hard, and before he could react, the men gagged his mouth and tied him to an ossified tree stump in a nearby cavern. The attackers were rough and methodical, binding him tightly with ropes that cut into his skin. On a whim, the leader decided to blow their captive to bits. Moi and his gang rushed back to the stagecoach to retrieve the explosives—a crude but deadly concoction he usually made in his cowshed. The plan was to leave no mortal remains of Mukund, erasing his existence completely. Before leaving for the market, one of them, with a cruel smirk, stabbed Mukund in the arm. The wound, deep and painful, began to bleed profusely.

Just then, Afzal Mian, in his bullock cart, happened to be travelling along the same shortcut. Ironically, years earlier, it was the Muslim farmer who had taught Mukund these rarely trodden, desolate routes. Afzal was a familiar and comforting presence in the community, his cart laden with freshly harvested jute—a symbol of his hard work and dedication.

Despite the blood loss, Mukund laboured to loosen the gag on his mouth. Each movement was agony, but he persisted, driven by a will to survive. Managing to free his mouth slightly, Mukund moaned as loudly as he could. The sound was faint but carried through the stillness of the forest. Luckily, the trail's only traveller at the time, Afzal, heard the desperate call for help. His ears perked up, and he stopped his cart, listening intently. Sprinting to the cavern, the farmer found his master's son tied and bleeding. Without a moment's hesitation, his strong hands worked quickly to untie the ropes. Covering Mukund's body with his wife's spare burqa, he took him to his modest mud house. This proved to be a life-saving move, the burqa concealing Mukund's identity and the bloodstains.

A few hours later, when Bhabesh's men returned to the cavern and realized that their captive had escaped, they began an all-night manhunt. The assailants angrily stormed into the homes of almost all those who worked for Keshav. They raided some of the Muslim homes as well, tearing through belongings and shouting threats. However, due to reasons known only to providence, they did not force their way into Afzal's cottage. Perhaps it was the burqa, perhaps it was divine intervention, but Mukund remained hidden.

Mukund lived in the farmer's barn for the next two weeks until his wounds healed. It was a simple and rustic place, but Afzal and his wife made it a haven for the injured youth. Afzal's devoted wife, a gentle and skilled healer, nursed Mukund round the clock, her hands moving with practised care. Knowing Sheela's fragile and worrying nature, Keshav, who had been discreetly notified about the incident, told her nothing about the violent attack on her son—he claimed that Mukund's prolonged absence was due to an assignment in Calcutta related to their estate's jute business. It was a convenient lie, one that kept Sheela's worries at bay.

Deeply grateful for Afzal's bravery and care, Keshav gifted the farmer 10 pure gold coins from his ancestral chest of gems—a chest that lay buried in a cellar under his kitchen. The saintly jute farmer accepted the reward only after great persuasion from Keshav and Flanagan. It was a humble exchange, a token of gratitude that spoke volumes about the bond between them.

When Mukund fully recovered, Flanagan brought him back to the estate. Mukund craftily hid his scars from his mother, always conscious of her watchful eyes. He no longer lazed at home without a kurta or an undershirt, concealing the reminders of his ordeal. From day one, he angrily and secretly whispered in his father's ears the fiery wish to avenge his near-death experience. The desire for retribution was ignited within him—a fire that refused to be quenched. Mukund, with a new resolve, began training under Flanagan's rigorous guidance, honing his skills and sharpening his mind for the inevitable confrontation.

Sensing the turmoil within his protégé, Flanagan offered wisdom and counsel, urging Mukund to temper his anger with strategy and patience. 'Revenge is a dish best served cold,' he reminded the young man, echoing the ancient adage. Mukund nodded, internalizing the lesson, though his heart still throbbed with a yearning for justice.

Days turned into weeks, and Mukund's strength returned. He spent hours practising with weapons, mastering combat techniques and studying the movements of Bhabesh's men. He learnt their strengths, their weaknesses and, most importantly, their routines. Each day brought him closer to his goal.

One evening, as the sun dipped below the horizon, casting long shadows over the land, Mukund stood before his father, his eyes burning with determination. 'Baba, the time has come,' he declared, his voice steady and resolute.

Keshav, seeing the fire in his son's eyes, clasped his shoulder firmly. 'Remember, Mukund, we fight for justice, not vengeance. Let your actions be guided by honour.'

With his father's words echoing in his mind, Mukund set out to confront his enemies. He moved silently through the night, a shadow among shadows, guided by the stars and the teachings of his mentor. His heart pounded with anticipation, every step bringing him closer to the showdown.

In the still of the night, Mukund approached the hideout of Bhabesh and his men. The moonlight cast an eerie glow over the scene, illuminating the faces of his adversaries. Mukund took a deep breath, steeling himself for the battle ahead. He knew that this confrontation was not just about avenging his suffering but about protecting his family and the people of his village from further harm.

The encounter was swift and brutal. Mukund, with his newfound skills and unwavering resolve, fought with the ferocity of a cornered tiger. Bhabesh's men, taken by surprise, fell one by one under Mukund's precise and lethal strikes. In the chaos, Mukund found himself face-to-face with Bhabesh, the man who had orchestrated his kidnapping.

'Your reign of terror ends tonight,' Mukund hissed, his voice low and dangerous. Bhabesh, sensing his doom, tried to flee, but Mukund was faster. With a final, decisive blow, he brought Bhabesh to his knees.

As dawn broke, painting the sky with hues of pink and gold, Mukund stood victorious. He looked around at the defeated gang, their threat now neutralized. The villagers, waking to a new day, found themselves freed from the shadow of fear that had loomed over them for so long.

Mukund returned home, his heart lighter but his resolve just as strong. He had avenged his suffering and protected his family, but he knew that the journey was far from over. There would always be new challenges and new battles to fight. With the support of his family, the guidance of his mentor and the strength of his spirit, Mukund was ready to face whatever the future held.

Chapter 10

A Father's Plea

KESHAV WAS A DESCENDANT OF THE SAGE BHARGAVA. Forgiving and forgetting were not part of his nature; fair retribution and justice were principles he held dear. One evening when Sheela was visiting a neighbour, the zamindar decided to counsel his son, who had narrowly escaped death at the hands of old family foes. Leading Mukund to the marble steps of the family deity, the zamindar made his son swear an oath.

Keshav spoke as softly as he could. 'Keep your voice down. Not just your mother…even the maids do not know about the nearly fatal attack on your life.'

Mukund nodded, his face a mixture of determination and frustration, 'Yes, Baba.'

Keshav's gaze hardened. 'They must be severely punished. If the district court does not act, we will erase them from this earth when the time is right. But right now, focus on getting the shackles off our motherland. Dedicate yourself wholly to this cause.'

Keshav, though still grieving, had deliberately cast aside the brutality inflicted upon his beloved son into a numb, distant place. The lines around his eyes and mouth had deepened, etched by the weight of his pain.

Mukund's muscles tensed with resentment. 'You mean I should run away from my immediate challenge? Hide like a rat behind some pile of lumber, firewood or a palm tree?' The ghoulish, celebratory faces of Bhabesh and Nobin's men in the cavern haunted him like an obnoxious toothache.

Keshav's voice was calm but firm. 'No. Your need for revenge will be addressed some day. But for now, you and Flanagan must use my printing press to awaken the thousands of youth emerging from this land.'

Mukund, still angry, demanded, 'Why must I do that?'

Keshav, suddenly transported into a realm of unbridled dreams, grabbed the end of his russet-coloured dhoti. 'Many more presses and voices must rise in this vast subcontinent. With time, their hearts will fill with the hope of self-rule and equality. And we must change the corrupt judicial system.'

Mukund looked sceptical. 'Will that be enough to ensure sovereignty?'

Keshav shook his son's shoulders almost violently. 'No. When the time comes, you and your progeny must find the right band of mates. You will have to do much more to gain freedom.'

Mukund avoided his father's gaze as he replied, 'I wonder sometimes how many more generations it would take before such a day dawns...'

He glanced out of the window, watching the day fade into dusk. Spurring his flagging mare, his accounts clerk happened to be going home, cantering past a mud-filled bog just outside the boundary wall. Twisting in the saddle, he looked back just once.

Keshav braced himself, preparing to say something that weighed heavily on his heart. 'Remember one more thing. You are our only son. Your mother will never forgive me if those ruthless hoodlums manage to kill you.'

With age, Keshav's face had grown sallow and pinched.

Mukund's robust confidence superseded everything else. 'That will be the day. It will never happen.'

Keshav said warily, 'A few days ago, if not for Afzal Mian's timely interception, they would have almost killed you. Should you fritter away your life trying to get even with a bunch of low-life rogues?'

Confusion besieged Mukund. 'What are you saying, Baba? Are you—'

Keshav cut in decisively. 'I am saying that if you put your life on the line, do it for a great cause. Something your parents will be proud of. Fret for the greater good of a nation, not just a village.'

Mukund sighed, his frustration evident. 'At first, why not aim low?'

Keshav's eyes bore into his son's as he replied, 'In some walks of life, initially aiming low works quite well. But not in the affairs of a long-subjugated civilization. If you aim for the sky…you might get to the roof. If you aim for the roof, you might barely clear a field rat.'

Mukund, intrigued and somewhat amused, prodded grimly, 'Where did you learn these sayings?'

Keshav's face softened slightly. 'From my long-deceased grandmother. Hopefully, you will live to see India become independent. Meanwhile, as for retribution against those murderous, self-centred beasts, you must bide your time for the most opportune moment. Look at Afzal Mian…the way he handled a tough situation when he saved your life. How deftly he replied each time Bhabesh's and Nobin's heavily armed men enquired if he had seen you of late.'

Mukund lowered his head, the weight of gratitude pressing heavily on his shoulders. 'There is no question that I owe my life to him, a man among men. Even you do not know all the details about how he not only rescued me but also nursed my wound in his house for two long weeks…risking his own life and his wife's.'

Keshav reached forward and briefly ran his hand through his son's hair. 'Then at least listen to Afzal, if not me. This morning, I talked to him at length. He wants you to do the same thing I want. For now, stay away from trouble caused by petty people.'

The zamindar slumped on a nearby divan, hunching over as a sense of foreboding gnawed at him like a bloodthirsty worm. Sweat began to build upon his brow, and he fanned himself with a palm-leaf fan. His red-veined eyes could not belie his anxious, sleepless nights. A very long silence ensued, interspersed only by the ticking of a hallway clock. A breeze rose from the river. Keshav wondered if he would finally fall asleep easily that night. The youth's meditative expression seemed hard to read.

Keshav licked his lips nervously. 'I have not yet heard your answer. You know how your mother loves you more than anyone else in this world.'

The silence continued as Keshav warily looked around for his wife's return. 'She will be back any time now. Do I have your word that you will not go after Bhabesh's men or Nobin with weapons?'

Mukund's square jaws hardened, imparting a look of eerie strength. He remembered the sweetness of his mother's post-breakfast kiss on his forehead every morning and the way she hummed his favourite songs between her teeth. Could he do without her even if death promised him a heavenly afterlife? Never.

Mukund relented. 'Yes, Baba, I promise. But I hope you never rue this day.'

The relief the zamindar felt was palpable as he jumped up and hugged his son with abandon. 'No, I will not.' Tears of joy filled his eyes as he stared admiringly at his son.

In the years that followed, Mukund and Flanagan were destined to score a few key victories against injustices overlooked by the imperial government's legal system. They stood up before an administration too vast and unwieldy to grasp the nuances of complex discrimination issues. However, the zamindar and the Irishman never got over their failure to convict the killers of Nontu. Besides collaborating on issues of the freedom struggle, Mr Broad and Mukund worked together trying to ensure that the publicly funded freshwater wells in the villages of Madaripur and the rest of Faridpur district were accessible to Hindus of all castes and Muslims alike.

A few months later, Sheela passed away in her sleep.

Pandits trotted into the temporarily canopied foyer to exalt the pure soul's departure from the earth without the slightest suffering in the last days of her life. At the onset of the tragic days that followed, Prachi and Flanagan were among the first relatives to arrive at the Madaripur mansion.

Keshav, overwhelmed by the loss, looked to Flanagan for support. 'Flanagan...Prachi knows all our customs about how to bid farewell to a deceased soul. Since Mukund is still learning and my mind is in one big haze, I suggest you take charge.'

Flanagan, respectful and solemn, responded, 'Do you mean... Prachi will be the planner and I...the executor?'

Keshav nodded, his grief palpable. 'Exactly. Is that all right with you?'

Flanagan placed a reassuring hand on Keshav's shoulder. 'Yes. I will do whatever it takes.'

Struggling with her fondest memories of her departed sibling, Prachi agreed, silent tears streaming down her cheeks. For several days, the Irishman ran between Kulin Brahmins' homes, consulting with great gusto to ensure all the rituals expected on the 11th day were properly arranged. For the first time, a grief-stricken Mr Hall closed his medical chamber for a day. Mukund took it upon himself to redirect the patients to another doctor a few miles away.

Sheela's death sent a wave of deep sorrow across the village and beyond. People of every caste, faith and colour came to bid her farewell. No one was turned away; both Prachi and Flanagan saw to that.

Crestfallen and a mere shadow of his once-fiery self, Keshav grieved for months. Eventually, taken by the wiles of a matchmaker, he began to search for a bride for Mukund. Assigning Jimut other tasks, Flanagan volunteered to be his coachman.

Part II

Chapter 11

Ties that Bind

DURGA PUJA OF 1892 HAD MIRTHFULLY PASSED IN MADARIPUR when Mukund's personal life took a complicated turn. Deferring to his father Keshav and the family matchmaker's predilections, he married 16-year-old Archana, who belonged to the powerful and prosperous Roy zamindar family of Pabna. After an atypical two years of back-to-back drops in rice and jute yields, her arrival seemed to have reversed Keshav's fortunes, bringing during the month of Poush a hefty winter harvest to the farmlands.

Father of many daughters but no sons, Bhabesh received the joyous neighbourhood news with envy. To upstage the mirth-filled atmosphere at Keshav's mansion, one late afternoon, he had Moi release a pair of caged and vicious falcons from his terrace. The birds promptly flew to Keshav's home and scared away, if not anyone else, a flock of sonorous birds, including several innocuous mynahs that converged every day around the newly-weds' second-storey bedroom balcony.

Within days of arriving at her in-laws' home, among other things, teenage Archana became fascinated not only by her husband but also by Mr Hall's fatherly care and warm stories. An endless source of creativity, Mr Hall often helped Archana refine her painting skills and took on the role of educating the latest addition to Keshav's household.

One afternoon, while Archana was painting a landscape, Mr Hall began one of his stories. 'You know, Archana, the Chinese are known for their incredible resilience.'

Archana looked up, her brush pausing mid-stroke. 'Really?

Tell me more, Mr Hall.' Tales about Chinese industriousness intrigued the 16-year-old.

Mr Hall smiled, leaning back in his chair. 'Imagine the seafaring men from the Orient reaching San Francisco to get a share of the East Sacramento Gold Rush. The pigtailed Orientals were in for a rude surprise. Except in a few camps, the white Americans often shut them out of staking claims to any of the gold mines speckled across the valley. Bathed in mud, these men were allowed to scour the already-excavated claims for any remaining gold dust left by chance, but only after the Yankees were done digging and panning in any given lot along the river.'

Archana's eyes brimmed with tears, much like her husband's had when he first heard the same story.

Archana pouted, her heart filling with sheer compassion. 'So, in the end, what did the Chinese fortune seekers, not allowed to dig, do for a living?'

Mr Hall pulled out a picture of an Oriental man from Shanghai with a waist-long braided pigtail. Archana stared long and hard at it.

'They spread out between San Francisco and the American River in Sacramento... And they did exactly what I would have done under the circumstances.'

Archana grew so animated that her chair nearly toppled backwards. 'What is that?'

Mr Hall chuckled, enjoying her enthusiasm. 'The Chinese bounced back from the affront by finding their niche. Instead of chasing gold, they quietly started business ventures in many small mining towns, such as in the Bayside neighbourhood of San Francisco. When imprisoned, the immigrants cut their long hair off to prevent lice. Not far from the telegraph posts, pine trees and piers, they set up laundry shops and restaurants. To please the miners, the toilers even learnt to cook bear meat. They took up laundering, sending the miners' soiled clothes all the way to Shanghai to be cleaned and starched.'

Archana's eyes widened with amazement. 'How long did it take for the clothes to come back?'

Mr Hall leaned forward, his voice dropping to a conspiratorial whisper. 'Hauled by Chinese junk boats, the pressed pants and bandanas came back in three months. Today, it has become the world's largest and most thriving Chinatown, even bigger than the one in Calcutta.'

After one such Sunday evening session of storytelling and dining, Keshav approached Mr Hall. 'Over the years, I have noticed that you have not only shared your stories with young people like my son but also with many of your women patients. Even with my late wife...'

Mr Hall nodded, his expression thoughtful. 'Yes. It is the mothers of today and tomorrow who will shape the future. So, what better way to instil a pint of compassion in the next generation than by talking heartily with these young brides?'

The man of art and inimitable conscience had an uncanny ability to be exactly where he was needed most.

Keshav's voice trembled slightly. 'God bless you, Reverend. With Sheela gone forever, I feel so alone. I'm so grateful you keep a watchful eye on my family. The people of Madaripur and I must have done something good in our past lives to deserve someone like you...'

Mr Hall caressed his scraggly beard, his eyes soft with understanding. 'I do not know what it is, but something in your son Mukund reminds me of my youth.'

Keshav faintly smiled, his heart heavy but grateful. 'That is nothing but our good fortune.'

Life in Keshav's household continued, marked by the rhythms of farming, the bonds of family and the infinite stories shared around the hearth. Mukund and Archana's bond grew stronger, nurtured by the wisdom and warmth of those around them. Despite the envy and malice of their neighbours, they found solace in each other and in the enduring legacy of love and resilience passed down through their family.

Chapter 12

Of Trials and Tribulations

ARCHANA'S EXTREMELY WEALTHY FATHER, ROY BABU, HAD long forsaken all selfless Kulin ideologies and become an amoral go-getter businessman. His family's fortunes had peaked four generations earlier when his ancestors profited heavily as ship merchants for the East India Company.

Keshav had erred in understanding the prenuptial terms of his son's marriage proposal. The agreement was sent as a written statement from Pabna, and Keshav, without thoroughly reading the addendum in small print, signed the document and sent back a carbon copy.

According to the legally approved and court-stamped proposition, six months after the marriage, Roy babu required his new son-in-law to live in his home. Thus, the newly married Mukund needed to move to the gigantic Pabna estate with his bride. The self-absorbed and wealthy Roy zamindar also wanted his daughter's husband to manage one of his large Burma teak lumber businesses, effectively making Mukund a *ghar jamai*, a son-in-law who lives in his wife's parents' home along with them.

The acid test for the newly married youth from Madaripur arrived sooner than expected. Two months after Mukund's marriage, Archana's mother suddenly died of *kala-azar*. The Pabna zamindar and his sons immediately insisted that Mukund honour his prenuptial agreement by joining their household within the stipulated four months. As Archana was Roy babu's only daughter, he saw her return as a partial solace for the void left by his wife's passing.

Meanwhile in Madaripur, the news of Mukund's imminent departure devastated an ageing Keshav. On the fateful day, his head throbbed like an ignited cannonball. Standing behind the zamindar, the cook, the manservant, the guard and Bonka cried silently. The zamindar helplessly watched from the mansion's second-storey balcony as Archana and Mukund's freshly repainted stagecoach readied to depart from the gravel-topped courtyard.

From her earliest memories of childhood, Archana's snobbish father came across as a remote and inaccessible telegraph pole amid a highland. Before her marriage, she had watched in quiet disbelief Roy babu's insistence on going to bed only in imported nightgowns and after smoking a European cigar. To date, she remained clueless as to why her father had watched silently while one of her brothers nearly whipped a petty pickpocket to death in their foyer for stealing a mere 25 paise coin—a theft committed out of desperation after two days of starvation.

Archana harboured deep resentment towards her father for disallowing her mother from visiting her ancestral home to be with her severely ailing mother just because the month was considered inauspicious for long journeys. As a result, Roy babu's wife never saw her mother again.

As they prepared to leave, Archana reassured her father-in-law, 'Baba, your home is now my permanent home. I will be back soon. I am a guest in my father's house, and as they say, like fish, houseguests begin to stink after three days...'

Keshav comforted her. 'Archana, take care of yourself. Do not worry about me. Now, travel safely to your father's home.' Inside, he felt like choking himself to death for uncharacteristically not reading every line in the agreement before signing it.

Though her husband was duly accompanying her, and she was returning to her own childhood home, the newly married girl's mouth felt dry, an unknown fear gnawing at her.

Keshav, overwhelmed with emotion, suddenly broke down in tears and cried out to his beloved daughter-in-law, 'Oh, Archana, my little mother, who is going to take care of me? Who will cheer me up with my favourite songs?' His dispirited frame was wracked with the sharp return of painful gout.

Just then, an equally flustered Flanagan entered the balcony.

Mukund turned to his father's erstwhile pressman and typesetter. 'In my absence, I hope you will take care of my father and everything else.'

'Of course. I am now your family, am I not? And there is Bonka, Afzal and Mr Hall.'

'You will also need to take care of Bonka and my horses.'

'Yes, yes, do not worry. I will be shuttling frequently between my home and yours.'

Mukund tried to console his father. 'We will not stay in Pabna for too long. Between Archana and I, we will somehow figure out a way to escape the contract. In the meantime, Baba, will you be able to manage...all alone?'

Keshav pensively waved his progeny goodbye, his voice tinged with resignation. 'My son, do not fret about my well-being. The mistake is mine for not fully reading your father-in-law's legal agreement.'

Archana fell at Keshav's feet and lamented, 'My father has tricked you miserably... I do not wish to leave this home and live in his.'

Helping her up, Keshav gazed at his daughter-in-law with great affection. 'My child, you are completely innocent. I know that. The trouble is, I momentarily forgot one silly, unchanging reality about life.'

Archana looked up at him. 'What is that?'

'When it comes to both money and affection, no one is ever truly content with what they get from life. They always want more and then some more. Now go on... Jimut is waiting to take you to the boat.'

A warm blustery wind seemed ready to roughen the newlyweds' journey. Mukund opened the stagecoach door and helped his wife get in. They were headed to the river station, from where they would then take a *bajra* to Pabna.

As soon as Mukund settled inside the stagecoach, it took off towards the riverside. The bajra was scheduled to depart for Pabna shortly.

Flanagan and Keshav waved for as long as the cantering stagecoach remained in sight. Apprehending their protégé might fall into a life of laziness and leisure under the influence of his rich, controlling father-in-law, their hearts hammered like never before. News of Roy babu's ill nature and brutish behaviour had reached their ears only after the wedding.

From the day they arrived in Pabna, Mukund's life changed radically. He now lived with his wife's two brothers—Kanak and Suhash. Archana's long-deceased elder sister's husband, Mihir, also lived with them. Trained as a physician, Kanak was the only kind soul who treated Mukund and Archana decently. The rest were unkind to the bone, especially Mihir.

Mukund missed everything about Madaripur—the people, the activities he grew up with and especially his customized bajra. He also yearned to backpack and sightsee with his wife whenever he wished and to participate in the village plays. Though Mukund was blessed with a devoted wife, Mihir and Suhash maintained only a façade of civility and kindness. Whenever the Roy patriarch was not around, Mihir and Suhash adopted the subtlest of ways to slight the youth from Madaripur. At times, they grew bold enough to also throw darts at his young wife. Meanwhile, Roy babu and Mukund occasionally engaged each other in polite conversations.

Mukund quietly regretted his fate, for not being the master of his own castle, no matter how modest. He did not wish for a life of luxury under any circumstances, be it in the estate of either zamindar—his father or his father-in-law. Though inherently a free-spirited man, Mukund did feel deeply attached to his roots, which had lasted for nearly 300 years around Dhaka. The main trouble was that his father-in-law was endowed with a huge ego and rigidly set ways. If possible, the haughty Roy zamindar expected the whole world to assiduously follow his notions of robust personal habits, work ethics and recreational norms. For example, as part of an early morning wake-up call, a hooded hawk routinely came to his second-floor bedroom balcony.

Unlike Keshav, Roy babu did not waive his farmers' loans during occasional droughts. When wells threatened to run dry and crops died, no changes were made to the accounting ledgers to ease the farmers' woes. When the lands dried up, the farmers could only worriedly watch the skies and pray for rain.

Archana's ancestral mansion's central pathway was illuminated with lamplights imported from London, and the garden alleys were lined with sculptures and grottos. A curving, gradient-filled, wood-and-stone aqueduct delighted visitors and residents alike. At any moment, the towering Roy babu simply needed to lift his cane, and two willing servants would race to execute his next command.

In the Roy estate, every aspect of life was meticulously controlled. Each family member had a particular chair assigned to them in the living room, dining nook and even in the *majlis* hall, where overdressed singing girls with painted faces from Lucknow, Benaras and Allahabad were invited once a month. In the name of levity, nothing could be rearranged or disrupted even for a day. Archana's father's bad temper and rigid rules made every resident of the mansion live in fear and Archana terribly missed her late mother, who had been so accommodating and beautiful.

Mukund, too, felt the weight of this oppressive environment. At least twice a week, he was subtly pressured into joining the card game sessions with Kanak, Suhash and Mihir. The patriarch, inhaling from his gilded hookah pipe, silently watched the nightly frivolities. Mihir, who lived in the mansion as a parasite solely based on Suhash's patronage, seemed to be the secret mastermind behind many of Suhash's, as well as the ageing zamindar's decisions. Bucktoothed and curly-haired, Mihir had a singular obsession—to enhance his clout as well as Suhash's control within the Roy estate. Despite the opulent lifestyle, his skin seemed perpetually dry, like a drought-affected tree.

Kanak, the only principled and industrious son, was subtly undermined by Mihir and Suhash, who schemed against him to appear more worthy in the eyes of the zamindar. Both resented Roy babu's decision to make Mukund a live-in subjugated son-in-law, fearing another claimant to the family assets. Like his deceased mother, Kanak was a man of few words, often lost in his thoughts. His father did not rely on him for matters concerning the farms or the estate. After two local physicians left the village to practise in more profitable villages, Kanak took it upon himself to learn medicine, dedicating years to studying under a brilliant retired doctor. He selflessly prescribed medicines to the poor peasants who could not afford medical care.

On the other hand, before his marriage, Suhash conducted an unofficial, covert competition to deflower as many young daughters of peasants in the area as he could in one fateful year. Some of the girls, living in unhygienic hovels from the time of their birth, did not mind losing their virginity for a few months of luxurious living.

Nearly a century had passed since the faujdars, the *kannungos* and the *amils*, who were quite active in land revenue collection during Mughal and Pathan rule, had been replaced by British collectors. The walk from Roy babu's stagecoach parking spot to his mansion's porch was no more than 40 yards. Yet whenever the British collector from the Pabna *kachari* showed up at the Roy residence, a dark-skinned orderly invariably fussed with a parasol above the collector's head to shield him from the sun-baked day. While chaos reigned everywhere else in the mansion, Suhash typically ushered the collector into the living room, where they discussed the penalties likely to be levied on the Roy family for deliberately delaying paying land revenue taxes and other farming and fishery-related infractions.

Dressed in a burgundy vest and a dark Victorian frock coat, and flashing an emerald-cut solitaire diamond ring, the burly, moustachioed collector settled on the *malmal* and *reshmi* divan, shifting his weight from one side to the other. Later, he sent his final assessment in writing. All said and done, the effectiveness of the kickbacks discreetly arranged depended on the Brit's mood; sometimes it worked and other times did not.

During his early days in Pabna, Mukund tried hard to contribute to his father-in-law's estate. When some of the huge *beels* became shallow due to steady siltation, he proposed to have them cultivated by poor, unemployed sharecroppers in the area, believing it would benefit both his father-in-law as well as the farmers. But Suhash dismissed the initiative, even snubbing Mukund in front of the part-time farmers.

Mukund gradually came to know many of the farmers by name. Every day at dawn they took turns to drop off wicker baskets heaped with fresh vegetables and fruits at the mansion's porch. During the first week after his arrival in Pabna, he was often the only one up at that hour. Beholding the only son-in-law of the household at the crack of dawn, wilfully and cheerfully carrying the wicker baskets to the kitchen, one of the flabbergasted cooks dropped a bowl of freshly heated milk on the floor. Despite belonging to a family as wealthy as his in-laws, Mukund was used to being handy around the house. He gaped in utter confusion as the three female cooks broke into fits of giggles while watching Mukund bring in pails of water from the backyard well.

When the burden of being a cloistered ghar jamai grew too heavy, Mukund found solace in fishing with Kanak or sitting quietly with him and Archana by the pond overlooking a hillock. He found it hard to reconcile the excesses of Roy babu and Suhash's lifestyle with the harsh realities of the world outside the estate's walls. For example, on the same day that his father-in-law indulged in a 12-elephant parade on his birthday, a disabled leper seeking money for a new pharmacological treatment was turned away from the mansion's main door.

Whenever out in the woods, Mukund listened intently to the woodpeckers tapping on a tree as they searched for insects beneath the bark, occasionally hearing the louder knocks that signalled the birds were carving out a nest. Sometimes, Mukund crafted and flew colourful kites in the sky, but his attention often shifted to the plight of those around him.

When the scorching late afternoon sun beat down on overworked farmers' wives working in the rice and jute fields and they collapsed due to exhaustion, Mukund would scoop them up in his arms and take them home. On the day the mansion's washerwoman lost her only child to typhoid, she sat with her knees drawn up, rocking the lifeless body of her child, her moans eventually dulling into a low sorrowful hum. Unable to invoke a miracle that would alleviate her pain, Mukund went berserk and ran frantically around the mansion like a crazed bull, pointing his index finger skywards. Many such pathetic hazards plaguing the workers in the rural outskirts often devastated Mukund.

At night, when Mukund lay in bed, Archana wrapped her arms around her husband and tried in vain to comfort him. Whenever he was alone at home, Mukund found himself hallucinating. The countless British wall clocks, European oil paintings, pewter ware, wall-mounted showpieces, figurines, cutlery, chinaware and other expensive curios his father-in-law had collected over the years seemed to mock him and his apathy for imported luxuries.

If not for his loving wife, Mukund would have disavowed the contract that bound him to this life. He had tried hard to endear himself to the successful, self-absorbed traders, but even after three years of marriage, they were yet to make him feel at home.

Mukund regularly attended the monthly evening of jatra. Sometimes the overly painted faces of the male actors, disguised in the bright, loud costumes of heroic, melodramatic and historically rich female characters, brought comic relief to his oppressed soul. The histrionic laughter, romantic monologues directed at the moon, earth-shattering cries for help and the clanging swords of noble, saviour princes granted him a make-believe sense of hope. He was captivated by the way they strutted and performed on a knee-high square stage about 20 feet on each side, efficiently supported by an intricate truss of diagonally hitched bamboo poles, fastened by long nails and coconut ropes. Lost lovers, devilish traders, tragic, epic heroes such as Nawab Siraj-ud-Daulah, fearless warriors like Meghnad and Abhimanyu, the female bandit Debi Chaudhurani, the ill-fated Shakuntala, Kapalkundala, Bali, Sita, Prince Karna and even Raja Ravan—all found their share of ardent fans in the rapt, paan-chewing, spellbound audience seated on the matted ground around the square.

Finally, late in the cloud-scudded night, Mukund would walk back to his wife's house. He rarely took up his father-in-law's offer to use one of the several opulent stagecoaches; Suhash had never met anyone from an aristocratic Brahmin family who loved to walk as much as Mukund did. The lad from Madaripur particularly enjoyed walking upon the gravelly roads by the nearest railroad tracks. He would wondrously gape at the roaring iron horse with thick big wheels and an imposing smokestack as the steam engine's black smoke billowed high in rolling clouds and its loud whistle filled the air!

With very little work assigned to him, Mukund's in Pabna seemed to stretch endlessly, marked by reflection and growing disillusionment. He found himself reminiscing about his most recent train ride from Dhaka to Calcutta—the sagging telegraph wires, the rhythmic clatter of the rails and the swaying compartments, and the way the conductor, donning a black jacket with brass buttons, had checked everyone's tickets with a small hand-held metallic punch. As eight to ten connected bogies lurched at top speed, Mukund marvelled at how steam could generate so much power to pull the weight of hundreds of passengers along with the heavy bogies. He missed the familiar comforts of his home—Mr Hall's wide-brimmed straw hat with a blue ribbon, his mother's gentle chidings whenever he soiled his new shawl, and Flanagan's small mother-of-pearl pocketbook with little steel clasps in which he kept his money and the way the amazing Irishman turned down salary increases offered by his father.

Amid the grandeur of his wife's ancestral home, Mukund found himself trapped in a life of structured rituals and snobbish, self-righteous devotion. Slowly, his purpose and vitality began to wane. The only respite from the growing sense of despair came when he was all alone in the bedroom with his passionate wife. Their warm physical consummation of love at night kept his innermost spirits hopeful, offering a brief escape from the bleary days.

During Mukund's absence from Madaripur, Joggeshwar, Bonka and Afzal seemed to be doing a great job helping Keshav and Flanagan manage the estate. Before moving to Pabna, Mukund had briefed and transferred the daily sustenance tasks of his father's estate to these kinsmen and Flanagan. From time to time, under the guise of supervising far-off fisheries, Mukund sneaked a visit to Madaripur alone for a few days. He learnt that Mr Hall had started inoculating the peasants of Madaripur with newly invented tetanus and diphtheria vaccines. In fact, following a terrible accident, Afzal's eldest son had received a new lease of life owing to the timely tetanus injection.

~

Three long and difficult years passed slowly by. Mukund grew increasingly despondent, torn between his inner desires and the weight of his responsibilities, sometimes spending his nights visiting old ruins of temples and cremation grounds.

During this time, two sons were born to him and Archana— Aneek and Avirup—bringing joy into their otherwise difficult lives.

Although their marriage had been arranged, compounded by the prenuptial agreement, Archana, gentle and soft-spoken, loved Mukund unconditionally. Day after day, she quietly observed how her brother and Mihir slighted her husband. Even Roy babu sometimes jumped into the fray.

When Mukund wanted to help four flood-affected and displaced refugees from Rangpur by giving them part-time farming work on the Roy estate, Mihir opposed the idea and convinced Suhash to overturn Mukund's decision. The card game nights were the worst, and Archana always stayed away from the dreaded tables filled with steaming cups of tea, tubes of hookah and heaps of deep-fried snacks. Mukund bore these slights with stoic endurance, responding with monosyllables and ambiguous rhetoric.

One summer afternoon, Bonka made an unannounced visit to Mukund in Pabna. The latter's angst knew no bounds as he watched the blatant mistreatment his in-laws' extended family meted out to the tribal. The fact that he was Keshav's and Mukund's most trusted aide did not seem to matter. During Bonka's two-day stay, Suhash's wife offered him stale rice and an unclean, torn undershirt as a change of clothes. Mukund endured until one night when Mihir scolded Archana as well as one of the cooks for forgetting to add dates to the tomato chutney. Even Suhash's mild chastisement of his brother-in-law for the overkill did not help. For Mukund, his beloved wife being insulted by her siblings in her own home was the last straw—he could no longer honour his prenuptial promise to his zamindar father-in-law.

Archana, the ever-quiet girl, also broke down and began to vociferously plead with her father and brothers to release her husband from the agreement. Tears freely streamed down her cheeks as she moaned repeatedly, 'Do you not see what is happening to my husband? He languishes here, prey to the whims Suhash and Mihir?'

Kanak lost his customary gentility. Shaking with despair, he snapped, 'Yes, Baba. Have some mercy on our one and only sister. Let her and her husband go home to Madaripur where they belong. Let them go.'

One of the ageing female cooks, having the presence of mind, came forward to comfort Archana's children, who stood nearby, silently watching their grief-stricken mother's pleas, too young to understand the scene unfolding before them.

Seeing his only daughter crumpled at his feet, Roy babu's kinder sensibilities began to stir for the first time. At long last, his rigid exterior, moulded by years of aristocratic pride, finally cracked. He helped his daughter to her feet, and Archana wobbled into his arms like a toddler learning to walk.

Kanak was the only one who had sensed his sister's quiet suffering as she witnessed her husband's humiliation for years. Often at loggerheads with Suhash, Kanak had long strived to overturn his father's mind, hoping to reverse the zamindar's cruel and unrealistic decision. He seized the moment. 'What do you say, Baba? Is it not time to send Mukund, our long-suffering sister and our two nephews to where they truly belong—to Madaripur, their home, their family?'

Roy babu unexpectedly raised his arm, as if to calm Mukund's long-crushed hopes. He said softly, 'Mukund...is there something you would like to ask for yourself or your family before you return to your estate?'

Mukund responded, 'In matters such as these, I defer to my wife.'

Archana glanced at her husband and replied, 'You have suffered much more than I have. It should be your call.'

Wiping away tears of happiness, Archana knelt and touched her father's feet.

Roy babu then addressed Kanak, 'I am sure you will find great joy in arranging for your sister's return to Madaripur.'

Both Kanak and Suhash nodded approvingly, regardless of the latter's true feelings at their father's sudden change of heart.

The zamindar suddenly enquired, 'Where is Mihir? I have not seen him these past two days.'

No one knew his whereabouts.

Chapter 13

Homecoming

As promised, two weeks later, Roy Babu stood in the foyer, ready to bid farewell to his daughter and her family. Kanak had diligently arranged for Archana's return to her in-laws' home on a full moon night so that their bajra would not run into fishing vessels.

As their peacock-shaped bajra sailed past the familiar meadows of Pabna, a rejuvenated Mukund and his equally gleeful wife watched the star-speckled sky. Their two small children had fallen asleep in the most secure sleeping room of the vessel. The couple quietly slipped into the innermost chamber, away from the three-man crew and four guards armed with swords and rifles. Forever freed from the nosy maids of the Pabna mansion lurking just outside their bedchamber, they made love. Mukund's woes melted away as he lost himself in the warm valley of her bosom. In a single thrust, he embedded himself within her. He rode her hard and bloomed inside of her primal desperation for sensory delight. Mukund felt hungrier than ever. They went on until the bajra's woodwork creaked, before wandering out to the upper deck of the opulent bajra.

The night sky soothed their long-frayed nerves. The oarsmen and the guards, stationed far out of earshot, worked in companionable silence for hours. Occasionally, they broke into jovial laughter or sang riverine songs. At the other end of the boat, the youngest boatman prepared their meal over firewood carefully set on a sheet of cast iron to prevent any risk of fire.

The cook had packed food for the couple in a large tiffin carrier. After eating voraciously, they stretched out on a long lounge chair.

Seated side by side, Mukund could still smell the remnants of his passion on her as he held her close. By morning, they would reach the beloved waters of Madaripur. Mukund's homecoming companion, Bonka, slept on a cloth blanket at the forefront of the boat's deck.

Mukund gently cupped his wife's chin with his fingers. 'I'm so glad we are going home to Madaripur. How will I ever thank you enough for setting me free from the shackles of being a subservient son-in-law?'

Archana smiled. 'You'll clear your debt if you stay here with me as I gaze at the star-filled sky all night.'

Mukund was astonished. 'Are you suggesting that we sleep here...on the bajra's upper deck?'

Archana's eyes twinkled as she replied, 'Why not? This foot-long wall gives us privacy from the oarsmen's eyes...should any of them get curious.'

Mukund said, 'One more thing...I must resume...'

Moonlight danced upon Archana's breathtaking face as she asked, 'What is that?'

Mukund replied, 'Work with Flanagan to print and distribute nationalistic leaflets and mini newsmagazines.'

Archana's eyes lit up with enthusiasm. 'Yes! Did you work in your father's basement office? The cook told me that once a British Raj policeman raided the room. Is that true?'

Mukund nodded. 'Yes, there were two raids. I was barely a teenager then. My father was deeply involved in the cause.'

'At a glance, the room looks like a library during the daytime. The printers must be hidden in the annex behind one of the giant bookshelves, which is a sliding door. Am I right?'

Mukund smiled. 'Exactly. My father is willing to go to jail if that means seeing the freedom of his nation. But he is terrified for me. He knows of a few cases where budding nationalists were never seen after the initial incarceration.'

Knees raised and huddled near her chin, Archana played with her nose ring as the boat glided swiftly along the moonlit river despite a strong and persistent wind. She quietly snuggled to her husband, seeking warmth. Soon, covering themselves with a thick blanket, the couple fell asleep.

Mukund and Archana were rudely awoken by an ear-splitting explosion as the bajra lurched violently, nearly capsizing. The full moon night seemed to be in its last hour. The terrified couple saw the crew and Bonka running about the deck, tossing bizarre-looking jute bags overboard.

Alarmed, Mukund asked, 'Bonka, what are you throwing away?'

Bonka hastily replied, 'A boatman just found two bags of explosives. One of the other men set it on fire and jumped off the bajra.'

One of the three oarsmen cried out, 'I had a bad feeling about that traitor all along.'

Another hollered, 'He must have been set up by Mihir Babu to kill us.'

A light sleeper, Bonka had been quick to detect the smell of the inflammables immediately after the first ignition, and hence was able to throw most of the deadly home-made explosive bags overboard in time.

Archana began to cry silently, unable to believe that Suhash's brother-in-law would stoop to such wickedness. Recovering somewhat, she asked, 'We have left the mansion Mihir covets. Why can he not leave us alone? We are going home without any of the opulence my father has.'

Mukund sighed as he looked up at the unperturbed night sky. 'Get used to the fact that there are some people who feel so inadequate about themselves that they begrudge anyone who comes into their orbit. It does not matter that we have never harmed them or even intended to.'

'I think Mihir has been after our blood from the day you questioned one of our farmers' excessive drinking habits.'

Feeling much calmer, Mukund replied, 'It does not matter when Mihir's viciousness began. The important thing is that, thanks to Bonka's vigilance, we are alive.'

Archana nodded gratefully. 'Yes, just like Bonka's father saved your life when you were a child, now he has saved ours.'

'Indeed, Bonka must have been my brother in a past life.'

When they finally awoke the next morning, the sun had already risen over the emerald-green horizon. The river breeze had changed its direction, and the trauma of the night before seemed like a fading memory. Mukund suddenly sat up, his face serene yet immeasurably intense. A crew member had already served little Aneek and Avirup their breakfast of milk, flattened rice and date palm molasses.

By then, their boat had safely reached the riverside mooring of their village.

Chapter 14

A Race Against Time

A MONTH AFTER RETURNING TO MADARIPUR, MUKUND BOUGHT a new printer and resumed the production of nationalistic leaflets. The three-year hiatus when he was in Pabna had hardly dampened his drive. Despite cousin Joggeshwar's advice, Mukund refused to discard the old printer his father had first used, seeing it as a symbol of their legacy. Meanwhile, Archana, still reeling from Mihir's actions, decided to sever all ties with her father and siblings. The hiring of hoodlums by Mihir with the intent to kill her and her family was the last straw that broke the camel's back.

On a rainy dusk in July 1897, Mukund had just returned home after attending the first rehearsal of acclaimed writer Rabindranath Tagore's *Bhanusingha Thakurer Padabali*, a play written in the Brajabuli language to be performed by the village's jatra group he periodically sponsored. Everyone hoped that the team would have it ready for the upcoming autumnal festivities to celebrate the worship of Goddess Durga.

Shortly after his return, the estate's weathered clerk, or *gomosta*, arrived to provide a highly summarized weekly payment and income account of the estate. His russet face looked tense as he delivered the news to Mukund, not bothering to mince words. 'Chhoto Korta, Bonka's doctor says Bonka has tuberculosis!'

Mukund was appalled. 'What? Are you sure about saying such a terrible thing?'

The gomosta stood firm, his fingers briefly brushing his grey, nautical beard. 'I am sure. The *morol* came by my house to tell me about it.'

Born into an upper-caste Kayastha family, the clerk had come to Madaripur in his teens, working his way up from a farmhand during Keshav's heyday. It all happened suddenly after his own ancestral village in Kishoreganj had been partially washed away by an overflowing river.

Mukund eyed his subordinate as if he had never heard such ludicrous hogwash before. His face contorted in disbelief as he struggled to comprehend the weight of the news. He could feel bile rising in his throat. From the pocket of his kurta, he pulled out his Swiss-made Omega watch, glancing at the time. 'Is it too late to go and see him now?'

The gomosta nodded. 'The weather is too severe… It is certainly too late.'

Mukund was still absorbing the heartbreaking news. 'Only a month ago, Bonka saved our lives…'

The rain outside intensified, hammering down with a vengeful fury. As twilight faded and the darkness of the storm enveloped the porch, drenched leaves stuck miserably to the earth below.

Picking up a jade paperweight from the table, Mukund hurled it at the wall. Luckily, the ballast narrowly missed the multicoloured panes of one of the windows. After retrieving the paperweight to its original location, the gomosta looked at his master with terrified eyes as though he had just seen a river filled with piranhas.

'Is there anything else or can I leave?' asked the gomosta.

Mukund, his eyes wet and distant, dismissed him with a wave of his hand.

In the fading light of the day, Mukund eyes wandered across the sun-bleached bricks of the curved porch where tufts of weed had sprouted between some of the layers.

As the gomosta, unbothered by the downpour, bowed and stepped out into the rain-soaked courtyard, Mukund's mind raced. He must hire the best kobiraj and allopaths. He recalled reading in the *Calcutta Gazette* that tuberculosis fatality rates were declining. Bonka had saved his life a few weeks ago, and now Mukund must do the same. In his eyes, Bonka, the humble Bagdi tribesman, was nobler than most humans he knew.

The next day, as soon as the sun climbed over the front yard's mango tree, Mukund, sleepless and restless, bolted out of the front door. Mounting his brown horse, he galloped to Bonka's home. The TB-infected tribal's place was located not far from his estate.

Considering the risk of contagion associated with the disease, Bonka's young wife respectfully stopped their master at the door. In the far corner of the mud-thatched hut, Bonka lay on a *khatia*, a wooden cot meshed with jute ropes, staring blankly at the low, decrepit ceiling. Unable to speak, he turned his head slightly towards the large bamboo-propped skylight to catch a glimpse of the still-stormy sky. Tears oozed from his eyes as he saw Mukund crouch slowly within arm's reach. Bonka was dressed only in a loincloth, with a rough linen cloth draped over his rickety legs. His once-strong frame seemed to hold only half the flesh it had before. His sunken cheeks and protruding ribs revealed the full devastation of the illness—a shocking transformation in just a few weeks! Bonka's wife, fearing infection, had already sent their two daughters to stay with their uncle in a nearby hut.

～

Mukund had never formally studied medicine, though Keshav once had high hopes for him to do so. However, through his avid reading of medical journals, Mukund had kept himself well informed about most diseases and their remedies—old and new. As word of Bonka's condition spread in the local area, several neighbouring traders approached Mukund with the same demand—'Find a way to evict Bonka and six other families from our pargana.'

These were traders close to Mukund's nosy neighbour, Girindra.

One day at dawn, Girindra came over to meet Mukund and remind the latter of the infectious nature of TB. 'You know I checked with the British DMO (Divisional Medical Officer) at the Mitford Hospital in Dhaka.'

Mukund had just returned after praying to the sun god for Bonka's recovery from the terrace of his bajra, anchored along the river bank.

He ushered his neighbour into his study and slumped into a chair. 'What did the DMO say?' he asked.

Girindra replied, 'He said TB is caused by bacteria and spreads through the air from one person to another. And I am also told that presently, there are no solid cures or vaccinations available.'

Outside, the tinkle of cowbells filled the damp air. Roosters crowed incessantly as Archana stepped out to dip her feet in the backyard pond. Her pet frog hopped over and plopped under a spider web stretched between cattails. It was time for the hungry amphibian to catch flies from the web. An ageing, playful monkey repeatedly thudded to the ground from a banyan tree.

Mukund's patience wore thin. Girindra, despite his veneer of civility, had shown his ruthlessly selfish ways too many times. He was known for bribing his way through the kachhari, offering black rabbits to white bosses as well as the brown babus when they refused cash for favours. His sole focus was always on protecting his wealth and family, a trait that stood in stark contrast to his wife's more compassionate nature.

Mukund recalled an incident where Girindra's disregard for others had left a lasting impression. Mr Hall had snagged his toe in a wayside gunny bag and fallen from his bicycle. Despite seeing the injured man, Girindra had sped past in his stagecoach, pretending not to have seen the injured Englishman lying on the roadside just because he was late to pick up his newly arrived imported rifle from Calcutta. In contrast, barely days earlier, the medic had made a call to Girindra's house and helped the midwife deliver the latter's daughter, Koli.

Then there was the time Girindra's guards unleashed a brutal lathi charge on drought-stricken farmers protesting for tax relief—a promise Girindra had made and later retracted. The image of those peaceful farmers, beaten in Girindra's front yard, still burned in Mukund's memory.

Before Girindra could continue, Mukund cut him off sharply. 'I will handle this my way unless I am directed otherwise by the chief medical officer based in Dhaka.'

Having barely slept, Mukund felt utterly drained. He drew a ragged breath and continued, 'Let me assure you that I will isolate Bonka well enough so that no one else falls ill because of him.' His mind raced as he struggled to figure out the most effective way to contain this new bout of TB. The thought of life without Bonka, who had saved him not long ago, sent a shudder through him.

Mukund knew all too well that Girindra's concern for people was far from genuine. The well-off businessman's primary worry centred around the fact that some of his closest friends lived not far from Bonka's home. Mukund resented his neighbour's complete lack of empathy. Girindra enjoyed the luxuries of his auction-bought British stagecoaches and exploited low-caste labourers, showing no concern for anyone but himself. The businessman had bribed officials to get a road built near his granary and refused to contribute when rats overran the adjoining fields, leaving Mukund and others to foot the bill.

Girindra remained unyielding. 'All it takes is for Bonka to cough or sneeze near someone, and that's enough to spread TB,' he said, his thinly veiled smile more exasperating than ever

'I have already isolated Bonka in my disused stable during his treatment. Have you even visited him? He has been coughing up blood for the last six days.'

Girindra ignored the question. 'No matter how much you downplay the risk, I will be forced to file a complaint with the DMO's office if you do not immediately isolate Bonka in a remote shanty.'

Mukund, now seething but hiding his irritation, was flooded with memories of Girindra helping spice trader Nobin in a price-fixing scandal. He knew the conversation could easily spiral out of control if it continued. Hiding his aggravation, Mukund stood and showed his guest the door.

Bonka was kept in isolation for 40 days. Every day at dawn, Archana chanted the ancient *Mahamrityunjay* mantra in Sanskrit, praying for Bonka's recovery. She observed nirjala fasts on every ekadashi—the 11th day of the moon—while Mukund insisted that Bonka receive both allopathic treatments and ayurvedic herbs and roots.

Bonka fought his illness with remarkable fortitude, bearing it like a man accustomed to facing grave dangers since childhood.

Casting his robes, suits and bow ties aside, the smock-clad Mr Hall laboured tirelessly in his medicine lab. Despite his exhaustive attempts—rummaging through shelves of thick, heavy jars filled with dark-tonic remedies—none succeeded against Bonka's worsening condition. The Englishman, desperate and disheartened, found himself grasping at straws as he searched for a miracle cure.

Mukund and Flanagan took turns to disburse endless rounds of medication they managed to source among the TB-afflicted patients of Madaripur. They shuttled among various British doctors in Dhaka, Calcutta and even Patna. The young zamindar and the Irishman roamed far and wide, scouring dense, bustling markets and remote fishing villages in search of hope. On frigid nights, they often found themselves resting in humble shanties made of woven straws, where their impoverished hosts gathered around sputtering fires for warmth.

Despite the spectre of Bonka's death looming upon them, there were rare moments of levity, like when Flanagan wore his thick woollen socks as earmuffs. Another time, Mukund scraped a rare variety of barnacles off the bottom of one of his fishing boats, hoping to extract a rare remedy suggested by a travelling medicine man, but still, nothing worked. As Bonka's health continued to deteriorate, Flanagan penned letters to the divine, leaving them in the care of Mr Hall, pleading for celestial mercy to spare Bonka from the grip of death. Meanwhile, Archana spun the cotton wheel obsessively, tears flowing freely as she tried to cope with the possibility of losing Bonka. She wept silently, pouring her grief into the rhythmic spinning to ease her heavy heart.

At night, Archana whispered tender reassurances to her husband, who had vowed to sleep on the floor until Bonka recovered. Mukund cradled Archana's face in his hands. Moments after kissing her forehead, the travel-weary man went off to sleep. After a few nights, Archana too deserted their marriage bed and joined him on a jute mat spread out on the cold marble floor. As a sign of her devotion and grief, she gave away her most prized saris, embroidered with delicate blue corals, to homeless women near the ghats.

On certain days, nudging the cook aside, she prepared *rui* fish with spiced yoghurt for Mr Hall and a few mendicants who passed by her garden gate. The self-absorbed gomosta, who did not care for Bonka, made a face whenever Mukund went to check on Bonka's health or the zamindar's wife cooked for him. However, neither of the two stopped their diverse efforts to please divinity and earn a new lease on Bonka's life. Nothing worked. Death still lurked around Bonka and the other Bagdi homes.

One day out of the blue, a hermit from Haridwar arrived at Mukund's doorstep. Renowned for his ascetic powers, it was said that he could endure the harshest Himalayan winters through his mastery of pranayama and yogic exercises. His skin, smooth and glossy, defied his age, and with a swift flick of his long hair, his carbuncle-like eyes sparkled with an inner brilliance. Whispers followed the hermit's arrival—some claimed he could stand on his head for hours; others said he had withstood the cold like no man alive. Mukund welcomed him as custom dictated, hoping that this enigmatic figure might hold the key to Bonka's salvation.

The swamiji observed Mukund carefully and said, 'It seems there is something on your mind.'

Mukund put his hands inside the pockets of his hand-printed batik kurta. 'Yes. I have never asked any ascetic for anything to meet my family's needs and wish lists before.'

Swamiji nodded. 'I know. That is precisely why I have come to visit your home when the opportunity presented itself.'

Mukund, feeling desperate, said, 'But today, I will break my rule.'

Swamiji assured him, 'And I will help…if I can. I know what you will ask. It is about seeking a tribal's recovery from a grave illness.'

Mukund's eyes widened in disbelief. 'How do you know? Did someone tell you about our Bonka?'

Sitting serenely, the Swamiji's posture was one of calm yet sharp attentiveness. 'Nobody told me about Bonka. But as I was heading your way, a detailed vision came upon me. In it, I saw Bonka's battle with a life-threatening illness.'

Dumbfounded, Mukund fell to the swamiji's feet. 'How do these amazing truths come to you so easily?'

The octogenarian Swamiji smiled, gently lifting his host back to his feet. 'I wish I knew. All I know is that my twin brother had the same powers as I do. But soon after he tried to use them for personal gain, he lost his healing powers as well as his speech forever.

Mukund implored, 'Please help Bonka to live… He is not

related to you by blood or in any other way.'

'I know that too. Why do you think I have come here after declining requests from many a wealthy landowner of Dhaka and Barisal?'

Mukund clasped his hands in reverence. 'It must be the Almighty's mercy.'

'It always is. It is also because of your recent austerities. Like you, the God I serve has no caste or creed.'

Mukund was quietly elated by the Swamiji's words. 'How do you know all that?'

'I wish I knew how I know such things!'

Swamiji reached into his satchel, retrieving an assortment of herbal roots he had brought from Gomukh, the source of the Ganga River, along with a scroll of detailed mixing and serving instructions. 'Just follow these directions carefully and Bonka will not only live but outlast you for sure,' he said with unfathomable conviction, as the sandalwood tilak comprising three vertical stripes shone on his wide forehead.

Mukund exhaled in relief. 'May he just do that. By the way, I will not wash my hands for a very long time.'

Swamiji, with a hint of amusement, asked, 'Why not?'

'Because I have just touched your hallowed feet with these coarse, unworthy hands. Who knows whether I will be so blessed ever again!'

The ascetic touched Mukund's forehead for a moment. The next day before dawn, the Swamiji vanished as swiftly as he had arrived. Mukund's desperate mission proved worthwhile. Bonka gradually recovered from TB and most of the Bagdi families also survived the outbreak.

Chapter 15

Ashes of Deceit

MUKUND'S OLD FAMILY FOE NOBIN HAD BEEN SOWING THE seeds of discord by spreading vile rumours among the local populace, particularly targeting six- and seven-year-old primary school children. He claimed that anyone who came near a Dom would be struck by incurable diseases. His manipulative tactics aimed at turning the village's sentiments against Mukund, who supported the Doms. As fate would have it, however, life's calamities have a tendency to strike in tandem, and Mukund's mortal journey was no exception.

After Mukund managed to reopen the district court case against Nobin over the wrongful death of Nontu, he began receiving anonymous letters threatening his life. But Mukund refused to withdraw the charges against Nobin.

Meanwhile, the case against Moi slowly moved from the lower appellate of faujdari and *diwani* to the district court. In 1895, however, the district court judge suddenly dropped the case. No one knew why. The grapevine speculated that the inaction resulted from pressure upon the judiciary from the ultra-affluent government quarters of the Dhaka Collectorate. It seems that at will and at any time, Nobin could get the married but occasionally adulterous deputy collector from Farnborough to do anything.

This shakedown came about after the collector made the mistake of sleeping with the promiscuous native daughter of Nobin's business partner, a fellow spice wholesaler. Somehow, with the possession of the bundles of amorous letters written by the Englishman to his youngest lover, Nobin seemed to be in the driver's seat. The deputy collector was desperate. To keep the unscrupulous Nobin's mouth shut and prevent blackmail, he wrote to his erstwhile classmate and now the Dhaka district court judge to drop the case against Nobin. After all, his tough-talking, gun-carrying wife, an heiress of a Scottish castle, had given him one last chance to stop philandering.

Being exonerated of the pending criminal case did not comfort Nobin enough. He now sought revenge against Mukund because of the negative publicity the lawsuit had caused.

Nobin's opportunity arrived soon. As far as the village knew, Moi still worked for Nobin as an overseer. He had grown obscenely rich from a variety of dubious ventures. Wearing a sherwani, having shaved off his beard and moustache, and his curly hair hidden in an expensive turban, the Arakanese hoodlum was now hard to recognize. Nobin's associates had even taught Moi to talk like a Babu, in urban vernacular as well as bits of English. Most importantly, Nobin decided to make use of Moi's insider knowledge.

One afternoon, when Mukund's fields were filled with ripe grains nearly ready to be harvested, Nobin sent Moi to meet Mukund. Accompanied by two smart-looking mates, a well-disguised Moi introduced himself as Nobin's business partner in the spice trade.

Mukund completely failed to recognize Moi, the reckless fisherman he had once caned for endangering his pregnant wife's life by gambling and drinking. As a sign of goodwill, Moi presented Mukund with a beautiful parrot, a symbol of renewed friendship that the simple-minded Mukund accepted with pleasure. Trusting in nature, Mukund did not suspect any foul play in the warm gesture.

After Archana and Bonka personally served the guest and his three aides a delightful lunch, Moi made an unusual request.

The erstwhile fisherman pointed to the main road where several cartloads filled with new brass utensils, dhotis and saris stood waiting. 'If it is all right with you,' he began smoothly, 'can

I swing by some of your farmers' homes and personally distribute the gifts my business partner Nobin Babu has sent with me?'

Mukund glanced at Archana, who stood quietly in the patio, before answering, 'I do not have any objection to that.'

Bonka quickly offered, 'I will be glad to accompany you and guide you through the winding village glens.'

Moi's lips curled into a thin, serpentine smile. 'That will not be necessary,' he insisted. 'I know the area well.'

A flicker of unease crossed Bonka's mind. Moi's belligerence, though veiled in politeness, triggered a feeling of mistrust, but he could not imagine the magnitude of the visitor's sinister intentions. Bonka had always found the former fisherman distasteful—loud, obnoxious, and prone to foolish jests.

Moi nervously looked around. As Keshav's erstwhile employee, he did know the area well. He cautiously readjusted the silk turban. Moi knew that he must ensure his identity-concealing wrap did not dislodge itself from his head, thereby exposing his all-too-familiar and excessively curly hair. Pretending not to have heard Bonka, Moi and his three mercenary gangsters hurriedly left the compound.

That evening, many of Mukund's farmers gathered to sing and dance by the riverside. In preparation for a feast, three goats were being beheaded near a small pond. While Moi met and greeted the farmers and their families, he quietly added a soporific and narcotic mixture into their large earthen pots filled with date palm wine. Later at night, when all Mukund's farmers fell into a deep, drugged slumber, Moi's aides fanned out in various parts of the fields and quietly set them on fire.

It was well past midnight when Moi returned to Mukund's mansion, his face partially obscured by an indigo-dyed tagelmust scarf. In a final act of betrayal, he set the mansion of his erstwhile master on fire with his own hands.

By the time the sleeping farmers stirred and realized the

magnitude of the incident, the multiple fires had already spiralled out of control. Despite his as well as his servants' best efforts, Mukund had to endure the agony of seeing his ancestral mansion succumb to the flames. By the wee hours of the morning, the mansion was largely gutted and Mukund's fields of cash crops and grain lay in ruins. His groves, orchards and plantations were also reduced to ash. As dawn broke, some of Mukund's frantic staff could be seen crawling through the debris, desperately trying to salvage any valuables they could find. By daybreak, Flanagan joined the round-the-clock efforts to salvage the estate's landmarks.

Miraculously, Keshav, Mukund, Bonka and all others in the household remained unharmed. They had escaped through an underground tunnel built by Mukund's grandfather, taking refuge in their smaller, modest house hidden in the thickets about a mile away.

The fire burned the crops so savagely that the scorched earth remained barren for several seasons. Additionally, someone had poisoned Mukund's main fishery while bizarre, fruit-destroying insects invaded his orchards.

The damage extended to his printing business, with one of the presses destroyed beyond repair. Their hapless days began to blur together with deep despondency as Mukund's cash reserves began to dwindle.

Almost middle-aged by now, Flanagan offered to take up two jobs to help Mukund in his darkest days but Mukund firmly declined his offer.

To make things unimaginably worse, Mukund's eight-year-old son, Avirup, was diagnosed with blood cancer. Mukund and Archana sought treatment from several European doctors in Calcutta. Suddenly, Mukund found himself financially reduced to dire straits.

Well educated in schools and colleges of Calcutta, Mukund had, till now, not found it necessary to work for anyone but himself. For the first time, Mukund was forced to seek new sources of revenue through teaching and ventures other than his ancestral farms. Nobin's vengeance and Avirup's inexorably expensive medical treatment ushered in such a day.

Despite exhausting all that they had left on medical treatments, their younger son's health continued to deteriorate sharply and within a span of eight months, Avirup passed away in a Dhaka hospital.

Barely a month after Avirup's death, the family moved to their only surviving home, located on the fringe of their three-mile-long estate in Madaripur.

For months, Archana mourned Avirup's loss. One day, after completing an ekadashi fasting ritual, she abruptly stopped talking about him. Whether she also stopped grieving in the quiet recesses of her heart remained unknown to those around her.

Chapter 16

Rising from the Ashes

THE RAMSHACKLE HOUSE MUKUND AND HIS FAMILY WERE forced to move into was made habitable through the concentrated efforts of Bonka and the farmhands. Despite being financially wiped out by the arson, Mukund managed to keep paying his employees' salaries with coins, ornaments and the gold chest they had pulled out of the mansion's kitchen cellar before escaping. Tucked away in the thickets, their new home had a large peepul tree nearby—the only thing Archana liked about the long-neglected house.

Nine-year-old Aneek dealt with his suddenly disrupted life by sitting by the barn's trough, tossing corn bits to the ducks that had survived the fire or casting overripe bananas to the cows. The lad also helped the pushcart labourers bringing in replacement bricks and paint supplies for the house's exterior makeover. Overnight, their grand family mansion had been reduced to ashes. Leaving her home, Bonka's wife stood by Archana's side almost all the time. Ageing Afzal Mian's four sons and five other Muslim farmers also scoured the countryside to recover Archana's veena and sarangi, which had been stolen in the fire's aftermath.

Meanwhile, Bhabesh, Nobin and Moi, the triumvirate of malice, continued their nefarious alliance, but not without spasms of internal envy. As united as they appeared in their burning desire to hurt Mukund, they periodically encountered schisms of ego. When Bhabesh showed off his growing prosperity through imports of Virginia tobacco or Canary wine, Nobin countered with acquisitions of French porcelain and Chinese tea. Moi competed by indulging in Havana cigars and the fanciest spices from

Ceylon. Their ostentatious displays came at the expense of their constituents—mostly hand-to-mouth farmers. Now and then, they hired portraitists from Dhaka and Calcutta to capture their opulent lives on canvas, preserving their insatiable greed for posterity. Unwary British invitees watched their extravagant flamboyance in awe during holiday lunches, dances and wedding banquets.

Mukund began to earnestly look for employment in the various departments of the British Raj, extending his search into the private sector as well. Flanagan, too, faced the need to find a stable job. With both of his printing presses destroyed in the fire, the Irishman's work was impacted as well. A few weeks later, he landed a lucrative employment offer at the collector's office in Mymensingh district. However, considering Mukund's monumental difficulties, Prachi advised her husband to decline the position. Consequently, Flanagan stayed close to Mukund and helped the latter salvage and rebuild whatever was possible of the charred printing press, groves and farms.

Like every weekend, on the third Sunday of January 1900, old Mr Hall arrived in Mukund's stopgap home. Despite his age, he still rode his bicycle with the ease of a teen. He approached the situation with a veneer of normalcy, cheerfully enjoying the lunch prepared by Archana and her cook, as if only a minor misfortune had befallen Mukund and his family.

Despite cutting back on many luxuries, including food, Archana continued to prepare a special Sunday meal for Mr Hall, ensuring even small details like two halves of lime, pickled carrots and two sizzling green chillies found their place near the rim of his brass plate heaped with his favourite vegetable curries.

Since the night of the fire, Mr Hall had laboured every day to save at least two dozen homeless children from outbreaks of various diseases. Many had been caught between flaming logs and heavy bamboo posts that once held their cottages together. Now their limbs needed to be amputated to save them from gangrene. Nature, too, had simultaneously unleashed her share of tribulations in the form of diphtheria, typhoid, malaria, yellow fever and other maladies.

One native doctor from Manikganj had joined Mr Hall's frenzied effort to save lives from the aftermath of the arson. The doctor, along with Mr Hall, tirelessly treated the injured, using anything from chloroform to pyocyanase—one of the first antibiotics precursors. The smells of burnt skin, disinfectants, and the foul odours of infection no longer fazed him. In his selfless dedication, Mr Hall, for the first time in decades, looked more like the suited-up medical doctors he had gone to college with in England, the same doctors who now drove in sleek cars and made house calls to the wealthy neighbourhoods of Calcutta.

Producing a recent newspaper cutting from the folds of his white robe, Mr Hall insisted Mukund apply for a job opening in Darbhanga. Robert Weatherilt, an Englishman who worked as the senior property manager for Maharaja Rameshwar Singh of Darbhanga, had advertised the position.

The estate, located in Mithila, a few hundred miles north of Calcutta, was reported to have annual earnings exceeding Rs 3 million. The maharaja was seeking a deputy property manager and Mr Hall believed it was the perfect opportunity for Mukund.

'Mukund, you are like a son to me. This is the opportunity I have been telling you about during the last few days. Look ahead.'

The Englishman had apprised Archana beforehand, who wholeheartedly endorsed the suggestion. Staring into her husband's eyes, she implored, 'Yes, yes, please look at the ad. It will not cost you anything to consider it.'

Devastated by the arson, Mukund blurted out, 'Indeed. But tell me…where are Bonka and Aneek?'

Archana replied, 'Our son has accompanied Bonka to buy some

new medical supplies for Mr Hall from a pharmacy in Dhaka.'

Mukund's gaze turned towards the open window, where the remnants of his once-grand estate lay in ruins. He stared at the scorched land, burnt bricks and shattered glass, holding the newspaper cutting between his long fingers. He remained silent for a long time, his square jaw clenched in simmering anger and a sense of revenge. His ulcer, exacerbated by his stress, throbbed with renewed vigour.

In the distance, Mukund's displaced farmers had set up countless canvas camps. No one knew how soon the temporary shelters could be dismantled and the planters devoted to him could rebuild their clay, bamboo and straw cottages. One of Mukund's unscathed farmers, carrying a shoulder bag of repair tools borrowed from his master, watched his young son, slightly bruised from the fire, wash his face at the river's edge. Together, they trudged back to work on their damaged hut. A public works department operative had left behind a wooden sluice box on the river's edge, while another out-of-work farmer raked through cartloads of debris and rubble. Nearby, a few of his deadbeat companions slumped listlessly by an irrigation stream. Mukund could also catch a glimpse of the farmers, hungrily devouring their lunch in his barn.

In the past two weeks the zamindar's wife had struggled with an uneasy acceptance of the world's treacheries and the spite of vindictive people like Moi and Bhabesh. Sick to her stomach, she too glanced briefly outside at the heaps of dried-up rubbish left by the fire.

Since the night of the arson, Archana had hardly eaten. In utter solitude, she hopelessly grieved for her deceased son and the home they had lost, drawing away from everyone, even her husband and elder son, Aneek. At dusk, she would retreat to the abandoned fields, crying miserably. After a few minutes, she would return with a renewed facade of composure.

From dawn till dusk, Archana remained busy feeding nearly half of the farmers whose cottages had been razed as well. While fleeing the fire, some of the croppers had unknowingly dropped their life savings into marshy ditches. Some of the cattle suffocated and burned where they stood. Overnight, these once-prosperous peasants had been reduced to homeless destitutes.

Archana had been urging the distressed wives of the croppers to find new ways to support their families. They needed to survive first if they ever hoped to reclaim their former lives. Heeding her advice, some of them had begun working as washerwomen and utensil cleaners in the wealthy homes of the neighbourhood.

But Mukund continued to brood. Moi had managed to set ablaze every *bigha* of the rectangular land Mukund owned between his temporary home and the burnt-down mansion. Even the ubiquitous ants and beetles that once crawled under the slushy, verdant rice and vegetable fields seemed dead. The once-fertile land was now covered in a thick, impregnable cover of black soot. While destiny had allowed Archana to save some of her jewellery, her best saris were now tainted with the lingering stench of smoke.

Finally, Mr Hall broke the silence. 'Well, Mukund, what do you say? Are you ready to go to Calcutta for the interview?'

Mukund broke the tension in the room with a surprising statement—'Why not! I will go to Calcutta and interview for the Darbhanga job.'

Mr Hall clapped loudly and Flanagan looked pleased. Jimut also nodded happily from the doorway.

The Irishman assured Mukund, 'While you and your family settle in Darbhanga, Bonka, the gomosta, Jimut, Mr Hall and I will ensure your farmlands are slowly restored. We won't let anyone squat or take over your property. From my own coffers, I will pay your two remaining guards' salaries until you get a job. I will also donate my two heavy-duty hunting rifles. With their assistance, along with Afzal's help and Girindra's three armed guards, I will hold fort while you are gone. My days of duck hunting and going to the Dhaka rifle range are long gone.'

Mukund was sceptical. 'Since when has Girindra started caring about the people around him?'

Mr Hall, ever the optimist, replied, 'Oh, come on! Think positively. Girindra is gradually reforming. Give him a chance… will you? His *paiks* will watch over your property.'

Mukund asked, 'Will that be enough?'

Reassuring him again, Mr Hall said, 'Yes. Girindra will not be alone. There will be Afzal Mian Joggeshwar too! And why on earth do you forget me?'

Mukund was still worried and pressed on, 'But if my wife and I are gone from here…who will take care of my sick farmers?'

Mr Hall's voice rose, 'Just this morning the village kobiraj and I saved five of your men from further infection. Who knows more about medicine—you or I?'

Mukund quickly bit his lip and lowered his eyes. 'Mr Hall, yes, I will move to Darbhanga. I must earn well there…and recoup.'

'Yes. Then return and rebuild your mansion and all other buildings. I will stay right here with Joggeshwar and Afzal's sons to make sure that the collector's office does not auction off your landed assets as abandoned property. I am sure Flanagan will be more than ready whenever I summon him.' Mr Hall added, 'For now, you must immediately apply for the job.'

Mukund nodded. 'Better yet, I will go to the telegraph office now and send a telegram to Mr Robert Weatherilt, informing him that I will meet him in Calcutta for the job interview.'

Mr Hall tried injecting a shot of self-confidence into his ex-student's veins. 'Great move, Mukund. You will get the job. For years…I have taught you the Queen's English, civics and maths.

Besides, your Grecian looks and presentability will charm all of Darbhanga.'

Two weeks later, Mukund's telegram and application earned him a face-to-face meeting with Robert Weatherilt. Born and raised in India, Weatherilt was due to arrive in Calcutta the same day to interview Mukund on the maharaja's behalf.

Before dawn, Mukund boarded the Narayanganj–Calcutta steamer, arriving at Dalhousie Square by late afternoon. It was the most bustling mercantile-cum-administrative block of Calcutta. Accompanied by Bonka, Mukund waited inside a dark and dingy coffee shop. In his interview letter, Robert Weatherilt had specified the rendezvous to Mukund. To give his master a heads-up about the Englishman's arrival, Bonka waited just outside the small eatery.

After an exhaustive three-hour interview, Mr Weatherilt selected Mukund as the new assistant property manager of the Maharaja of Darbhanga.

Chapter 17

Bets and Bonds at the Maharaja's Estate

WHILE WORKING FOR THE MAHARAJA AND ROBERT, MUKUND began to learn not only the intricacies of his new job but also much about the men he reported to. The maharaja belonged to the Mithila Brahmin dynasty, which had amassed considerable wealth over six centuries, living near the India–Nepal border. Despite the region's tumultuous history, including Muslim invasions from Afghanistan and later the Mughal Empire's rise, rulers like Emperor Akbar had unexpectedly patronized their dynasty by granting them the kingship of Mithila. Prior to the 13th century, Mithila had adhered to the Hindu norm of being ruled by Kshatriya kings.

For Mukund, whose zamindar ancestors had never worked directly under either Mughal or British officers, this new arrangement was life-altering. He and Robert formed a perfectly odd pair of colleagues, initially cautious with one another but gradually evolving into a more amicable and productive camaraderie.

Robert and Mukund worked closely together for four eventful years from 1900 to 1904, shuttling through the busy, cattle- and cow-dung-filled backroads of Darbhanga, the maharaja's many trading offices, car-servicing garages in Bhawanipur, sports grounds and crowded auction houses of Dalhousie and Chowringhee.

Smartly handling his role at the estate as well as his side businesses, Robert had accumulated significant cash savings. Years earlier, he had married an 18-year-old Cynthia, whose British ancestors had settled in India in 1755. Now in her 30s, Cynthia still retained a Venus-like charm and beauty. She and Robert had two children—Hubert, a teenager, and another son who had died in infancy, succumbing to the tropical heat of Bihar.

Within months of moving to Darbhanga, Mukund developed a fine friendship with the Englishwoman, primarily through their shared love of chess and their habit of reading the daily newspaper with a fine-tooth comb.

After starting his job in Darbhanga, Mukund, with Robert's help, was able to secure a job for Shanu's nephew in the government. The youth moved to Calcutta and became a young orderly in the Writers' Building—the huge administrative juggernaut secretariat of the British Raj. Living in a modest, tiled shack near St John's graveyard on Park Street, the 20-year-old faced a major turning point six months later. One night, while walking home, armed with a well-hidden *bhojali*, he apprehended a pair of hoodlums who had just robbed and desecrated a grave in St John's graveyard. The grave happened to be of an eminent officer of the erstwhile East India Company. After all the facts were uncovered, the outcaste youth was recognized for his bravery and promoted briskly. In a few years, he became the chief security guard at the Writers' Building.

More than just a full-time job, the duo of Robert and Mukund managed numerous aspects of the huge Darbhanga estate. Their duties extended beyond cars to include overseeing paintings, sculptures, building maintenance, livestock and even managing disputes. When visiting Calcutta, Mukund occasionally dabbled a bit in rugby with Robert and his friends in Royd Street. On holidays, if they happened to be in the big city, the odd pair would rent twig- and hay-littered boats idling on the banks of the Ganges River. Leasing a downstream sailing vessel at Re 1 per day from overworked farmers who worked in the verdant rice fields near the Jagannath Ghat steamboat station, the duo would then cruise towards the Bay of Bengal. On more than one occasion, Mukund had to give his somewhat inebriated friend a few pokes to wake him up. As they cruised quietly down the river, they watched fishermen cast their nets into the water—some from large, aristocratic ships owned by zamindars, and others from simple wooden rafts.

During other trips, Robert and Mukund would stroll from the Great Eastern Hotel to the artificial lake in Eden Gardens. Sitting on a bench and munching on freshly roasted peanuts, they would quietly admire the pagoda that British soldiers had brought after they defeated the Burmese in the war of 1885. When Mukund found himself alone in the big city, he often visited the three-storey Indian Museum. Standing by the ashes of Lord Buddha's bones or antiques excavated from Mohenjo-daro, he would observe the people around him.

One morning, on behalf of the maharaja, the two men arrived at a grand auction house in Chowringhee. The intent was to buy a rare painting by Sir Joshua Reynolds. However, upon arrival, they learnt that they were a day too late. Mukund grew increasingly anxious about how they would face the maharaja back home.

Holding the black wrought-iron handrails of the Victorian mansion, a dhoti-clad Mukund stood on the long veranda on the first floor of the mansion. Worried, he asked, 'So what do we do now? How can we return to Darbhanga empty-handed... Without the painting?'

Robert replied, 'For the last two weeks, we tried our best, did we not?'

'Yes.'

'The head auctioneer gave us misleading information about the auction's date, did he not?'

Mukund sighed. 'Yes. Last time we were here, the chief manager at the auction company told us it was happening today. Today, he is not even here, and his deputy is running the show,' replied Mukund, dejected.

'Next time we are here in the city for any reason, remind me to wring the auction manager's neck. It will bring me great joy to personally punish him for his extreme callousness or deliberate favouritism.'

Mukund was curious. 'What do you mean?'

'I think he deliberately misled us about the date of the Joshua Reynolds painting auction.'

'But why?'

'I believe he has a close friend who wanted the painting. It was likely auctioned to him.' Robert continued, looking around, 'In any case…let's enjoy Calcutta and this blessed day.'

Mukund asked, 'And where will we go?'

'You tell me. Though I personally see nothing wrong with a visit to the Calcutta Racecourse, name your preferred destination.'

'How about the Calcutta Public Library?' suggested Mukund.

'All right. They recently renamed it "Imperial Library", did they not?'

Mukund's ears reddened instantly. 'Yes, they have. Lord Curzon has finally opened it up for public use.'

By now, Mukund felt close enough to his boss to freely express his concerns about his growing notions of nationhood. 'I hope these cannons will not be used against Indians if we were to speak our mind about freedom.'

Robert concurred, 'I pray so. From what I have heard from my informers at Raj Bhavan, Lord Curzon seems to be a consummate imperialist. He is already talking about how the Nizam of Hyderabad must cede! But you may be wrong about one thing…'

'What is that?'

Robert inched closer to his deputy. 'Regardless of what is in my blood, this land called India is mine as much as it is yours. Do not forget that I was born here just like you.'

Mukund stood his ground. 'Yes, of course. Perhaps you may like to prove it someday. But why is the British government always talking about dividing this land?'

'What are you getting at?'

'Have you not heard the whispers coming from Curzon's Raj Bhavan that Bengal needs to be divided?'

'Yes, some...' admitted Robert.

Mukund pressed on, 'And Darbhanga, the land of the legendary Maa Sita and our current source of employment, is to be taken out from Patna division? Lately, why is there only news of the partition of states, divisions, districts, *sadars, mahakumas* and parganas? Is nothing served well through unity and consolidation anymore? Do you need more examples?'

Robert, ever patient, replied calmly, 'No. But when I hired you, did I promise to give invincible explanations for every action taken by hundreds of senior officers of the British Indian government?'

Mukund simply nodded in acknowledgement.

Robert continued 'And do you think I know what rapport the deputy commissioner has with the powerbrokers in Raj Bhavan as well as Writers' Building? Who am I? I am just like you. I drink to the hilt, play nine-hole golf and yes...I like the racecourses, horseracing and steeplechasing. When offered a chance, I admire the fine-looking ladies at the Tolly Club and Rangers Club. Since I am a married man...most of the time...I try not to do anything more. But let me tell you, many women at these places are so persistent!'

Mukund paced up and down with disgust.

'You will not tell Cynthia about my drinking or my fondness for women, will you? Please be careful with your tongue. This is just man-to-man talk.'

Mukund could almost see Cynthia's cheerful figure and even smell her peppermint fragrance, her red scarf flapping brightly like a banner as she ran after her son. He could not help but like her Indian mannerisms—the way she tucked her legs under her when sitting down and how she expertly rolled the last mouthful of bourbon around her mouth with flair.

Robert resumed the conversation, 'What do I know of politics and administration? I do not snoop around Raj Bhavan or the exclusive clubs in Calcutta. My skin may be white and my accent may resemble King Edward VII's, but in the end, I am just the property manager for the Maharaja of Darbhanga. And he could let go of me at any time…despite my white skin!'

Mukund interrupted him, 'King Edward VII is a kind man.'

'Really?'

'Yes. In many letters he wrote to his friends or relatives, he criticized how native Indians are treated by British officials. He once said: "Because a man has a black face and a different religion from our own, there is no reason why he should be treated as a brute."'

Robert tried to soothe his conscience. 'Embarrassing… I did not know our king shared sentiments like me. Where do you read such stuff?'

Mukund replied, 'From an old British magazine shipped to you from Bristol. Last month, you discarded it one evening after three glasses of single-malt Scotch!'

Robert grinned as they climbed into the grey, two-row, ribbed seats of a brand-new five-passenger car, imported from the Premier Motor Company in Indianapolis. Barely a month earlier, the maharaja had personally sought out the best agent of American exports in the Dalhousie area and overseen the purchase of this vibrant crimson vehicle with a pressed steel frame. It was meant for use by his senior-most staff whenever they were sent to Calcutta. Robert always ensured that the automobile was stored in a rented, fully covered garage in Kyd Street before leaving for Darbhanga.

Though based in Darbhanga, Robert and Mukund frequently visited Calcutta. Much of the maharaja's investment and business interests were in and around the capital of British India. Over time,

Robert became increasingly drawn to the afternoon horse races at the city's racecourse. Occasionally, he would commission Mukund to handle tasks with the Premier while he hopped onto an electric tram for a quick peek at the racecourse thrills. Sometimes, he bet heavily and lost. Before long, he grew into a compulsive visitor of the Calcutta Turf Club whenever the maharaja dispatched him to Calcutta on business.

Cynthia was somewhat aware of her husband's gambling habits. For a while, a small and unscrupulous band of Italian gamblers, veterans of Monte Carlo casinos, had created a powerful nexus that Robert joined. These men lived near the only Armenian Church in Calcutta. Armed with extensive insider information about the racehorses, they seemed mostly unbeatable.

After a string of losses, Cynthia began to admonish Robert, but without much success. Burdened by raising a young son and supporting a huge orphanage, she desperately sought Mukund's help, pleading with him to keep Robert away from the racecourse.

Mukund devised ways to minimize Robert's wagers so that even when he lost, the impact was minimal. Despite his best efforts to curtail Robert's gambling, Mukund one day succumbed to the same temptation.

A novice in betting, he lost a significant portion of his savings in a single day at the Calcutta racecourse. Distraught, Mukund returned home immediately and confessed his grave financial indiscretion to his wife.

Archana cried out, 'Oh my God! Just a year ago, the fire destroyed our farm and home. You promised Joggeshwar you'd help him pay off his loan. How could you squander our precious money meant to rebuild our mansion?'

Mukund's eyes grew misty with grief. 'Robert swept me away. Never again will I gamble. Nor will I ask the maharaja or Robert for additional money.'

Archana rarely scolded her husband, but this day was one notable exception. 'How could you have wasted so much of our cash reserves? Especially after the arson...'

Mukund pleaded, 'Forgive my foolishness... I was hoping to recover some of the losses from the fire. I will make up for it.'

Archana remained firm. 'No matter how hard-pressed we are, we must still help Joggeshwar.'

'Yes. But how?'

Amid the odd aftermath of her husband's rare but sheer recklessness, she calmly offered an unexpected proposal, 'Our *kansari* has given me a fine suggestion.'

Mukund looked up sceptically and asked, 'What has he recommended?'

'He travels much and is savvy about the latest market demands. To get out of our tight monetary spot, I have decided to make and sell soap. People are leaning towards buying cheaper soaps made in our land.'

'You must take care of your frail health first.'

'Don't worry, I will be fine. Flanagan has sent a fair amount of money too.'

'Where did you get the idea about making soaps?'

Archana smiled. 'Who else but your eternal well-wisher—Flanagan.'

Mukund's face lit up with admiration. 'Amazing human being! Never running out of ideas or hope or the desire to help even strangers. Despite his white skin... Nowadays, Flanagan also does not make all that much...working for the government.'

To rescue her husband from monetary troubles and his inability to financially help Joggeshwar, Archana hurried to her only maternal uncle's home in Barisal. Her uncle's estate clerk helped her accumulate an ample quantity of shell lime, sesame oil, Fuller's soil, goat fat and salt. Thereafter with the help of the family chemist, they came up with a customized soap-formula. As soon as Bonka heard, he wired his desire to volunteer and showed up in Barisal three days later. Once a week, Bonka and his aide began to take batches of the home-manufactured soap to a *haat* in the town's main market. Scores of boxes were quickly sold out.

Within six months, Archana made enough profit to fulfil her husband's commitment to pay off Joggeshwar's loan. The day the amount of money was raised, Mukund rushed to Barisal and brought Archana home. Joggeshwar symbolically thanked Archana by gifting her one *pasari* of sugar molasses, sweets and fragrant wax brought from Bhawal, a thriving locality near Dhaka.

After returning to Darbhanga with her husband, Archana resumed her role as a housewife as if nothing had happened, pretending that she had returned from a long vacation. No one besides her maternal uncle ever came to know about her soap-making venture.

Both Robert and the maharaja remained oblivious to Mukund's lapse into gambling and Archana's subsequent short-term business that had saved them.

However, Mukund, true to his promise, never gambled again.

Observing his British boss, Robert, Mukund steadily learnt the intricacies of his job. With sheer amazement, he also noted how elaborately layered the Indian division of labour seemed to be. Robert had a driver who chauffeured him everywhere, whether for business or personal trips. A servant always opened the door for him every time, while a peon loudly announced his arrival. Even for short trips, perhaps just a furlong away, the driver insisted on driving, and Robert was never allowed to carry so much as a parcel, no matter how light.

Mukund also accompanied Robert and the maharaja of Darbhanga on hunting expeditions in the Terai jungles. The royal hunting party travelled in their imported cars along rustic, makeshift roads and trails until the terrain became too rough, at which point they switched to riding ornate elephants hired from pre-selected local scouts. The rattle of the snare drums during the hunts fascinated Mukund, and he watched in awe as a pistachio-green parrot remained perched firmly on the maharaja's shoulders. Bonka timed his visits to Darbhanga well to join the hunting trips. Being an excellent lancer, he was an asset to the marksmen during reconnaissance trips. Barking hounds followed the slow-moving party with ease. While the king and his regal retinue looked for tigers, in some cases, they often returned with a fox. On more accessible trails, the maharaja used cars fitted with extra-wide footboards for servants to stand on. High-powered lamps were also used to dazzle the eyes of the tigers, making them easier targets.

Over time, Mukund's and Robert's families grew close, often travelling and vacationing together. Their young sons, Hubert and Aneek, developed a deep bond of friendship.

It was not only the maharaja of Darbhanga who led a luxurious lifestyle—by the early 20th century, Indian rajas and maharajas collectively purchased nearly 850 Rolls-Royce cars, a testament to their opulence. Witnessing and catering to such grandeur for four years seemed enough for Mukund. His uneasiness steadily grew, and he felt that his country had far more pressing goals to achieve.

Throughout the last decade of the 19th century, Swami Vivekananda, a renowned monk from Bengal, had awakened the world with his message of universal brotherhood. His legendary speech at the 1893 World's Parliament of Religions in Chicago had left a deep impression on Mukund. Vivekananda, a mystic and nationalist, had proclaimed that no nation could prosper— spiritually or industrially—while under foreign rule. Liberty, he argued, was the first prerequisite for progress in any domain.

This message resonated deeply with Mukund, and the idea of freedom began to stir within him like a chronic arrhythmia. Restless and increasingly dissatisfied with his role, Mukund quit his job as the maharaja's property manager in mid-1904. However, Robert and Cynthia remained his lifelong friends.

Chapter 18

Unspoken Desires

MEANWHILE, ROBERT AND CYNTHIA'S MARRIAGE BEGAN TO show irreparable cracks. By the end of July 1904, Mukund learnt from his Darbhanga colleagues that the Englishman had moved permanently to London and was living with a mistress half his age. Robert had failed to return from a two-week trip to England, where the maharaja had sent him to negotiate and purchase imported goods. Both Mukund and Cynthia were aware of this fact.

Thanks to the four years of a generous salary and bonuses from the maharaja, as well as the unwavering support from Bonka, Flanagan, Mr Hall and Joggeshwar, Mukund and Archana had mostly restored their fire-ravaged Madaripur mansion, along with its farmlands, fisheries, orchards, lakes and ponds.

In August 1904, steeped in melancholy, Cynthia arrived at Mukund's home to find out the latest news about her estranged husband. After all, Robert was Cynthia's first love. Mukund had no new information to share, except that Robert's mistress was a young lawyer in the UK. Archana insisted that Cynthia stay for lunch, to which Cynthia readily agreed. Ever since they first met and lived as neighbours at the Darbhanga estate, she and the zamindar's wife shared a complex mix of envy, admiration, scepticism and wonder about each other. During lunch, they politely enquired about each other's sons and praised each other's paintings with great gusto. After the meal, Cynthia departed.

A week later, Mukund visited her home in Calcutta. Cynthia did not hide her joy at seeing him.

Mukund hurriedly said, 'I have come to give you some money the maharaja owes your husband as salary.'

Cynthia sighed, accepting the large envelope. 'I see. Is that all? Did you not want to see me?'

The old pendulum wall clock in the living room ticked with quiet indifference. Cynthia's once-soft face was already lined with wear, and she smiled wanly. The loss of one son in infancy and the strain of caring for her surviving, sickly son, Hubert, did not make her life easy.

Unbeknownst to Mukund, Cynthia had harboured an unspoken affection for him over the years; their perspectives aligned and they had grown close in thought and spirit.

Mukund composed himself and said, 'There is one more thing. You once asked me about selling your Darbhanga home. I came to ask if you still plan to do so.'

'I do.'

'In that case, I have a potential buyer you may want to meet. But perhaps you should wait until Robert returns from London. You might also want to consult one of the British officers stationed at Fort William, or maybe your sister's husband, Shawn, who is a senior officer at the Lal Bazar secretariat.'

Handing him a plate of shepherd's pie that he had grown fond of during the Darbhanga days, Cynthia declared her true feelings. 'You are a nice chap. These are attributes money cannot buy. You once saved Hubert from falling off a horse when I wasn't around.'

Mukund was surprised. 'Who told you that?'

Cynthia smiled. 'I have my sources. Over the years, I have come to trust you as much as any fellow Englishman—perhaps even more. But tell me, when will you stop calling me "madam" and use my first name?'

The married zamindar blushed for a moment. 'Thanks for your vote of confidence.'

Cynthia moved forward and hugged Mukund joyfully, while the latter squirmed, uneasy. Then she dropped a bombshell. 'It is now confirmed that Robert has found a mistress in London. If his heart can stray, why should mine lag behind? I have decided... I am going to keep you for my pleasures. Do you mind?'

Mukund was taken aback, unsure if the Englishwoman was kidding or not. Cynthia had never been so direct. A long silence ensued.

Not wanting to be the sole passive recipient of her bold statement and to play it safe, Mukund replied politely, 'But I am a happily married man with a wife who would come after you with her kitchen knife if I were to loiter. You do not know Archana fully yet.'

Cynthia laughed, dismissing his caution. 'You mean she does not submit to your will all the time?'

'No. For both our sakes, you better believe it. Besides, there is little left of my will these days.'

Cynthia teased, 'All right then. Beneath that big, tall frame, it seems you have degenerated into a chicken-hearted man. I never expected that. But you better come and see me in Calcutta whenever I write to you.'

Mukund nodded and quickly headed home.

Some time passed. By this time, Cynthia had moved into her new home, and when she sent a telegram summoning Mukund, he visited her again.

From the terrace of the new Belvedere mansion Cynthia had purchased, she and Mukund watched Diwali fireworks blaze in the cool night sky. Suddenly, tapping his shoulder, the tall woman whispered, 'Mukund, I have something to tell you.'

Mukund, still peering at the semi-dark street below, saw firecrackers intermittently illuminating the scene. A sputtering Opel 1900 sedan rattled down the road, its thick black plumes blending into the night.

Mukund asked cautiously, 'What is it?'

Cynthia hesitated for a moment, then decided to hold back her original thoughts. 'Nothing. Just give these new paintings of mine to your talented wife.'

Mukund responded, 'Is that why you called me here? Or are you still worried about the speeches Viceroy Lord Curzon is giving in Dhaka, Faridpur and other places to justify the long-talked-about partition of Bengal?'

Cynthia shook her head. 'No. I have a far more personal query. Do you still consider yourself happily married to Archana?'

'Yes. I have never really measured happiness in my personal life. Our Eastern ways are a bit different, and you know that. All I know is that to maintain amity when I am wrong, it's best to admit it. When I happen to be right, it's better to stay quiet.'

Cynthia shifted the conversation. 'By the way, I hear Bonka has yet another job. A few years ago, when he got a position as a signaller for the Indo-European Telegraph Department (IETD), was it you who dissuaded him from joining?'

'No, it was Archana.'

'She is rather possessive about her loved ones, isn't she? She wants them near her all the time.'

'Yes. I suppose so...since it would have required Bonka to move far away, even beyond Afghanistan.'

'What will Bonka do in his new job?'

'Telegraph signalling. The British Raj established the IETD in Persia 50 years ago to keep tabs on Russian advances into Central Asia. Now they are looking to increase staff.'

Cynthia, looking puzzled, asked, 'Why?'

'The British Raj hopes to strengthen its communication network in its peripheries and secure a psychological advantage in its long-standing cold war with Russia. According to Bonka's appointment letter from IETD, he has been posted deep inside Iran, near the Russian border.'

'From what I have read in the newspapers, even Englishmen are declining jobs in such remote places. You are the root cause for Bonka being picked for this in the first place.'

Mukund, taken aback, asked innocuously, 'Why?'

Cynthia smiled. 'Why did you have to teach the poor tribal so much English?'

Mukund smiled back. 'For his good, so that he can communicate with people around him, I suppose.'

Though deeply troubled by the Englishwoman's increasingly lonely existence, Mukund quietly took his leave. He headed for the steamer station to head back to Madaripur.

Chapter 19

Whispers in the Rose Garden

Two months passed. In February 1905, Mukund received a telegram from Cynthia, which read: 'Please come and see me again. I am dying of a rare blood disorder.'

Taking the first available steamer from Madaripur, Mukund rushed to Calcutta. As he settled into the mahogany armchair beside her bed, Mukund looked around the room, which echoed the grandeur of the Darbhanga mansions. Large glass windows let in the soft afternoon light, while ribbed columns and marble floors gave the room a cold elegance.

Cynthia lay in bed, frail and misty-eyed, too weak to get up. An untouched plate of soft-boiled eggs, boiled asparagus and sliced cucumber sat on the bedside table. Hubert's sports trophies filled the wooden cabinets, yet the house felt like the saddest place on earth.

'Cynthia, why did you not tell me about your illness when we met last time?'

'Thank goodness you have finally called me by my first name! It is high time.'

Mukund's eyes welled up, his voice thick with emotion as he rasped, 'Answer me. Why did you not tell me earlier about this horrible ailment?'

'The doctor was not sure back then. I hid my periodic morphine consumption from you as well. Stop crying, you grown man!' In the hope of delaying his departure, Cynthia asked her visitor, 'Do you remember, back in Darbhanga, you helped Hubert with maths?'

Mukund nodded. 'Yes, I do remember. Where is Hubert? Have you not told him about your illness?'

Cynthia ignored his query. 'I am dying soon. So, you have to stay with this forsaken Englishwoman for a while.'

Mukund glanced at the ill-fated woman. 'All right. This time, I will stay for two days. But I must first send a wire to my wife.'

'You can stay in the guest room on the far side.'

Impatiently, Mukund asked, 'What is the doctor's latest prognosis?'

Cynthia slowly wiped her dry lips with a damp washcloth. 'I could live for a day, a month or maybe even a year. Did you bring my favourite red pumpkin from Madaripur...from the village lit up by Petromax lamps?'

Digesting the shocking news, Mukund felt as if he were standing atop a powder keg of explosives. A rare smoker, he took out a cigar from a silver box left behind by Cynthia's brother-in-law Shawn.

'Yes, I did bring it from the Madaripur market,' Mukund said, stepping out to the veranda momentarily. He returned with a bulging burlap handbag and Cynthia beamed. Refocusing on her, Mukund exhaled slowly, feeling an uneasy hunch rising within him. 'Is there any other reason you called me?'

Cynthia looked around before whispering, 'Yes. Come closer. I called you to resolve a mystery that has haunted you since childhood.'

'Which one of the many unanswered questions do you have an answer for?'

'Remember you told me long ago about one of Mr Hall's two preteen sons, who ran away from home?

'Yes.'

'Well, that older son was kidnapped by a rascal who was on parole from Dhaka jail. The boy was sold twice by crooked agents and eventually ended up in a decent home in Wales, where a childless couple was looking to adopt.'

Mukund was in utter disbelief. 'You must be joking!'

'No. Shawn is none other than the elder son of your childhood teacher! The younger son died of dengue, right?'

Mukund's mind spun, trying to comprehend the gravity of this revelation. 'How do you know that Shawn is Mr Hall's son? What a twist of destiny! Please go on.'

'The little boy's kidnappers in India sold him to a crook in London, who immediately sold the boy to a blacksmith in Kent. But that blacksmith, lured by the chance to make more money, sold the young boy to a kind doctor in Wales. Though Shawn grew up in a good home, he never fully recovered from the trauma of being sold three times. His temper and sudden outbursts make much more sense when you understand the scars left behind.'

'How can you be so sure about what you are saying?'

'Wait a minute. There is one photo that the little Shawn managed to hold on to through all his turmoil and change of homes.'

Reaching over to her bedside table, Cynthia carefully opened a drawer and pulled out an envelope. From it, she withdrew an old, frayed picture and handed it to Mukund. It was an unmistakable photograph of Mr Hall, Mrs Hall and their two boys, taken on the family's Madaripur house porch.

With trembling hands, Mukund grabbed the picture and turned it around. Written on the back, in faint ink from a fountain pen, were the words: 'My parents and us, weeks before we left home.'

Mukund put the picture back inside the thick envelope and asked, 'Where did you get this?'

'I temporarily stole it from Shawn just to show it to you. You might recall I had seen this very photo in Mr Hall's home when I visited Madaripur once with you and Robert.'

'Yes, I remember that trip.' Mukund paused, and then added, 'Just last month, an old friend of Mr Hall, the district magistrate of Faridpur, came by to check on Mrs Hall's latest condition. She's nearly lost her mind.'

'And what did he say?'

'He's considering sending her permanently to the mental sanatorium in Ranchi.'

'Did he ask for your opinion?'

'Yes.'

'What did you say?'

'I agreed. I am glad they will send her to the Ranchi sanatorium.'

'Good. Hopefully, someday she will come to Calcutta and spend her remaining years in her son's home.'

Mukund deliberated, 'When I return to Madaripur... I wonder if, as a consolation, I should tell Mrs Hall that her elder son is alive, and is an Indian Civil Service (ICS) officer now, happy and married.'

Cynthia nodded. 'I think you should. That is why I told you. I will ask Shawn to see her, and if possible, bring her here.'

Uncertainty clouded Mukund's face. 'But what if he has an outburst again...if he finds out that she was unfaithful to his father?'

Cynthia sighed and looked out the window. 'I think, in the long run, he will forgive his mother. She has already paid dearly for her sins.'

Mukund could not help but agree. 'I think you are right.'

His eyes were drawn to a new painting on Cynthia's wall. Drawn by Emmeline Pankhurst's tireless efforts in seeking voting rights, and social and economic equality for women, Cynthia had become a long-standing admirer of the middle-aged widowed activist from England. As a tribute to her, she had recently painted Pankhurst's portrait based on a newspaper cutting. After being repeatedly manhandled, heckled and arrested, the women of the Women's Social and Political Union, formed by Pankhurst, had resorted to aggressive measures, shattering windowpanes of shops and slashing various trains' leather seats.

Mukund looked away for a moment. He knew that similar

days of violence would soon erupt as close as in Calcutta, wherein freedom-seeking youths might resort to the same tactics. A new wave of hope surged within him.

He handed Cynthia a glass of water, helping her drink. She glanced around to make sure that none of the servants, her sister or her family members stood within earshot. Then with an unexpected boldness, she raised herself slightly from the bed and said, 'I may have only a few more days to live. Why should I hesitate to tell you what I have felt for you for so long? Let me openly express my truest emotion…even if it is for a day…not to the entire world… but to you.'

Mukund, acutely embarrassed, scratched his face and averted his eyes. He responded ambiguously, 'Who said emotions ever followed logic or reason?'

'With each passing year, we realize the people we love become less and less humane. We are often reduced to little more than desperate, apocalyptic animals…'

Mukund, suddenly feeling like a knight bound by an unspoken code, added, '…With only an occasional pang of remorse or kindness in the heart.'

'Since Robert left me, every time you and I have met, instead of me, it is you who sounds bitter.'

Mukund sighed. 'It is because the predicament I see you in is more rampant than you think. And it bothers me.' Without elaborating further, he nervously fidgeted in his chair. For long, he had found Cynthia attractive, but nothing beyond goodwill nourished his synapses. A deeply ingrained sense of loyalty— perhaps genetic—kept him from straying from his monogamous life.

Cynthia resumed speaking with difficulty 'Can we, just the two of us, disappear into the flower garden my uncle still owns in Kurseong? If you must still desist, can we at least have a platonic picnic together, just once, before I die? Can we not smell the roses together, for this one and only time?'

Mukund replied gently, 'Cynthia, it might be best for you to stay quiet and rest. Maybe if you take this medicine, you might live on for the next 20 years. I can do anything for a dear friend and his wife.'

Cynthia interrupted hurriedly, 'You mean Robert's abandoned wife...just that...nothing else... I am not your friend.'

Mukund looked away. 'Did I ever say that?'

His heart ached to comfort the fragile, beautiful woman before him, who seemed to yearn for a tender embrace. Yet despite his intense temptation, he could not bring himself to cross the boundaries often conceived by the writers of passionate romance novels.

Eyes welling up, Cynthia struggled to swallow the doctor-prescribed tablets. 'With such ailments, both physical and mental, who wants to carry on for 20 more years? Certainly not me. Perhaps my heart did not wish to stop beating until I saw you and bid farewell one last time.' Struggling to breathe, she continued, 'By the way, I do not wish my siblings to claim any of Robert's property here in India. Make sure Hubert gets this, and distribute the rest to the native widows' rehabilitation mission I used to run in Darbhanga. You will remember to do that much for me, won't you?'

The Englishwoman pulled out a legal, 8.5-inch by 14-inch document from her study table drawer and placed it in Mukund's hands. Sighing, she said, 'This is my will. The details of my wishes are all written here.'

Mukund took the document. 'It will be executed. You should not worry. I will always keep an eye on young Hubert. But I expect you to live on, for a long time—the young boy still needs your love and support.'

'Yes. I should not neglect Hubert just because Robert has left me for a younger woman. But for now, can you help me to the backyard garden?'

Mukund nodded and carefully carried her outside. The garden was large, enclosed by a sturdy wall, and her old gardener lived in a makeshift den at the edge of the compound. The native stoked a fire in his clay oven to cook a meal for himself, dark smoke billowing around him. Cynthia looked at the scene fondly, her eyes crinkling at the rising exhaust. Nearby, the security guard was securing an outdoor storeroom with a padlock, singing a devotional song in his Bhojpuri dialect.

Settling into a monsoon-stained hammock next to a bush of roses, Cynthia continued to ponder. 'Have you seen a rose or jasmine bud just as it opens its petals?'

After a brief silence, she mumbled again, 'I want to die here—smelling the best roses in the world. Not in a hospital bed.'

Holding her hands, Mukund said softly, 'You are talking too much about death. You are so selfish.'

'Selfish? You must be joking!'

'Only selfish people try to secure their goals by lamenting their fate. At this very moment, as much as you want me to, you know that my inability to hold you in my arms has nothing to do with my wife's qualities or shortcomings. It is about the values I have learnt to imbibe from very early in my life.'

'Do you not care for me at all?'

'As absurd as it may seem, I could flout the values even if my parents were to appear before me at this very instant. If it is any consolation, I hold an indescribable everlasting goodwill for you in a way I have never felt for anyone.'

Cynthia chided herself, 'Only fools like me do not know when to shut up.'

Mukund looked around. 'I do not see Shawn today. Where is he?'

Visibly tiring, Cynthia spoke slowly, 'Shawn has just been demoted and transferred from Writers' Building to Madras. This happened right after he hurled verbal abuses at his war veteran boss.'

'Where is Linda, your sister?'

'Working as a court writer in the high court. I hardly see her or her kids nowadays. She seems busy with the woes of living alone in her mansion and managing her life in Calcutta. But once a week, she brings me the necessary groceries, which I pay for in full. Her children are cared for by an Irish governess who lives nearby.'

'It seems Hubert is doing well in academics. I have been writing to him at his boarding school and visiting as often as possible.'

'I know all about your benevolent help. Hubert mentions you all the time in his letters.'

'Has the divorce between you and Robert been finalized?'

'Yes, a marriage that began with much gusto when I was barely 18 is finally over at 35.'

'Has anyone seen Robert's new bride?'

Cynthia's voice dripped with sarcasm, 'No. But besides the final decree, he has gallantly sent me a picture of his lovely new bride from Surrey. I have it in that drawer. Do you want to see the photo of his new woman?'

Mukund shook his head in disappointment. 'No. The devil has besieged Robert's head. How drastically people change sometimes. How could he play Casanova after creating a family with you?'

Cynthia shrugged. 'Your guess is as good as mine. Even amid the worst of tiffs, not for a single day of our marriage did I make him sleep on the living room couch or deny his need for physical intimacy.'

'Mrs Weatherilt, you still look so beautiful. Does Robert know you are critically ill?'

Cynthia sighed. 'No, I did not tell him. It does not matter. My earthly time is running out quickly.'

Mukund urged, 'Please stop saying that.'

'Forget about Robert…will you?'

'Sure...what do you want to talk about?'

Cynthia, figuring it was useless being a shrinking violet, said, 'The obstinate Hindu that you are, my pounding heart tells me that you and I will meet again in another life.'

Mukund sighed. 'As much as you are beginning to believe in the cycle of birth and death, I have my doubts from time to time.'

Devoid of inhibitions, Cynthia grabbed his thick dark hair with her feeble but elegant hands. 'I hope it is not due to Robert's bad influence, is it?'

Mukund replied, 'No. It seems that all human lives are burdened with their share of misery.'

In a poignant tone, Cynthia, said, 'Soon I will be gone, and none of this will matter. I was a young virgin when I met Robert. Sometimes I wonder why I saved myself for a lecherous chap like him... You crazy man, I have a secret to share. All these years and countless meetings, my hands perspired whenever you came near me. Without ever touching you, I have considered you my secret lover. But you don't care...'

Mukund nearly choked at this sudden admission of her love. But he responded with compassion, 'You have just changed a part of me forever.' Then, in an abrupt shift of topic, he asked, 'What have you been doing lately?'

'Inspired by your wife's amazing paintings, I have been trying to paint too, instead of just buying those pricey ones. Some paintings are here in this room while the rest are in the mezzanine room...' Her voice suddenly trailed off.

'That is wonderful! I will have to see them before I head home. You are evolving from a patron of art to being a budding artist. Well...I think I am making you talk too much.'

Cynthia gently interjected. 'No. I am enjoying every bit. Can you please take me to Kurseong? I want to revel in its natural beauty one last time...meet those quirky, enchanting hillbillies.'

The Madaripur zamindar could no longer turn down the dying woman's wish. Getting to his feet, he said, 'All right. You and I will take a trip to Kurseong. I know Archana will understand. Now, take a nap. In the meantime, I will drive down to the reservation office and get us train tickets.'

Cynthia's eyes lit up. 'Oh yes! One more thing I must tell you—something I have never told Herbert or my husband. This will give you an idea of how deeply I feel about you.'

Mukund's heart pulsed like a marathoner's. 'What?'

'Can you lock the backyard door so no one stumbles upon us?'

Mukund complied and returned to her side. 'Is there anything...I can do?'

'Yes. Hear me out...it is about a painful event in my early life.'

A long, heavy silence followed before she finally began, 'When I was only 14, my mother's brother took me and my brother on a camping trip to the jungles of Topchanchi. My alcoholic uncle had the porters build three separate tents, one for each of us. Late at night, when my brother Paul was fast asleep in the adjacent tent, my predator uncle gagged and raped me.'

Shaken to the core, Mukund held his head with both hands. 'Did you not expose his crime to your mother?'

'No. He threatened to kill me and my mother if I did. At 14, I was convinced that he would carry out this threat.'

'And then...' Mukund's voice trailed off.

Cynthia continued her account, 'When I became pregnant, I told my mother everything. Without informing anyone, including my father, she whisked me away to an obscure little town in Scotland. We lived there for a year.'

Mukund gently said, 'I am guessing no one there knew you or your mother.'

Cynthia nodded. 'Yes. Before leaving India, she told all the folks that we were going to Britain for an extended period for her operation. After placing my firstborn son in an orphanage, we came back as if nothing had happened. Thankfully, my uncle became a supervisor in the Post and Telegraphs department in Indore and moved away. My mother died soon afterwards. So, the secret has been mine to bear ever since.'

Her hands trembling, Cynthia took out a crumpled piece of paper. Handing it to Mukund, she said, 'In this sheet, you will find the orphanage details of where my firstborn was placed. Hubert must know about him, not before I am dead.'

Completely overwhelmed by the weight of her revelation, Mukund asked, 'Cynthia...why do you want to contact your firstborn son after all these years?'

She firmly gripped his right hand and gazed into his eyes as though they were the last two lighthouses left on the planet. 'My inveterate friend, when death is near, many old equations come to the fore. I want to give my eldest son what I have received from my recently deceased father's estate.'

Mukund asked with concern, 'Can someone later malign you by saying that it is unfair to Hubert?'

'A dying woman like me does not worry about such issues any more.'

Mukund nodded.

Cynthia carried on, 'My proud mother wanted to protect her ancestral family's reputation by not exposing her brother's terrible sin. I have not been able to do anything for my first child all this time. Let me help him now—should he need it.'

Mukund glanced towards the mansion's veranda, thinking carefully. 'Should I somehow find your firstborn son, what do I do...if he refuses to accept the money?'

Cynthia sighed. 'Then give it to the poor as you see fit. And give him this letter I wrote for him long ago.'

Mukund, trying to lift her spirits, said, 'Now we are going to take an electric tram and get to the railway station. I bet you have not taken a ride on one of those amazing vehicles.'

Cynthia clapped her hands like an excited schoolgirl. 'And then?'

'And then we are going to head for Kurseong. Show me where your closet and suitcase are... I will pack a few essentials for you. Before anything else, I must send a telegram to Archana.'

Cynthia purred softly, 'Yes, I need a long train ride; just you and me. But let me rest for a while. You have driven my ecstatic brain nerves to the tip of Everest.'

She closed her eyes, attempting to rest. Mukund, still bewildered, quietly wondered what had driven Robert to leave such a beautiful and loving woman for someone else.

Chapter 20

A Journey to Remember

A FEW HOURS LATER THAT EVENING, MUKUND AND CYNTHIA arrived at the Sealdah Railway Station. Navigating the zigzagging crowd on the bustling platform, Mukund hunted down their designated bogie, clutching the Englishwoman's small suitcase in one hand and her medicine chest in the other, while his own leather bag straddled his right shoulder. A few steps behind, two porters carried Cynthia in a wooden chair. In the rush, one of the porters accidentally dropped Cynthia's delicate white ostrich-feather hat on to the ground. Mukund dashed back to retrieve it.

Minutes earlier, after much debate and citing Cynthia's illness, Mukund managed to secure permission from the stationmaster to accompany her in a nearly empty first-class compartment. This crucial concession came from the almost all-white operational staff at the railway station after the duo presented several pieces of evidence that established Mukund as a former officer in the Darbhanga estate. He suffered through racial humiliation simply because of his loyalty to Cynthia and the grave uncertainty about her longevity.

Finally, they settled into their seats in the first-class bogie of the night train to Kurseong. Exhausted, Cynthia sank into her cushioned seat and gazed out at the bustling station, which was teeming with life, busier than ever with the recent surge in coal production from the Jharia and Raniganj coalfields that had turned railway stations in and around Calcutta into frenzied hubs of activity.

The train was gearing up for departure. Tearful relatives pressed close to the barred windows of the rust-coloured coaches, bidding farewell to their loved ones. The train guard, leaning out from the rear bogie, made eye contact with the driver, signalling the impending departure.

A stray but contented-looking dog seemed to have extended its afternoon nap on the platform, not far from the reservation office. Built like a prize fighter, a Railway Protection Force chowkidar guarded a rolled-up canvas holdall and a steel trunk with the alertness of a village sentinel patrolling a mango grove during harvest. The luggage belonged to a smart-looking uniformed officer of the Royal Navy waiting to board a train. For now, he happened to be getting his spanking new shoes polished by one of several shoeshine boys.

Cynthia broke the silence first. 'Did you notice that not just the ticket and reservation officers who accosted us, but even the engine driver is still a white man?'

Seated in the seat directly in front of her, Mukund sighed. 'Yes.' He lifted her and moved her closer to the window so that she could look outside easily.

She felt even lighter than foam. For a fleeting moment, there was a flicker of girlish gaiety in her eyes, as though some last hope for a chivalric romance had sparked. But the harsh reality of her fate quickly extinguished it. Sensing each other's rapid breathing, they both looked out the window together in perfect harmony. On the platform, a middle-aged beggar, drunk and blissfully unaware of the world around him, danced erratically. Nearby, a group of mixed-race college students, freshly arrived from a missionary school in Shillong, bustled past in their tailored blazers and polished shoes.

After a while, Mukund resumed the conversation. 'Since you have raised the issue, a British driver still manning an East Indian Railway train is but the tip of the iceberg. The government's policies are such that even some of the bids on the key coach and engine repair materials are still presented to the India Office in London.'

A brief silence followed as Mukund helped Cynthia gulp down some bitter-tasting tablets, tilting a water bottle gently towards her lips.

Cynthia mumbled, 'Maybe God will let me die in peace, if not live in peace—'

Mukund interrupted with great concern. 'I can run to the train's guard and ask him to delay the train and get the station doctor to see you? He can give you a quick injection of morphine to ease the pain.'

The highly erudite and socially conscious Cynthia retorted despite her ailment, 'No. Let us talk about anything other than my bodily woes.' Her face had a haunted, hollow look—like the last tree standing in a field after a devastating storm.

Mukund complied. 'That is just fine with me. What is the latest insider news?' He deeply admired her determination to stay abreast of current affairs despite being mired in personal tribulations.

'During his final Saturday evening drinking binge before being shunted to Madras, Shawn divulged to me that the Tata Company tried repeatedly to compete for such orders from the government department and failed each time. The earls, lords and undersecretaries at London's India Office are repeatedly awarding the new contracts to British or American companies.'

Mukund sighed. 'The newspapers hardly cover such events. It's surprising that Shawn, of all people, would let such information slip. The Tatas will succeed but it will take some more years and the spillage of more blood.'

Gently placing Mukund's hand in her lap, Cynthia queried, 'Did you know how Jamshedji Tata's projects in Jamshedpur first began?'

He smiled at her, inches from her face, as he tenderly brushed a stray wisp of hair from her cheek. 'How on earth do you know?'

Cynthia replied with a hint of reproach, 'In recent months, you hardly came by. So, to pass my solitary days, I befriended one of the Belvedere physicians. He told me about a chance meeting between Jamshedji Tata and Swami Vivekananda 18 years ago.'

Mukund nodded. 'Yes, I remember hearing that they had met on a steamship during an overseas trip. Is that right?'

'Yes, Jamshed was heading out to the UK to strike new business deals for his company when the monk told him to explore his homeland and make the best use of the natural resources in Chhota Nagpur.'

A young, handsome British army officer strolled repeatedly past the compartment's narrow corridor. His eyes lingered a little too long on Cynthia each time he passed, drink in hand. Sensing the man's intentions, Mukund quietly stood up and closed the compartment door, leaving it unlocked. For a moment, a flicker of jealousy crossed his face, though Cynthia simply smiled weakly at the situation.

Her gaze returned to the window, watching the bustling platform outside. Vendors continued to push their wooden carts along, selling tea and various goods, calling out in animated voices.

When a preteen, swarthy, skinny boy stuck his tiny begging bowl through the bars of the window and into the compartment, Cynthia took out a handful of four-anna coins from her purse and nearly filled the boy's bowl. The child's eyes widened in astonishment at the unexpected generosity, and he quickly darted towards his blind father. Standing with his back against the station's commercial supervisor's office, the haggard man with sunken cheeks was playing a shoulder-strapped harmonium and singing a soulful song.

Cynthia tore her gaze away from the middle-aged singer, deeply disturbed by the display of abject poverty. She turned to Mukund with a request. 'Can you please buy me a comb? In the rush to catch the train, I forgot to pack it.'

Mukund sprang out of the compartment and onto the platform with the speed of a young cheetah. After purchasing the most expensive comb the station could offer, he hurried back to the train.

Struggling to retain focus, Cynthia lapsed into silence as if she had begun to feel the beginning of the end. Abandoning any pretence of modesty, she clasped Mukund with her slender arms.

Reaching into Cynthia's medicine chest, Mukund handed her an oral dose of sedative. Lethargically downing the tranquillizer, Cynthia's gaze drifted towards two burly water deliverers marching up and down the platform, offering fresh drinking water to the outbound passengers. One wore traditional Muslim attire, and the other was dressed in traditional Hindu garments. Their service seemed to be still based on the religious faith of each customer seeking their help.

Feeling the life slipping away from her, Cynthia sighed. 'My dearest man, not much has changed here during my lifetime. But I still hope that this blessed land soon gets to see better days.'

Mukund replied softly, 'Indeed.'

The ticket checker completed his pre-departure routine, and the guard blew his loud, high-pitched whistle, waving the green flag. With a rumbling clatter, the train began its journey, pulling out of the station and into a six-mile-long embankment. Deeply embedded at the terminus, this embankment was arduously built to bring the main railway line into the station by passing various canals, roads and pits in the central business district of Calcutta.

As the train moved forward, Cynthia wasted little time. 'Mukund, please lock the door.'

Mukund asked, 'But why?'

'Soon I will cease to exist in this world I have failed to fully fathom.'

'You must not harbour such negative thoughts.'

Cynthia pressed on, 'In memory of our amazing friendship, this dying abandoned woman is commanding you to make love to her.'

Mukund was momentarily stunned, and then hurriedly locked the door. 'But what about my scruples... What about hurting Robert and Archana?'

'Lecherous Robert and I are divorced. And as for Archana, I will draft the most beseeching letter asking for forgiveness.'

'Can we talk about something else...like Hubert's plans?' Mukund tried to deflect.

Cynthia ignored his attempt to change the subject. 'Some of your long-gone ancestors had three to four wives. Isn't that true?'

'Yes,' Mukund sluggishly admitted.

Cynthia's voice took on a pleading tone. 'I will posthumously request Archana to grant me the joy of being her co-wife, albeit for a few weeks. Now...come closer...and give this dying, lonely woman a kiss.'

Mukund felt as if the four walls of the compartment were closing in on him. During his 10-year marriage, he had never been unfaithful to Archana. His only other intimate encounter was with a briefly visiting widowed cousin, which had occurred unexpectedly before his wedding. Unlike many of his peers, he nested no secret concubines or visited any whorehouses. He also did not follow the tradition of Kulin Brahmins, who maintained multiple wives in various villages.

Softly kissing her forehead with the care one shows while placing flowers at a deity's feet, he whispered into her ear, 'May divine mercy easily grant you a hundred more years. May you be crowned the most compassionate citizen of the world.'

'What a sweet thought. But that kiss is not enough. I need much more.' She reached out and caressed his smooth face. Despite the years, Mukund's skin was spotless, like the surface of an unspoiled, virgin pond.

Mukund nervously eased back. He had had no clue of this solicitation for physical intimacy when he had offered to take his friend's ailing wife for a change of place.

Cynthia asked in a seductive tone, 'Do you not find me desirable, my handsome landlord?'

Mukund felt out of breath. 'Yes, I do. But...'

'There are no buts today, especially with my days numbered! Not after all the ordeals you have gone through for me over many years. Even if you must tell Archana some day...she will understand.'

Mukund instinctively continued to fight the amorous invitation. 'You have forgotten that I despise the four-century-long landlord era in my lineage. It was mostly corrupt, greedy and self-serving.'

Cynthia groaned, frustration evident in her voice. 'Here I am trying to get in the mood for the last glimpse of mortal love, and you are lecturing me yet again about the excesses committed by the powerful.'

Mukund's gaze softened as he looked at her. Despite her frailness, she still looked beautiful and desirable. For the first time, Mukund took the lovesick, ill-fated and abandoned wife of Mr Robert Weatherilt in his arms, holding her as if she were made of glass. Her kiss was tender but insistent, and she gripped the back of his head with surprising strength.

In a whisper, Cynthia confessed, 'I have loved you for a long time.'

'But you are sick... How can you be thinking of romance right now?'

'My illness is bizarre. The discomforts are highly cyclical! For instance, I am feeling great right now. I have no clue if my pain will return in one hour, tomorrow or next week. Yes, when I am down, it is a terrible feeling. But at this moment, I feel fine.'

Mukund suddenly stood up. 'What are you getting at?'

'Let me be your barge-wife for the shortest of whiles as you journey down this mysterious blue river back to your loving Archana.'

Mukund tried one last evasive action. 'We are not in a barge… but in a train.'

Cynthia cooed, 'You are unpoetic! The compartment is locked like a highly secluded room. I command you to make love to me. Can't you see I may not be around next week to badger you?'

Mukund, despite his inner turmoil, found himself unable to refuse the terminally ill woman's plea. His final resistance crumbled away like dust in the wind. Cynthia eased out of her lilac sari with the practised, sinuous moves of a courtesan. This was the first time the faithful woman embraced a man other than her husband. She pulled her breast free from the lacy confinement of her brassiere. Mukund's lips gently kissed the warm mounds and coral nipples. He slid his hands down and cupped her now-bare buttocks. She responded with a throaty purr, pressing her breast against him. Then her lips took him beyond paradise. The air in the compartment thickened with the scent of lavender as desire flowed between them like warm honey. The last nudge of conscience dived deep into oblivion. He draped her thighs over his shoulders and slid into her, his hands firmly supporting her hips as he lifted her to him. He kissed her eyes tenderly as he lost himself within her.

After they made love tenderly and endlessly, he braced himself above her and gazed at her contended eyes and bare bosoms with unqualified love.

Cynthia's long fingers lightly traced the contours of his muscular arms. 'I know what you are thinking right now.'

'What?' Mukund asked as he caressed her still-bare breasts.

'You are feeling guilty about betraying your innocent wife.'

Mukund nodded quietly. She snuggled close to his broad, hairy chest. The Englishwoman had hit the nail on the head. Mukund felt as though he had plummeted from a great height. He confirmed his guilt with his restless gaze, Archana's face vividly present in his fractured, conflicted thoughts.

Putting her clothes back on, Cynthia pulled at her sari to make it sit properly over her blouse and petticoat. She leaned back on the plush cushions of the compartment and looked out of the window. 'You must not worry. This transgression will not happen again, even if I were to miraculously live for the next 50 years. I will easily live with the memories of this journey with you. It is my fault to have lured you into infidelity. But soon I will be dead... and it won't matter.'

Mukund's lips came down on hers tenderly for one last time. He placed a finger over her mouth, a silent plea for her to stop speaking of her impending death. As he quickly dressed, Cynthia folded her knees and began to nervously count her toes.

Cynthia mumbled, 'But you know I could tell that your mind was not fully upon me as I clung to you. You were thinking about your wife. How lucky she is.' An unpleasant twinge of guilt shot through her.

Mukund gaped at her with a lost look. He felt disoriented, struggling to distinguish between duty, compassion and personal desires. 'I am sorry if you found me distracted.'

Cynthia sighed. 'It is all right. It was too abrupt on my part. But I loved every moment...despite the distraction. And what else have you not done for me in the last few years.'

A deathlike pall hung over them. Mukund felt the weight of his actions, both physically and mentally; Cynthia, on the other hand, reflected on her life, marred by a broken marriage with a self-absorbed and money-hungry gambling addict. She also quietly relished the secret consummation of complete joy that only this good-looking, introspective native of Madaripur could have brought her. His kind, caring eyes haunted her every time she looked at him.

As the train slowed down to stop, Cynthia turned to Mukund with a request. 'If Robert ever returns to town, you will urge Hubert to forgive him. Won't you?'

Mukund answered slowly, 'Yes, I will. I think you were an exalted sage in your last life.'

'Yes, I bet I was your wife along with Archana.' She looked around the swaying compartment, feeling the train's rhythm match her inner turmoil. Then she shifted her focus, her mind racing. 'You know I am highly fond of your wife. I will not write a cruel letter to her asking for forgiveness. Let us do better. Please do not ever tell her about what just happened. If you do…it will crush Archana. I never meant to lead you astray… This premature rendezvous with death has clouded my mind.'

Mukund gently kissed her on the forehead, his half-smile hiding his anxiety. As Cynthia smoothed the wrinkles in his khaki kurta, she fell silent, listening to the rhythmic sounds of the train and the night. Mukund retreated into a book on the French Revolution, trying to escape the emotional storm.

After a few hours, Cynthia's voice cut through the silence. 'I am feeling stuffy and hot. That sick feeling is once again crowding my head.'

Mukund carefully helped her lie down on the berth. Once she was settled and had drifted into a restless sleep, he wandered through the violently rattling coach's corridor. Finding a quiet corner near the closed toilet, he lit a cigarette. The dispossessed, erstwhile zamindar searched for solitude.

The vast darkness outside the train window was punctuated only by the encroaching fog. The distant farmlands were swallowed by the night, leaving Mukund alone with his conflicted thoughts. The aroma of parboiled shrimp seasoned with butter and lime juice permeated from the adjacent pantry compartment. Such fine dining was meant only for white travellers.

The images of his son Aneek crowded his mind. How happily and securely his young son rested in his arms whenever Mukund returned home. He felt a surge of unprecedented remorse. A counterbalance lurked as well. What could he do after the heart-rending way she had spoken of her ardour for him? Already blessed with plenty, the happily married dreamer did not need Cynthia's love and emotional support. But she desperately did. He could easily slog and sweat to death for the Englishwoman to help her with the onerous chores of her life. However, having just slept with her had shaken the watchdog pegs of his conscience.

As Cynthia's condition worsened overnight, Mukund's concern deepened. When the train reached Kurseong railway station the next morning, Cynthia collapsed in his arms, her plea for comfort barely audible. All she could mumble was, 'Hold me tight…hold me tight.'

Mukund waved away the coolie keen to take their bags and instead arranged for her to be taken to the local hospital. A few days passed, during which the Kurseong doctors could do little. Wretched to the core, Mukund did not know what to do next.

Desperate for better medical care, Mukund secured a return ticket to Calcutta and transported Cynthia back, hoping against hope that the Calcutta physicians might offer a solution. By the time they arrived at her Belvedere mansion, she had lost most of her consciousness.

At the next daybreak, Cynthia passed away. Crying silently, Mukund ran to the Alipore telegraph office and sent a telegram to Hubert. Abiding by her last wish, he found her Bible and placed it in her hand during the burial in Chinsurah, a town she had chosen.

Ironically, two days later, Robert arrived from London, hoping to reconcile with his ailing wife. Instead, he was faced with the news of her death. To Mukund's great relief, Hubert did not misbehave with his devastated father.

The news of Cynthia's death also left Archana shaken for months. Yet she never queried her husband about the Englishwoman. Mukund, for his part, kept the secret of their last encounter to himself.

Years later, with Shawn's help and persistent efforts, Mukund finally located Cynthia's firstborn son. After being adopted by a childless vicar and his wife, Cynthia's firstborn, Patrick, had bloomed into an eminent lawyer in Aberdeen. After Patrick declined to recognize any ties or even accept money from his ignoble past, Mukund donated Cynthia's money to the Red Cross.

Chapter 21

Transitions and Tides of Renewal

Between 1904 and 1905, a restless Mukund often shuttled between his Madaripur estate and the district of Rajshahi. Having left his comfortable job in Darbhanga to restore his family farmlands, he periodically taught in Rajshahi. In an effort to shake off the tragic losses of Cynthia, followed by the gomosta's wife, who succumbed after 10 childbirths, Mukund turned his attention to the matters of his extended family.

Meanwhile, Flanagan had built a two-storey burnt-brick home, complete with a balcony, to please Prachi, the love of his life. It was only a mile away from Mukund's mansion in Madaripur and in an affluent section of the village.

Late at night after they made love, Prachi loved to hear about the rapid advancements in commercial shipbuilding from her untiring husband. Nestled against his arm, she marvelled at faraway inventions such as the screw propeller, the compound engine and the triple expansion engine. Burying his face in her long, scented hair, he would elaborate on how these innovations had made transoceanic shipping safe and economically viable.

For brief relief from his internal turmoil, Mukund often joined his fishermen by the riverside, casting giant fishing nets. When the monsoon rains peaked, he headed out to the dangerous strip of land between the swollen Jamuna and Hurasagar Rivers. Despite returning with chronic dysentery, Mukund still managed to help some of the farmers there survive the perilous floods.

One fateful day in Madaripur, Bonka's younger wife went to meet a cousin, taking their teenage daughter Shukla with her. Just then, at home, stomach cramps gripped their younger daughter, Shitala. Scared by her symptoms, Bonka's older wife rushed off to fetch the village physician. The childless stepmother wholeheartedly loved each of Bonka's children. In her absence, an intruder broke into the cottage. The ruthless son of a ganja addict solicited sex from the young girl. Promptly refusing the demand, Shitala declared that she preferred death. After tying up her hands and feet, the enraged intruder, instead of raping her, killed her with a spade lying in the next room.

A month later, at the special judicial session where the British judge was about to sentence the criminal to death, Bonka sprang a surprise. He informed the judge, 'I met my daughter's killer five times last week.'

The judge looked stunned. 'Good heavens, Bonka! Why did you do that?'

'The murderer wept and repented each time. Abused by his handicapped uncle throughout his childhood, he is filled with more remorse than anyone I have ever met. Please let him be in jail forever, but do not kill him.'

'But why?'

'A life filled with remorse, locked in prison, is far more painful than death. I want him to suffer for years and not escape through the gallows. Besides, the killer's death will not bring my daughter back.'

Mukund, the judge and every observer in the court sat dumbfounded by Bonka's remarkable act of forgiveness. Mukund and Archana had never felt prouder of the generous tribal. After his daughter's death, Bonka's exuberance faded. He became a pale shadow of his former self, his spirit dulled by grief.

Archana handled her husband's frequent absences by travelling as well. During Aneek's school holidays, she visited Aunt Prachi's home, staying there for one or two days at a time.

During the weekends, Prachi and Archana joyously watched Aneek and Prachi's two older sons frolic together in the mansion's garden and yards. In the afternoon, the young trio invariably extracted the fullest amusement as they banged the porch swing's iron chains, hurling themselves to dangerous heights under the warm sunshine. The mothers, despite their love for the boys, could do little but groan in disapproval at their more reckless antics. The boys often playfully pushed one another down from a wheelbarrow to claim their turns on the unusual vehicle, racing over tickly grass and molehills, their bare heels dusted with green specks of grass. Joyfully, they dipped their toes in puddles and bumped into each other when the monsoon gale struck without notice. Torrential rain and monstrously howling winds chased them inside Flanagan's gardening shed where cobwebs clung to the walls, and the air smelled of wild mushrooms and earth potatoes.

The absence of Mukund's hefty salary from the Darbhanga estate was now but a faint and unimportant memory in Archana's mind. As her husband's printing business earnings grew sporadically, the continued string of bumper crops from their revamped farmlands in Madaripur helped the devoted wife run the household the way she had hoped.

At times, local issues in and around Madaripur gripped Mukund's attention and led him into dangerous territories. One of his newsletters, encouraging young native men to resist joining the Royal Army or the Royal Navy, hit a raw nerve in the Dhaka office of the home ministry. Despite this, Mukund continued his work, though he quietly missed Cynthia's weekly letters, which had once inspired him endlessly.

Unbeknownst to Mukund, Aneek had been secretly involved in several nationalistic skirmishes in Dhaka. From 1904 to 1905 Aneek had been shuttling between Ramna in Dhaka and Madaripur. During this period the youth had already diverted much of his secret grants from Flanagan and pocket money (extracted from Archana) into a leather business in the Ramna area. This enterprise, selling shoes and handbags, served as a front for raising the operating expenses of the freedom fighters.

One day, an ageing, newly migrated farmer on Mukund's estate disowned his son for marrying his sweetheart in a temple without seeking permission from his father and without accepting any dowry. To teach the greedy father a lesson, Mukund waylaid the tyrannical sexagenarian behind a karamcha bush, where Bonka gave him a thorough beating with his own hands. The following day, the terrified farmer dropped all financial claims he had levied against his new daughter-in-law's parents. Earlier, the same fat-necked man had locked his wife indefinitely at home for disobeying him and siding with their son. Learning of this, Bonka and Mukund concocted a clever ploy by breaking a massive beehive right in front of the house, causing chaos. In the confusion, the woman escaped after 12 days of captivity and moved in with their son and his new wife, never to return to her oppressive husband.

During more peaceful times, Mukund stayed home and became a devoted provider for his family. On one occasion, Archana's favourite cow stopped producing milk after the loss of its newborn calf. To alleviate his highly aggravated wife's concern, Mukund fashioned a straw-stuffed replica of the calf and presented it to the recalcitrant beast. Within a day, the cow's udders overflowed once again.

On quieter days, Mukund would stand on the partition between the rice fields from dusk to dawn, lost in thought, philosophizing like a solitary iceberg that had stood unmoved for millennia.

Chapter 22

A Long March Towards Freedom

On 19 July 1905, the British announced the partition of Bengal, setting off waves of anger and protests throughout the region. Two days before the announcement, Archana, anticipating unrest, had sent Aneek to a friend's home in Barisal, fearful that the teenager would slip away to Calcutta and get hurt in the potentially volatile demonstrations. While she had managed to send the nationalistic juvenile away, she could not stop her husband.

In the midst of this political turbulence, the only significant and heartening news that both Mukund and Archana rejoiced over was the fact that within weeks of Cynthia's death, her younger sister Linda had reunited with her estranged husband Shawn. Most importantly, he was no longer the foul-tempered racist man he used to be. Linda, inspired by her late sister, picked up the habit of frequent letter writing. Thanks to the rapidly improving Railway Mail Service, it did not take long for letters mailed from Calcutta to reach the developing Madaripur.

Through her correspondence, Linda remained well connected with Mukund and his wife. In her letters written to Linda, Cynthia had urged her sibling to resolve all differences with her well meaning but headstrong spouse. Additionally, in keeping with Cynthia's wishes, Mukund masterminded Shawn and Mrs Hall's loving reunion and reconciliation. At Linda's behest, Shawn topped it all off by changing his job and returning from Madras to Calcutta. Most importantly, he invited his long-separated and mentally unstable mother to live permanently with them in their Calcutta home. Linda also proudly shared that her husband was now a very senior ICS officer in the British Raj.

As July neared its end, Calcutta erupted into riots and processions protesting the Partition. One such day, throwing aside his usual caution, Mukund joined thousands of marchers in a demonstration that stretched across the city. Barefoot and dressed in simple white attire, he began the long walk from the home of his brother-in-law Kanak—who had shifted from Pabna to Dumdum—accompanied by his trusted companion, Bonka. It was the longest walk of his life, taking him past the first electric power generating station near Prinsep Ghat by the Ganges River.

As they walked through the rain-soaked streets, the smell of pigeon droppings and cow dung mingled with the scents of the reawakening motherland, creating an oddly invigorating atmosphere. Mukund felt an extraordinary sense of belonging as he marched alongside people from all walks of life, united in their defiance of British rule. Meanwhile, horsebound, strait-laced British policemen in white uniforms, and their native counterparts with conflicted hearts, tailed the marchers ominously. To create a deterrent for any violent outburst from the massive crowd, they fired several rounds in the air with their Lee-Enfield Mark I rifles from time to time.

Throughout the day, whenever Bonka urged his master to leave the procession, Mukund replied, 'In one more mile.' Mukund not only liked his perennial mate but had grown to admire him. Having quit the Railway Mail Service, ever restless at work, Bonka now had become a trusted apprentice in one of the first automotive repair shops in Madaripur. His renewed proximity pleased Archana immensely as well.

Drowning his perpetual sidekick's objections in endearing, good-natured profanities, Mukund trudged along. The stony roads they walked were strewn with debris—brickbats, discarded sal-leaf cones from roadside food vendors, decaying leaves, twigs, animal droppings, trashed papers, torn placards, manholes and potholes, challenging the marchers. At the crossroads of summer and monsoon, Mukund and Bonka veered from one gritty road to another.

Among the sea of marchers, they passed crumpled cycles belonging to roughed-up protesters lying on the footpath. Nearby, a baton-ravaged skinny rickshaw puller was threatening a British policeman by tearing off all his clothes in public. Notoriety was his chief form of defiance. A native *daroga* quickly stepped in, delivering a blow to the exhibitionist in the mouth. The damnable crime immediately drew a roar of disapproval from the sea of people marching down the road. But no one hit back at the artless daroga babu; their eyes were transfixed upon the sheer magnitude of the protesters on the street. Even the most hardened pedlars stood and watched.

Shaken totally out of their wits, road cleaners and shoeshine boys watched as well. A ragamuffin walked with the flag of the Indian National Congress (INC) wrapped around his bare chest. A British storeowner in a loud checked coat and a quiet laugh in his eyes watched the unhurried procession. Self-assured, he seemed unimpressed by the display of such futile energy and enthusiasm by the masses. Carbon copies of half-finished trading memos floated in the air, and amid the chaos, an old woman succumbed to convulsions and bouts of vomiting.

As the colossal convoy of vociferous men passed by, panicked stall owners hurriedly slammed their wooden doors shut. Pushcart labourers stopped their tasks of stuffing wares into their two-wheelers, pausing to watch the unfolding demonstration.

Before long, passing a closed meat market still reeking of raw meat, Mukund chanced upon a frenzy-filled huddle incessantly screaming on one side of the road. A teenager had died after falling into a half-open manhole. To make matters worse, a native daroga of Calcutta Police had stood by apathetically while a fellow native had taken advantage of the unending melee to drag a 19-year-old female student into a closed machine shop shed and raped her.

Mukund quickly approached the only food hawker he could spot. The workaholic had dared to stand his ground under the abandoned wooden canopy at the crossroads of two major streets. His dark beehive-like hair was mostly hidden under his cap—a part of his uniform. Vintage automobiles and stagecoaches honked impatiently as they navigated through the throngs of people.

Resting his tiring legs, Mukund slumped on the foot-high platform atop which the cop stood and asked him, 'Have they caught the man who assaulted the girl?'

Completely ignoring the question and the background din, the cop continued wiping down the black-and-white base with a discoloured rag. Before Mukund could repeat his question, a peanut hawker appeared from nowhere. Huffing amid the chaos, he offered all the answers, 'Yes, they caught him. He was a fellow Indian, like you and me. According to a passer-by I met, the criminal worked as an undersea telecommunication cable layer.'

Mukund asked, 'Why would a man stoop to such a terrible crime?'

The hawker sighed. 'Who knows? All I know is he was a middle-aged man, fired recently from his job.'

'And what about the victim?'

'She was an ace student from Bagnan,' the hawker replied. 'She had come to the big city for the first time.'

Mukund's lips quivered with anger. 'What an inhuman, cowardly deed... Who brought her to Calcutta?'

'She trusted her guide—the rapist himself. He was a neighbour she had known for years and thought of as a brother.'

Mukund let out a bitter sigh. 'What is new? Sometimes, we are hurt by the ones we love and trust the most.'

At that moment, the impassioned and collective cry of *azaan* filled the sky, echoing from a nearby mosque.

Bonka turned towards his mentor. 'Yes, yes. I still remember how that arsonist we relied on razed your farmland.'

Mukund's eyes snapped toward Bonka, a sharp reprimand in his gaze, as if to tell the tribal not to revive those painful memories of the treacherous fire. The latter complied. Meanwhile, twirling their rosary beads, a group of mullahs in the thick of the parade filed past the intersection. Women in light blue burqas followed them quietly.

Expertly lodging a pinch of snuff into his nose, the peanut hawker continued, 'Arriving in the big city barely two days ago, she came, like many, to protest the partition of Bengal. Now she is scarred for life.'

Bonka asked, 'How did the rapist manage to find a secluded spot?'

A strong odious smell of tear gas began to fill the thick air.

The peanut hawker, with a grim expression on his face, explained, 'The disgusting cable layer was familiar with the area. He knocked the girl out with a chloroform-soaked handkerchief and carried her into a dark, windowless shed while everyone was busy trying to save the boy who had fallen into the manhole. The shed was a disused machine shop with several rows of lathes.'

Mukund inquired, 'How did he get caught?' His gaze briefly lingered on a kite trapped in a telegraph pole stacked on the top with six rows of white ceramics.

The hawker continued, 'The rapist got caught when he tried to assault the girl one too many times. An angelic 13-year-old daredevil boy accidentally helped in catching the dismissed cable-layer.'

Bonka asked, 'How?'

'While trying out a bidi, by sheer chance, the teenage boy sauntered into the machine shop right where the assailant was. He caught a glimpse of the rapist sitting on top of the barely conscious girl, groping and thrusting...'

The effect of the tear gas released by the cops was starting to subside.

Though the victimized girl was a stranger, Mukund felt sad and enraged at the same time. Not interested in any more of the gory details, he slowly pressed forward.

His eyes briefly and disapprovingly rested on a European variety store's glass-covered showcase filled with toiletry goods. An Anglo-Indian guard stood nearby, a new Webley self-cocking automatic revolver hitched to his waist belt. He nervously looked down the street, his hands fiddling with a yellow zinc-carbon Eveready flashlight sticking out of his baggy pants' side pocket. Despite the store being closed due to the forewarned public agitation, a string of lighted carbon filament bulbs glowed meekly inside. The bulbs, filled with soot on the interior, provided minimal illumination to the neatly stacked items like toothpaste, soap, hairbrush, shampoo, cologne, and other daily necessities—all made in England. The wall cabinet racks teemed with hats, belts, halters, hand-blown carafes and whisky glasses.

Meanwhile, some of the marchers were still in a circle, demanding answers from a white police officer as to why a manhole was not fully secured, which had led to the tragic death of a young boy. A rifle-carrying British police sergeant responded by disciplining the most vehement complainers, shoving them into a narrow alley. Cursing in the vernacular and thrusting his bayonet, Sergeant Tait threatened the crowd to retreat. In the process, he became isolated from his patrol—a large group of horse-riding cops who had been circling the street corner.

Seconds later, Mukund found himself intervening when a section of the angry mob lunged at the sergeant, pinning him to the ground. Snatching the Englishman's rifle and revolver away, three enraged men from the crowd began to stamp his hands and feet in the murky shade of a blind lane. They yanked off every shred of clothing from his body except his hat and underwear. Just then, Mukund whacked the lead assailant's face so hard that the man fell into a dry sewer.

Heaving himself from the dust and gathering his torn uniform, Tait glanced at Mukund and all the others with a mixture of disgust and gratitude. Amidst the roar of hundreds of angry onlookers, Mukund's voice cut through the uproar. 'Enough, enough!' he shouted to the crowd 'You have humiliated the sergeant enough. He is not responsible for the boy's death or the girl's rape. For many decades, other Brits have done much worse. If freedom is what we are truly after, we must look beyond Tait and corner the schemers and the masterminds first.'

As Mukund glared at the mob's leaders, they reluctantly loosened the circle around the Brit and made way for him to escape and save his life.

From the fringes of the crowd, a hostile voice shot back, 'Whose side are you on?'

Bonka, stepping in to support Mukund, retorted in his rough eastern dialect, 'If you care to listen, our goal is the same as yours.'

As an angry protester elbowed Bonka in the ribs, Bonka, undeterred, jostled back and continued, 'If you have the guts, the resources and the planning, target the top-ranking policymakers. It is the viceroy who has ordered the partition and not his salaried minions or the lowly nobodies in the totem pole.'

Mukund added, 'We are marching for freedom, but not to lose our dignity over the idiocy of petty, loose-tongued men.'

Not everyone in the crowd was convinced by Mukund and Bonka's arguments. As tensions remained high, a sudden shriek from Bonka warned Mukund just in time. Two of the assailant's cronies had tried in vain to strike Mukund on the back with a wooden rod. Momentarily wincing with anger, Mukund and Bonka somehow broke away from the dhoti-kaftan- and kurta-clad cartel, managing to catch a ride on a handcart pushed by a coolie.

Minutes later, the duo resumed their march. Mukund's mind frantically, overwhelmed by the ruthlessness and its sudden display in human hearts on both sides. In the heat of the moment and the immensity of the day, he did not realize that he had sustained permanent physical damage. For the remainder of his life, his long upper torso would lean marginally forward, and his gait would forever diminish, albeit slightly.

At noon, the procession reached Creek Row, an area of opulent British bungalows guarded by turbaned, moustachioed sentinels wielding lances and rifles. Outside one of these grand residences, a modest roadside eatery had been set up, offering spicy mutton, puris, and a drink made from fire-cooked mangoes. The owner, coerced into service by off-duty native cops, served the hungry marchers.

A few hours later, Mukund arrived at the intersection of Harrison Road and College Street, home to some of the city's most prestigious academic institutions. Though his back throbbed painfully from the wound, a peculiar trance in his psyche prevented him from abandoning the march.

Nearby, a two-wheel, single-horse *tanga* sat idle, its young, sour-faced and bearded owner unhurriedly feeding grass to his horse. Abandoned by their operators, scores of hand-pulled rickshaws stood leaning against a wall that was being used by some as a urinal. Starving protesters who had arrived at dawn from the suburbs had stopped to purchase a quick bite from an enterprising Chinese pedlar with a wooden hand-pulled food cart. Carrying a varied mix of home-made chicken chowmein and chilli fish, the second-generation immigrant from Shanghai had been trying to cash in on the hungry wave of people walking down the street.

In front of a jukebox store, its antiquated Anglo-Indian owner strummed his guitar, nursing the nearly impossible hope of drawing in customers. His teenage grandson deftly played the mandolin beside him. For a fleeting moment, Mukund saw the city as a reflection of its tumultuous history, a rebellious and unruly entity evolving from its colonial past into something unpredictable and vibrant.

Chapter 23

United in Dissent

MUKUND COULD HARDLY BELIEVE HIS EYES WHEN HE SAW Shawn and a few of his erstwhile fellow English colleagues from Dalhousie Square standing on the doorsteps of a closed bookstore. They held a placard demanding the revocation of the partition of Bengal. The posse's headcount was small compared to the total number of Anglos employed in the Writers' Building and other administrative offices in the area, but, Mukund had not expected any Brit to protest on behalf of the Indians.

Before Mukund could say anything, Shawn stepped forward. They stood near the fissured trunk of a leaning palm tree. Hugging Mukund, Cynthia's brother-in-law greeted him with the warmth typical of a high school reunion. Personifying a showcase of modesty, Shawn seemed a wholly different man. The once-boorish Brit's rough edges seemed to have disappeared into the wilderness of interstellar space.

Mukund was struck by Shawn's transformation since their days in Darbhanga. The man who had once used profanity and shown disdain for natives now seemed to carry the weight of recent hardships and new awakenings. Shawn had come to terms with his identity as Mr Hall's son and was striving to align himself with his father's noblest values.

In a flash, Mukund set aside any lingering acrimony. He also forgot the times he had wished to crush the bureaucrat's every bone with a heavy-duty hammer.

'What are you doing here?'

Shawn grinned unabashedly. 'You are not going to believe it... I am agitating for India's freedom. Mr Hall...my father's innermost spirit is finally kindling in me.'

'I heard you left your government job in Madras.'

'Yes. I also quit the Writers' Building ICS job last week. Besides…it is wonderful being with my mother after so many years. She has gotten a lot better. I am helping Linda run a flower shop, raising our daughter and keeping an eye on Hubert.'

Mukund could not help himself from being nosy. 'Shawn, you seem to be a changed man. What sparked this newfound sympathy for the masses of this land, beyond reuniting with your family?'

Lighting a cigarette, Shawn mused, 'It is a long story…'

Gently nudging Shawn away from his mates, Mukund enquired with near-drunken elation, 'I do want to know.'

Shawn continued cordially, 'You could say Mr Hall's remarkable genes have finally taken over my heart.'

'What about the other Englishmen with you?'

Shawn sighed. 'They, too, are tired of the British Raj. Each has lost a sibling in the Second Boer War in South Africa. Do you know when it will end…this unending desire to colonize?'

'I wish I knew. What was the last straw that made you quit the coveted ICS post?'

Shawn's face immediately darkened with grief. 'Some of my college classmates, who had been missing in action since the Second Boer War, have been confirmed dead.'

'It seems this era is plagued by dramatic miscommunication all across the empire.'

Shawn wiped away beads of sweat from his baked-red face. 'Indeed…' He briefly leaned against a Victorian lamp post to ease his tired legs, handing Mukund a flyer. 'The flower shop you visited is on sale. Some other day, please visit my new eatery near Chowringhee for a complimentary lunch or dinner.'

'Linda and your daughter must be delighted to have you back home.'

Shawn nodded his head vigorously. After shaking Shawn's hands, Mukund and Bonka returned to another wave of the protest march. Shawn joined his handful of poster-carrying white friends supporting the freedom-seeking revolutionaries.

A large INC banner and handbills from various covert nationalist organizations lay scattered on the dusty street. The INC poster had likely been dislodged during the police charge and tear-gassing following the chaos triggered by the rape incident.

After hours of walking, Mukund's calves, knees and heels were in excruciating pain. Yet, he felt no desire to stop. Another Londoner, the owner of a 100-year-old bakery store, stood impassively and watched the human spectacle. Even several petty but rich rajas joined the parade, accompanied by pet cats, duly anointed with long names. Destitute poets, skinny students, buxom housewives, masons and carpenters—all joined the civil disobedience. A few inceptive European cars sputtered along.

Coolies, grocers, labourers, potters, estranged couples, lovers and tan-coloured clerks accompanied the march as well. Realizing a higher, noble call coming from within, even amoral traders who peddled black-market goods in shanty-like stalls gave up their moneymaking spree for the day. Bunking work and holding hands with their sari-clad sweethearts, fiery-eyed young pedlars joined the procession. Ultra-fit spinsters who sold cosmetics to housewives by endlessly walking from door to door comprised the procession's fore.

It was a day when even some of the most pompous zamindars trudged for miles. Oblivious to the bombastic titles granted by the British governors, these elites grabbed and hugged strangers on the road. Even an obese and money-minded grocery shop owner whom Mukund knew walked for hours with his protruding, overhanging stomach jiggling under the blinding sun. Everyone seemed to march with a sense of purpose, united in their common and long-delayed cause.

After aeons of being drowned in foreign rule, the populace finally seemed ready to collectively defy their oppressors with the force of a rocket escaping Earth's gravity. Some of the older men, unused to such demonstrations, became afflicted with diseases like flu, diarrhoea and malaria. The rest, including Mukund, pressed on, fighting for the freedom they all envisioned together. From behind the barred windows of their tiny shops and apartments, the more cautious Calcutta residents earnestly watched the march. Some handicapped individuals, seated along the narrow verandas of smelly and crammed boarding houses above cheap eateries, peered down at the tram-lined streets. It was a transitional period, with horse-drawn trams gradually giving way to electric ones.

Bonka's eyes nearly popped out with outrage at a young self-absorbed Bengali babu nonchalantly marching alongside him. The man wore a rugby shirt, double-pleated haltered pants and brand-new Lotus shoes imported from Stafford, England. Bonka was an ardent supporter of Swadeshi—buying and using Indian products only. Even the handkerchief he carried in his white kurta pocket was home-made, with hand-painted borders crafted by his younger wife, who was good at handicrafts. When Bonka picked up a brickbat to hurl at the youth, Mukund quickly restrained him. Watching the marchers go by, a group of 12-year-old boys scribbled words of protest upon a bright red mailbox. Far less forgiving than Mukund, they taunted the overdressed babu with stinging catcalls.

A column of athletic young villagers ran alongside the marchers, distributing drinking water from large leather jugs reinforced with tar to retain some shape. In the midst of this, a heavyset grocery godown guard with coarse skin seemed to accost an old, frail woman for allegedly stealing a small bag of rice.

Suddenly, a new melee erupted when a stagecoach horse accidentally trampled an octogenarian dissenter. It happened in front of a department store billboard displaying a painting of

Houdini shaving with a newly marketed British razor. In the exaggerated artwork, the magician's eyes glowed like gemstones and his teeth shone like the sun.

Bonka asked Mukund, 'Why was the old man so incensed that he forgot to watch for traffic?'

'I think he may have been far more resentful than you about buying essential goods from British companies.'

Above them, a golden langur leapt playfully across the roof of a two-storey mercantile office. The building belonged to a Parsi travel agent who handled commercial and passenger steamship bookings from Calcutta Harbour. Carrying tonnes of coal, tea, jute and countless other freight back and forth, the ships regularly travelled mostly to Bristol and London. The edifice was almost buttressed against the Eastern Shipping Company office. Only a few years earlier, Robert and Mukund had sought the Parsi agent's advice regarding shipment matters relating to the Darbhanga estate.

As Mukund surveyed the scene, a young activist, speaking through a loudhailer, directed the frontline marchers about the imminent turns and emergency traffic-related pauses they ought to take.

Bonka said, 'Your father once told me that perhaps we wouldn't be dealing with the British if, in 1715, the British physician Dr Hamilton had not operated on and saved the life of Farrukhsiyar, one of the last Mughal emperors.'

Mukund replied, 'Yes. As a sign of gratitude, the Mughal emperor issued a royal farman in 1717, granting the East India Company the authority to trade all over India without paying taxes. He even gifted 38 villages surrounding Sutanuti, now known as 24 Parganas, including this very land we are treading today.'

'From what your father told me, the seeds of the Mughal Empire's demise were sown in old Farrukhsiyar's thankfulness and his obsession with marrying Ajit Singh's daughter. Life is full of so many ironic and momentous what-ifs. Is it not?'

Mukund mused, 'Yes, if Dr Hamilton's surgery had failed, perhaps India's destiny would have taken a different course, and we wouldn't need this protest march. But speculation is pointless, especially in hindsight.'

Peering into the double-glass door of a pastry shop, Bonka quickly agreed. 'True. Reflection on the past only serves to alert us about the mistakes not worth repeating.'

As they marched, a roadside cobbler worked swiftly to repair the marchers' snapping sandals and Kolhapuris on the fly. Along the way, eager volunteers pitched greasy tarpaulins to periodically shield elderly demonstrators from the harsh summer heat. Sweating, bare-chested native cooks wearing baggy loincloths and shorts offered free food to the exhausted protesters while poor orphans and women crouched by the sidewalk, watching with sympathy. Even middle-class housewives afflicted with rheumatic fever stood in their second- and third-storey balconies and lent their voices. Clanging brass dinner plates with serving spoons, they loudly greeted the marchers. Every now and then, the marchers splashed their faces with water from roadside tube wells to cool down. Even beggars, from their disfigured aluminium bowls, handed over their day's earnings to the marchers in a show of solidarity.

Mukund could feel the heat rising from the freshly laid coal tar road beneath his feet. Nearby, a young mother hurriedly scooped her toddler's released faeces into a gunny sack and tossed it into a city drain. Clutching her baby tighter, she picked up her pace, determined to keep marching.

The national outburst for freedom had finally penetrated every corner of society.

As the momentous day of public dissent drew to a close and twilight's shadows began to cloak the city, Mukund realized that over 50,000 people had taken to the streets; out of immense pride and joy, he wept quietly. The verdant and restless roadside trees jostled each other like the large crowd still streaming along. A pack of the city's stray dogs too joined the march, instead of running after heaps of gradually increasing urban trash. Sickly little boys, weak and exhausted, either trailed behind their parents or lay on the dusty footpaths, watching the procession like spent vines in spring.

Mukund warily eyed a new column of policemen, both brown- and white-skinned, following the marchers on horseback. He turned to Bonka and queried, 'Why don't you abandon your plans to return to the railway postal service and help me rebuild the printing business?'

Mukund continued, 'As you have seen today, there's much more to be done. Besides, I want to shield Aneek from all this. He's growing into such a strong-willed boy—if he'd been here in Calcutta today he would have surely gotten killed.'

Bonka nodded slowly. 'Yes, I think I will help.'

'Yes, I did. But to hell with that idea now. At that time, I had only suggested it because I knew Shitala's would-be in-laws were asking for an outlandish dowry. Besides, you were unwilling to take even one paisa from me to help with it.'

'How could I? You have done so much for me already.'

Mukund's tone softened. 'Now that your daughter is no longer with us, you do not need to raise that impossible amount. Instead, our time and energy belong to Bharat, our nation. Just look at how the Brits rule much of the world! Their India Office does not bother to justify anything to anyone but a small group of people back in London.'

Bonka's ears buzzed. 'But didn't you say earlier that, by their own law, the British viceroy is required to present his reasons for the Partition at least to the elected members of their nation's panchayat?'

'Yes…hundreds of members of the House of Commons in London must agree before any decision becomes the law.'

Several hours had passed since the march began, yet it was still far from over. The air was filled with the rhythmic chants of the protesters. On the side of the road, a stoic old man who owned a mobile hair salon continued his delicate work—removing a tattoo from a lad's forearm. Despite the activist-announced 24-hour shutdown of commerce, a porter hurriedly pushed a two-wheeled wooden cart, transporting burlap bags filled with grain.

'Bonka, do you know anyone else these days who has two wives living in the same household and not fighting with each other? Instead, they are looking out for one another, for the co-wife's progeny and the husband?'

Bonka chuckled. 'It is not like they do not express discord or grind and claw their way through tiffs. But I have never seen them let their disagreements last more than 24 hours.'

The marching chorus grew louder. Hauling their children in wicker bassinets, young mothers also joined the controlled fray. Babies burping and crying from colic pain added to the din. Teaming up with various multidirectional marching groups, the duo from Madaripur eventually reached the Council House Street, where the Central Telephone Exchange had been relocated in recent years. They watched as a middle-aged citizen pushed a much older mate in a wheelbarrow. The latter seemed to have fallen ill due to the enervating day-long walk. The scene was eerily reminiscent of the wheelbarrows used by the municipality to clear away trash from the streets.

An unexplainable rainbow suddenly appeared in the darkening, ashen sky.

Bonka, overcome by the rousing emotion evoked by the glorious lyrics sung by the marchers, prostrated himself on the boulevard and kissed its long-settled dust. When Mukund tried to follow suit, the beating he had incurred while trying to protect Sergeant Tait from certain death in the afternoon prevented his acrobatics. His swollen and yet-to-be-evaluated wound felt like burning embers with each movement, stabbing at him as though a blacksmith's hammer was striking his flesh. The physical pain was unbearable, but the weight of his motherland's bonded misery continued to leech his already tortured mind. Her fate still felt uncertain, like a ghost lumbering and trampling upon a half-burnt field of wheat. But amidst this sea of oppression, he felt that a brave, resilient tugboat—small but determined—was ready to pull the mighty ship of freedom towards the horizon.

Bonka finally grasped the severity of Mukund's injury. Fatigue and pain were etched on Mukund's face, his lips parched and eyelids heavy. No longer heeding Mukund's refusal to quit, Bonka quickly hired one of the few two-wheeler horse carts still operating on a day when most of the city was paralyzed by a near-total shutdown.

Firmly tugging at Mukund's sleeves, Bonka announced, 'Enough is enough! I have abided by your dictums all day, but not any more. Before your gory laceration becomes worse and turns deadly, we must reach Kanak dada's house.'

Archana's elder brother, Kanak, had left their father's huge zamindari in Pabna and moved to Calcutta to join the freedom movement.

'Yes, that is a good idea,' Mukund agreed.

Bonka helped Mukund, wincing with pain, onto the cart. Though the pain from his injury was evident, Mukund offered no resistance. For the first time that day, he allowed himself to sit, his weight relieved from his feet. He looked over at Bonka and, with a weary smile, said, 'Do you not wish to end your ultimatum with your standard closing statement?'

Signalling the sinewy cart driver to stop for a moment, Bonka quickly bought an unripe green coconut from a street urchin. The young hawker expertly hacked it open, readying the fruit's delicious milk to be consumed immediately.

Since the landlord had acquiesced to undertake basic treatment, Bonka simply smiled. Both knew that Mukund's gash must be stitched and bandaged at the earliest. Bonka quietly urged the driver to speed. The horses neighed in the warm and humid evening. Swatting away mosquitoes and gnats, they headed towards Kanak's home in Maniktala, where Mukund would receive treatment and, if needed, they could retreat to the more secure underground home of Shawn.

Chapter 24

A Secret Mission

Two days later when Mukund and Bonka reached home, they found a highly emaciated Archana shut in the mansion's prayer room. The chamber, which Archana had designed herself during the final years of their time in Darbhanga, was a sacred space lined with painted mirrors, positioned in such a way that Lord Krishna and Goddess Kali could be seen from every corner. Terrified about her husband's well-being during the potentially violent protest, she had retreated to seek divine intervention. Throughout Mukund's absence, she had survived on a once-a-day intake of khoi and plain yoghurt.

With Aneek also being away, her anxieties had peaked further. Bonka's younger wife had been regularly helping Archana with her day-to-day household affairs while Mukund and Bonka were away. Moreover, as the dutiful mother of Bonka's only surviving child, Shukla, she had also been overseeing the preparations for the teenager's marriage to a vaunted young clerk of the British-controlled Imperial Tobacco Company.

During the marriage, Bonka's first wife delighted everyone by gifting her prized chandrahaar to her stepdaughter as a wedding present.

Meanwhile, Mukund operated as a conduit of information for various activist groups, a secret known only to a few trusted colleagues, friends and relatives. An activist from nearby Barisal had been hanged, despite extensive legal efforts to save him, and Mukund financially supported the man's widow. Despite harsh societal criticism, he arranged for her to marry the estate's stable keeper, ensuring her security. During this period, Mukund met

Ambika Charan Mazumdar, an eminent freedom-seeking activist from Faridpur. It was also around this time that Mukund came across the luminary freedom fighter Surendranath Banerjee of Calcutta, who was ardently fighting against the British plans to partition Bengal.

One day, Surendranath came to Faridpur to meet Ambika Charan. Standing not far from a telegraph pole damaged by a humongous wave of locusts, Surendranath addressed his large and silent audience. 'Alone, each of us is merely a nuisance, like a single locust swaying in the wind. But together, look at the destruction they cause. Similarly, we must fight our battles with astounding unity—that is bound to overwhelm our opponents.'

Despite the mounting opposition, on 16 October 1905, Viceroy Lord Curzon carried out the partition of Bengal. Claiming it would improve governance of the populous province, Curzon split Bengal in two. The move was met with widespread resistance, especially in Calcutta, where people fasted in protest. Eateries shut down, and the streets emptied of horse-drawn carriages, rickshaws, pushcarts and bicycles.

Enraged, Mukund travelled to Calcutta for a few days. Vowing never to allow the separation to be effective, he tied a yellow ribbon—rakhi—on the wrist of his cousin Joggeshwar and his friends who now lived in the city. Later, swearing for a reunion, the two kinsmen dipped in the Ganges River and offered prayers to Goddess Kali at the Kalighat temple. With no firepower at their disposal, that is all the cousins could do against a highly organized ruler.

In the days that followed, Mukund joined thousands of Calcutta residents and much of India in fasting, sometimes for days at a time. Even the hat-check boys from the Grand Hotel and Great Eastern Hotel joined the movement. Eyes prickling with tears, sleepless mothers held their breath late into the night as they waited anxiously for their sons to return home. Meanwhile, on Dalhousie Square's marble staircases, white-shoe bankers and flaxen-haired British lawyers stood in stunned disbelief as they witnessed a long-overdue but immutable national awakening.

The repressed wives of alcoholic Anglo-Indians—many of whom Mukund knew—came down the spiral staircases of stuffed apartments and isolated attics. The Anglo-Indian folks sometimes harboured contradictions in their hearts, torn between supporting the British Raj and sympathizing with the burgeoning independence movement. Their husbands, often reeling from the effects of their addictions, began discarding the remnants of their vices, like beer bottles hidden under study tables, and some even started schools for the blind, deaf and mute in an attempt to redeem themselves. Undaunted by the sharks just under the blue sea of humanity, a wave of altruism swept through the peninsula. Then the time arrived when even mothers stopped shedding tears of grief or pity for their sons' indefinite incarceration for nationalistic activities.

The protest organizers urged only children and the sick to refrain from fasting. Throughout the day of partition, barefooted marchers, filled with resolve, traversed the city from one politically charged destination to another, including mills that had ground to a halt and secret hideouts where activists masqueraded as leather goods manufacturers. Housewives switched off all kitchen lights as if the mother of all mothers had just passed away. Rabindranath Tagore wrote a new song to commemorate this day, now named Rakhi Sangeet.

Before long, the freedom seekers established the Federation Hall in Calcutta. In a symbolic act of unity, Surendranath Banerjee tied a rakhi around the wrist of Sikh Guru Kunwar Singh, solidifying the bond between Bengal and Punjab, the two states leading the revolt against British rule. Organizers arranged replicas of such meetings in numerous villages of Bengal, Punjab, Maharashtra and the rest of India. Spokesmen opened their 'demand for self-rule' rallies by reading Rabindranath and Gandhiji's fiery letters and speeches. Select businessmen of Bara Bazar, indifferent about nationalism so far, invested every spare minute in battling the domination of the Indian market by Manchester clothiers. A native foundry owner from Baranagar, known for making Western cutlery, began to collect scrap metal to make knives and swords.

Eluding frequent raids by native police officers working for the British Raj, such as Basanta Chatterjee, Mukund continued his covert efforts to print information brochures for the freedom movement. He provided crucial support to underground operatives and activists like Ashwini Kumar Dutta of Barisal. In November 1905, Dutta circulated a memorandum condemning the export of cotton yarn to England, urging his fellow countrymen to avoid buying clothing produced by British mills that profited using the dirt-cheap raw material muscled out of its largest colony. However, Dutta astutely warned against preventing others from buying imported goods since it would be construed as illegal.

Propelled by Dutta's charm and his circular's clarity, people's committees were formed in every village of Barisal. Laikat Hossain, known for organizing the East India Railway strike, came to Barisal from Calcutta to vigorously support Dutta's cause. His fiery speeches earned him a four-year prison sentence. Nawab Muhammad Hussain of Natore also aligned with Dutta and supported the 'Buy Indian' motto. Dutta's flyer had been printed by Flanagan and funded by Mukund.

The Lieutenant Governor of the newly formed Eastern Bengal and Assam, Mr Fuller, immediately classified Ashwini Dutta's flyer to be seditious. In response, Dutta personally met with Fuller to clarify that his memo sought only to promote freedom regarding consumer choices, not to incite rebellion. As a compromise, Dutta agreed to take out a few words, and Mukund reprinted the revised circular.

To discredit Dutta, the district magistrate of Barisal publicized a distorted account of the exchange between Fuller and the Barisal activist. Fuller alleged that Dutta conceded the seditious nature of his circular. Dutta, undeterred, sought a correction of the magistrate's false claims. When silence followed, Dutta did what few natives at the time dared to do—he filed a defamation lawsuit against the British district magistrate. To the complete credit of an impartial British judge, Dutta won the case, resulting in the magistrate being fined Rs 120. Even English newspapers in Calcutta derided the magistrate's excesses.

Reports from Barisal villages about Hindus forcing Muslims into boycotting British-manufactured clothes reached the magistrate's ears. When the latter arrived at Banaritola village to investigate, a fracas ensued. He arrested a few students, and when he ignored the request to drop the petty charges, protesters reacted angrily by hurling bricks at the magistrate. The latter immediately wired to Fuller, who dispatched Gorkha soldiers and Assamese tribal police to curb the violent unrest.

Churning out a new flyer every night, Mukund and Flanagan worked round the clock to record the armed enforcers' atrocities. Singing nationalistic songs and promoting indigenous goods suddenly became criminal offences. British, along with native soldiers loyal to them, looted shops at will. Under the pretext of investigations, they entered homes, assaulted unwary residents and caused great destruction. Young boys were persecuted for expressing nationalistic sentiments. While visiting Dhaka, Joggeshwar was arrested for singing 'Vande Mataram'. When senior British officers showed up in Barisal, Assamese policemen battered whoever accidentally happened to be on the streets.

During the 1906 provincial conference in Barisal, prominent figures such as Surendranath Banerjee, Barrister Abdullah Rasul, Motilal Ghose and many others arrived in the violence-afflicted town. Mukund and Joggeshwar followed suit. The police pounded them and many other attendees with cudgels. Their apparent crime was wearing a badge that had the words 'Vande Mataram' inscribed on it. Mukund's left eyebrow was scarred for life. Most activists began to sing the banned nationalistic song as lathis struck them again and again.

Surendranath Banerjee, seeking to make a stand, approached Police Superintendent Kemp and courted arrest in lieu of some of the convicted youths. Hours later, when brought before Magistrate Emerson, Surendranath was denied the right to sit and fined Rs 200 for masterminding a procession without a licence and singing 'Vande Mataram'. A native barrister immediately paid his bail. Surendranath returned to the conference site and received a resounding reception from the large crowd. However, the next day, the police imposed a blanket curfew under Criminal Penal Code 144 on the conference attendees and effectively disbanded the masses. On his way back to Calcutta, Surendranath was greeted as a hero at each steamer station by villagers who hailed him as a martyr.

During his stay in Europe, freedom fighter Aurobindo Ghose had closely watched how a small group of Irishmen baffled the English using guerrilla techniques. Inspired, he sought to apply similar strategies in India. Aurobindo operated a nationalistic weekly journal in Bengali called *Bande Mataram*, which began to highlight the violent actions of Fuller and their effect on the people of East Bengal. Bipin Pal, an avid supporter of self-rule and the Age of Consent Bill (1891), had initially started this magazine. Mukund took upon himself the task of printing and distributing hundreds of copies of Aurobindo's and Bipin Pal's writings in Madaripur and Faridpur. Every word of Aurobindo Ghose's incendiary articles was written with a pen but sizzled with fire. Soon, the pen did not seem enough to him. He therefore took to militant means, along with his youngest brother, Barindra Kumar Ghosh.

Fuller's men also decided to prosecute Brahmabandhab Upadhyay, the editor of the paper, *Sandhya*, for sedition. Intrepidly defending his actions, Brahmabandhab died before the trial ended. Bipin Pal's English weekly, *New India*, also came under attack.

After the 1906 INC meetings, freedom fighters Bal Gangadhar Tilak from Bombay and Lala Lajpat Rai from Punjab began to visit Bengal regularly. Soon afterwards, the freedom fighters arranged a 'Shivaji Day' in Calcutta in remembrance of the indigenous ruler who had once successfully defied Mughal rule for years.

Mukund, despite being bedridden with whooping cough for a while, continued to secretly perform translation work (Bengali to English and vice versa) to further support the freedom movement. Rabindranath Tagore composed another legendary poem called *Shivaji's Utsav*. Even cunning, self-serving haberdashers and fancy launderers, who had fattened their pockets lifelong, now hid absconding activists in their storerooms and vat-filled cleaning rooms.

Racecourse gamblers in Calcutta stopped drinking and took up menial late-night jobs to contribute to covert fundraisers. The city's hawkers rapidly morphed into nocturnal artists, drawing anti-colonial graffiti, posters and murals. The head of the Calcutta Police detectives, Charles Tegart started a special branch to locate and arrest freedom fighters.

In October 1906, on the first anniversary of the Partition, cities like Dhaka, Calcutta, Faridpur, Pabna, Chittagong and Barisal saw complete standstills and processions. The Nawab of Dhaka, Khwaja Salimullah, also joined in. The protesters reiterated solidarity by singing 'Vande Mataram' yet again. Young and old unitedly promised to only buy and use indigenous home-grown goods.

Adamant on maintaining the division of Bengal on religious lines and weakening the nationalistic movement, Lord Curzon steadily worked on manipulating the most vulnerable side of human nature. He decided to lure away the key figure in East Bengal to his side by offering money in a creative way. To secure his long-term allegiance, the viceroy offered the Nawab Salimullah of Dhaka a loan of Rs 1.4 million at a next-to-nothing interest rate.

Thereafter, with Salimullah's unwavering help, more and more Muslims began to support the break-up of Bengal. The government's intent was communal or, at best, divisive, when it began to encourage the formation of a new political entity—the All-India Muslim League, which was finally formed on 30 December 1906 in Dhaka. Ethnic confrontations erupted in the province and in Comilla. The nawab patronized red leaflets urging fellow Muslims not to support the nationalistic Swadeshi Movement. Thus, the League dawned with the tacit supposition that the interests of Indian Muslims could not be served by the INC.

Tagore, observing the growing communal tensions, immediately wrote a caution to the nation: 'There was rarely any serious prejudice between Hindus and Muslims of India. Request our British rulers not to create division among us.' However, the inter-religious clashes began to slowly spread and swirl across various districts of Bengal.

At the same crossroads of time, to celebrate Aneek's 16th birthday, the teenager's grand-uncle Flanagan and grand-aunt Prachi visited Mukund's mansion. To alleviate his mother's worries and longings and to curb his own homesickness, the lad had come home for a few days from his new boarding school in Santiniketan. However, the day before Aneek's birthday, Bonka's first wife brought Mukund grim news: Gorkha troops loyal to the British had evicted 50 families from Banaritola and nearby hamlets, including a nationalistic relative of hers. Many of these families were on the brink of starvation.

Garnering whatever resources they could find, Mukund and Flanagan took the first steamer to Barisal. With help from local men, they set up eight tents at record speed and provided food—

rice, dal and squash curry—to the displaced families for 20 days until a lawsuit filed by a famed barrister allowed the residents to return to their homes.

Not to be outdone by Mukund in charity work for the oppressed, Nobin launched his own fundraising drive for the evicted villagers with the help of Moi. Most people in Madaripur and other parts of Faridpur pitched in generously, and the duo collected nearly Rs 50,000 from roughly several hundred farmers and the burgeoning middle-class meritocracy of East Bengal. However, Nobin siphoned off 80 per cent of the money under the guise of travel and administrative expenses, lining his own pockets.

Shiuli, a maidservant in Nobin's household, could not digest her master's corruption. She trotted for nearly two *kos* to divulge the ugly secret to Archana, clutching her master's fake balance sheet to her bosom, which she had taken from Nobin's special ledgers, concealed in a disused storeroom's subsurface alcove. Shiuli disclosed that Nobin had hidden the ill-gotten money in the same alcove instead of the highly secure iron vault he normally used.

Archana immediately sent long-retired Jimut's armed horse riding son to Barisal to inform Mukund. Nobin's wicked inclination to cheat even a small band of nationalist villagers cast into dire straits by lawless native troops incensed the zamindar deeply. He grew determined to somehow recover the stolen money.

Pacing in his hallway all night long, Mukund devised a plan with Flanagan to reclaim the Rs 40,000 Nobin held illegally in the secret alcove.

Before going to sleep, Flanagan had a chat with Aneek and then dragged Bonka to a secluded corner of the backyard. No one ever came to know about what exactly transpired out there.

But at dawn, as soon as Prachi headed to the kitchen to prepare breakfast, Flanagan dashed to one of the large storerooms in Mukund's mansion. He knew precisely what he wanted. Searching through the shelves that housed Mr Hall's spare medicines and medical supplies, Flanagan located a bottle of the colourless, sweet-smelling and dense liquid—chloroform. He grinned widely. Bringing the sealed bottle near his nose, he made sure of its contents with a quick sniff. 'This will work,' he murmured to himself as he slipped the bottle into his pocket. Without delay, he quietly ambled towards the main walkway in front of the house.

At exactly 5.30 a.m., while Mukund was still asleep and Archana was heading to the prayer room, Flanagan stopped her and whispered, 'I know Mukund is still sleeping and he thinks our daily work will start at 6.30 a.m. Just for today, make sure you and Prachi hide the handguns he has been personally carrying of late.' Then he turned around and with Bonka next to him, mounted the family's main carriage.

Pale as snow, Archana stood alone in the quiet morning, terrified as she watched Flanagan and Bonka prepare to depart. Just as the four-horse carriage was about to leave, Aneek dashed out from his room and handed Bonka a clothbag. Archana chose not to enquire about the contents while Flanagan, as if going for a joyride, gave a brief nod to the teenager and waved cheerily at Archana, who looked on worriedly.

Four hours later, Flanagan and Bonka arrived at the home of Mrs Rasul, a revolutionary activist in Barisal. With his customary flair, the Irishman talked the beautiful and naive Englishwoman into joining him for a worthy mission. Clueless of Nobin's deceit, Mrs Rasul saw great merit in encouraging Nobin's fundraising efforts and supporting the self-rule-seeking populace of Barisal. She readily consented to accompany Flanagan on a congratulatory trip to the spice trader's residence. As they approached the alley near his home, Flanagan dropped Bonka off at a teashop they knew well.

Around 10 a.m., Flanagan and his unwitting female companion arrived at Nobin's home. The spice trader had never imagined seeing the beaming face of the attractive British wife of nationalistic leader Abdul Rasul at his front door. This was Nobin's perfect opportunity to wipe out some of his notoriety and emerge as a compassionate leader in the community, and at the same time stuff his coffers like never before. Overjoyed, he welcomed Flanagan and Mrs Rasul into his living room. Within a few moments, Nobin's servants and his wife swarmed around the unexpected visitors, holding every golden plate of hospitality.

While Nobin was basking in the moment, Bonka, disguised as a naked, mad fakir with wild hair and an ash-smeared face, slipped into Nobin's vast two-storey manor through the back door. He pranced in and out of the rooms, including the living room where the Englishwoman was seated. Except Flanagan, the mastermind behind this idea, no one could recognize the intruder's identity. To avoid the inescapable viewing of his ash-smeared swaying genitals, the mortified women—the cook, Nobin's wife, the maids and even Mrs Rasul—rushed to hide in an underground storeroom.

Pretending to help Nobin track down the madman, Flanagan accompanied the spice trader through the house. The fleet-footed Bonka kept dodging, staying out of reach, keeping the household distracted just long enough for Flanagan to make his move.

As soon as Flanagan found Nobin's manservant isolated in one of the rooms, he swiftly overpowered him, soaking a kitchen rag with chloroform and pressing it against the man's face until he was rendered unconscious. With the servant out of the way, Flanagan turned his attention to Nobin.

Tiptoeing from behind, the Irishman wrestled Nobin down to the ground. But before he could gag his mouth with the chloroform-soaked-handkerchief, the well-built Nobin fought back hard. Like two mighty bears fighting over a large fish, they vied momentarily for control of the cloth. In the end, the spice trader succumbed. As Nobin lay unconscious, Flanagan scanned the house, calling out Shiuli's name. When he found her, he spared the loyal maid from the same fate.

Before long, Flanagan inflicted the same ordeal on all the maids as well as on Nobin's wife until they, too, passed out. When everyone in the inner chambers of the home except Shiuli lay unconscious, he summoned her eager help to retrieve the cash from the hidden alcove. Still oblivious of the well-intentioned burglary, Mrs Rasul sat patiently in the storage room.

Upon locating the stash, Flanagan stuffed the money into a cloth bag and quickly made his way out. Bonka, still disguised as the mad fakir, had already made his exit through the kitchen, pulling a dhoti off the clothesline to cover his bare loins.

The Irishman's insane plan had worked flawlessly. Within days, the evicted, hard-pressed families of Barisal received all the financial help they needed to return to their homes and rebuild their lives. Shiuli, fearing retribution from her master, disappeared that very day, never to be seen in Nobin's household again. Knowing the dubious, ill-gotten nature of the money he had just lost and of Flanagan's tough retributive temperament, Nobin chose not to file a lawsuit against him.

No one except Prachi came to know that her grandnephew, Aneek, had been an accomplice in the highly unusual heist. Not even his mother, Archana, found out that it was her teenage son who, on the fly, had supplied Bonka's disguise of long hair and face-masking ash, beard and moustache. All of it was once meant to be used in a play Aneek had nearly acted in at Santiniketan.

In the larger scheme of things, the primal relief the people of East Bengal felt by the end of 1906 was when the despotic Mr Fuller dug his own professional grave. In the height of arrogance, Fuller directed Calcutta University to force out two of its nationalist students known for organizing frequent agitations. This decision alarmed Archana, who feared that Aneek's own political involvement might someday attract the attention of British authorities, potentially jeopardizing his future.

At the time, Gilbert John Elliot-Murray-Kynynmound, better known as Viceroy Lord Minto, happened to be Fuller's boss as well as the chancellor of Calcutta University. The reform-minded 4th earl of Minto rightfully sought advice in this regard from the newly appointed vice chancellor of the university, Sir Ashutosh Mukherjee. The bushy-moustachioed prodigy of maths and physics and alumnus of Presidency College urged his Eton- and Trinity-educated superior not to disaffiliate the students. Drawing on his family's legacy of opposing tyranny, when Lord Minto's great-grandfather, Lord Gilbert Minto (Senior), had befriended Edmund Burke in their intense dislike for the oppressive actions of Warren Hastings, the first governor-general of Bengal, Minto agreed. He immediately instructed Fuller to withdraw the students' expulsion request. When the Lieutenant Governor refused, Lord Minto readily fired his fractious deputy from the high office. After Fuller's exit from East Bengal, the violence against citizens engaging in civil disobedience eased.

Meanwhile, Mukund busied himself in the search for erudite educators, keen on spreading learning in rural eastern Bengal. He looked for young men groomed by pioneering and premier colleges who also shared his vision. Travelling on foot, by riverboat, steamer and train, he met graduates from renowned institutions like Jagannath College in Dhaka, Ripon College and Presidency College in Calcutta, and several more. Eventually, he and his band of teachers founded many schools in various villages of Faridpur district. But the dream of self-rule, if not complete independence, remained alive and unremitted in the fondest nooks of his heart.

Between 1906 and 1910, when some of his friends joined the INC and demanded self-rule, Mukund continued to work 14 hours a day to publish numerous leaflets for local militant revolutionary leaders. At his own expense, he voluntarily reprinted and distributed a more economical concise version of the English daily *Bengalee*. He did this to better educate and politically awaken the residents of Madaripur, many of whom were learning English for the first time in their lineage.

During his school years, Aneek went back and forth between home-schooling, a local school in Madaripur and the newly founded Santiniketan boarding school. Rabindranath Tagore's newly established school was not too far from home. The monthly fees of Rs 15 covered all essentials, including tuition, boarding, medical support, grooming, laundry and food. However, Aneek's neglectful communication with his family became a source of deep distress for his mother, Archana. The absence of letters and his physical distance left her anxious and miserable. Before long, she exerted subtle but enormous pressure on her husband to bring their son home. Archana's health began to deteriorate, and she started talking to herself and goblins in the middle of the night, preferring plants over people. As she steadily lost weight, Mukund's resolve to provide their son with the finest culture as well as education buckled.

After spending six months in Santiniketan, Aneek once again returned to Madaripur. The revised plan was to have him complete his school and college education in the nearby town of Faridpur.

His return brought comfort not only to Archana but also to Flanagan and Mr Hall. The Irishman began to frequent the mansion once again, showering Aneek with insanely expensive gifts he could barely afford. Mr Hall even gave away his two pet parakeets that Aneek had long coveted. The uniqueness of these birds was that they never had to be caged.

One day, Mukund and Archana went to attend a distant cousin's marriage in Barisal, leaving their son for seven days in the care of Flanagan. On the very first day of his parents' absence, Aneek fell from his horse and badly bruised his upper arm. As the lad writhed in pain, the Irishman was filled with anxiety. He sat cross-legged on the marble floor, closing his eyes to think. His first instinct was to find the nearest physician, but something else took over his mind.

Abandoning the vial of modern medicine bought from a pharmacy, Flanagan decided to return to his Irish roots to heal Aneek's wound. Recalling his older brother's penchant for herbal remedies, he rummaged through his antiquated holdall and pulled out a bag of dried herbs. The mixture, made from willow bark and heartsease extract, was a remedy commonly used in the British Isles in days past. By chance, Flanagan had recently purchased it from a European general store in Calcutta.

One week later, when the teenager's parents returned home, the swelling had drastically reduced, and the nearly healed laceration on Aneek's arm did not attract Archana's maternal worry.

Part III

Chapter 25

Fragments of Freedom and a Mother's Woes

INDIA'S SWADESHI STRUGGLE, FOCUSING ON SELF-SUFFICIENCY through the boycott of foreign goods and promotion of indigenous products, continued with full vigour well after the partition of Bengal. The underground elements of the Indian populace were finally awakening to the possibility of deploying various strategies simultaneously, from ambushing key administrators of the British Raj to non-violent resistance, boycotts, strikes and non-cooperation. The cumulative effect of these efforts was slowly becoming apparent.

Mukund, now clad in a fatua and a folded dhoti, adhered strictly to a vegetarian diet, abstaining from meat and even fish. Every other week he would visit underground cells in Jinjira, Kidderpore or Chandernagore. Wearing silk or leather face masks, he always returned under the dark cover of the night. While these outfits had developed many young skilled sharpshooters, targeting high-ranking British officers, who often adopted unpredictable travel patterns, was proving to be a challenge. The fear of high collateral damage plagued the freedom fighters as well.

Archana, on the other hand, faced her own struggles. The physical ardour she once knew in her marriage had dwindled almost entirely, leaving her with a sense of disappointment. Her cooks also no longer allowed her to do anything strenuous or time-consuming in the kitchen. Sometimes, she wished her day would be more swamped so that she would have no time or energy left to drift into other longings. At times, the forlorn mother wished she had 13 children like one of her neighbours. But the zamindar's wife felt beset by fate to escape her destiny. She hurt the most when Mukund accidentally walked past her amid a roomful of freedom-seeking babus he gathered in their living room and sought donations for another printing press dedicated to nationalistic leaflets and booklets.

Once in a blue moon, when Mukund and Archana lay in bed together and he plumped the pillow behind her back, she grew hopeful, especially when her husband's hands accidentally grazed her breasts or her thighs. Alas, thereafter, he briefly held her in his arms, but with platonic affection. Archana's last hopes for intimacy decimated as soon as he turned on his side, snoring within minutes. Later, the sleepless wife would brush her fingertips across his warm forehead, feeling a deep sense of loss. She sometimes blamed ancestral bad karma for her husband's lack of interest in extending their quota of sensuality into their middle age.

Mukund's mind was determined to reject all joys around him relating to touch, vision and hearing—if that would somehow bring freedom to his motherland.

Facing the reality of her situation, Archana soon ceased to act as her husband's seductress and steadfastly learnt the intricacies of press operation. Their only apprentice seemed eager to share all he knew. Thus, during Mukund's and Flanagan's absence from Madaripur, she became the de facto press machinist. Slowly regaining a modicum of exposure, she became a workaholic of a slightly different kind. Even if she did not have a clue where her husband was obtaining the materials to be printed, she became an efficient mass producer. Although he never expressed much, Mukund quietly adored her for her vigorous support.

In 1907, a band of bleary-eyed babus working in the Writers' Building faked accidents to avoid work, intending to create home-made explosives. Their aim was to disrupt the early telephone booths that were appearing in the heart of Calcutta.

These were the times when the elite Englishmen avoided using their phones for long-distance connections, preferring instead to make appointments with the Calcutta Telephone Company and travel to special long-distance 'silence cabinets', equipped with four-wire telephones, to ensure clarity during their calls.

This period also saw communal Hindu–Muslim riots across the country, leading to significant bloodshed.

At this time, to Archana's utter dismay, Mukund became increasingly involved in Dhaka's newly formed freedom-seeking organization called Broti (the Missionary). Following the partition of Bengal, many such groups had mushroomed, with the Anushilan Samiti in Dhaka and Suhrid Samiti in Mymensingh being the most prominent. These groups focused their efforts on fellow natives, searching for activists who dared to voice aspirations of self-rule, and deliberately violated multiple militancy-based laws of the Indian Penal Code.

In the 150-year-old abandoned ruins of the Jinjira Palace, not far from Mukund's estate, where the Mughal governors of Bengal—Sarfaraz, Alivardi and Siraj—once lived, new activists including Mukund began to hold secret meetings in the middle of the night.

Every other day, late at night, Archana stared at the bedroom wall clock with consternation until she heard the familiar thud of the front door announcing her husband's arrival. On their way back home, each member would hide their pistols and small bombs in a narrow tunnel they had dug amid the Jinjira ruins. The months dragged on, and Archana, tense and worried, suffered the loss of two premature stillborn children. To liven up Archana, Mukund bought a renovated bajra from an open-air mart next to the Bharakar Canal in Bikrampur. Although it was not as fine as the ones his father Keshav once had in his fleet, he hoped it would lift her spirits. However, he knew how lovelorn Archana eagerly waited for him and not his gifts.

One day, while Mukund was away, the Calcutta Police tracked down his home and printing press. Before the white cops wearing white uniforms could enter and search the premises, Archana worked up a storm. She first tied a gamchha around her waist, and with the help of Bonka's two wives, quickly cleaned up all traces of controversial leaflets. Jimut's son and the mansion guards relocated and hid the printing presses in a cellar beneath the kitchen.

When the police arrived, the women, including the cooks, had transformed the mansion to appear completely innocuous. When one of the fastidious deputy inspectors still nosed around, Archana picked up an axe and chased him out of her home. His cronies breathlessly followed suit. No one from the law enforcement offices of Calcutta or Faridpur ever again entered her house.

Chapter 26

A Chance Encounter

AROUND 1908, MUKUND MET A YOUNG REVOLUTIONARY NAMED Jatindranath Mukherjee in one of the stenographer's offices at the Bengal secretariat in Calcutta. Mukund was visiting this spectacular red-brick office to submit a job application on behalf of his farmer's orphaned son. As the summer wind stirred the Union Jack atop the red multistorey building, Mukund noticed Jatin standing on the lower steps of the Secretariat.

Mukund, peering at the handsome clerk, asked, 'Jatin Babu, are you not the one taking stenographer's lessons from the famous Mr Atkinson?'

Jatin nodded in the affirmative before unenthusiastically gazing at the honey-coloured sunlight that had striped the main staircase.

'Can I please have a word with you?'

'Yes. But let us not chat here. Perhaps, we can get to know each other under that faraway tree?' Jatin suggested.

'Sure. But first, do you know the room number where I can submit this application for a worthy young man who has completed his matriculation with high marks?'

'If I were you, I would not submit the application in any secretariat such as this.'

'Why not?'

'A clerical job here would only lead to a life of relentless subservience,' Jatin explained. 'Tell your young man to come and see me. I will give him a different kind of job.'

'What kind?'

'Let us sit under that shady tree and continue this discussion...' As they walked towards the tree, Jatin added, 'Will the youth be ready to handle a few run-ins with the police? Can he brave the possibility of the harshest interrogations by inspectors in dingy jail cells where the daroga babus might pull out his toenails or teeth?

Mukund's anticipation grew. Had he finally met the embodiment of his ultimate dreams? Someone who was willing to risk his all for the seemingly unattainable dream—a sovereign India?

Perched on a sun-baked stump under the tree, Mukund pretended not to understand Jatin's pointers. 'What other kind of job do you have in mind?'

Standing close by and holding the end of his plain white dhoti in his hand, Jatin said, 'First, take off the sunglasses you are wearing.'

Sensing the distrust, Mukund complied but added, 'I assure you that I did not wear them to emulate the British; it was only to provide shade and relief to my weak eyes. Wait a minute...You are not Bagha Jatin, are you?'

'Yes, that is my nickname. I wanted to see your eyes clearly to determine if I could trust you.'

The tall revolutionary rose to his full height. His long, sinewy legs, hidden until now by the folds of his crisp white dhoti, came into view as he briskly stamped on a thick twig lying in the dust, effortlessly snapping it in two.

Jatindranath Mukherjee, deeply committed to India's freedom, had been secretly devising plans for months. His nickname, Bagha Jatin, had resulted from an incident in the jungles of Kushtia in eastern Bengal. A Royal Bengal tiger had been terrorizing nearby villages. Jatin and his cousin, along with a band of drummers hired to scare the beast, set out to kill the man-eater. When the tiger appeared, Jatin's cousin shot at it, only managing to graze its ears. As the tiger lunged at Jatin, he fought it off with a gruesome struggle, ultimately killing the beast despite being gravely injured.

Wiping sweat beads off his bushy eyebrows, Mukund gazed at the fine-looking youth with pure admiration. A few moments passed into the wombs of mysterious time.

Wide-eyed, Mukund whispered, 'My friends in the Anushilan Samiti and Bandhab Samiti tell me that you are the freedom-seeker who wants to acquire weapons from Germany and link up with the guerrilla units in Meerut and Ludhiana?'

Bagha Jatin smiled faintly. 'I am just a simple man, once thrown out of a railway carriage by a British Raj lackey because of the colour of my skin,' he said, his broad chest, draped in a beige Khadi shawl, rising with deep, oceanic anger. 'Now, I want to die fighting a fierce, open-armed battle so that our nation may awaken forever.'

He looked at the blue sky as if already dreaming about the deep sea and the ships bringing ashore the cartons of bullets and rifles he pined for. His large and eloquent eyes resembled an uncharted ocean breaking upon reefs miles away.

Bagha Jatin looked back at Mukund. 'You can put your goggles back on. I will answer your query.'

Mukund heaved a huge sigh of relief, but deep within, he felt something in his core had irreversibly changed.

Bagha Jatin continued, 'Yes, I am a freedom fighter who believes that the Brits would leave only after facing some level of violence. If you want your farmer's son to live a patriot's life, he can join my band.'

Mukund replied, 'Yes, I have heard about you. I have no trouble with adopting such a route. But what drove you to such extreme militancy? Tell me more.'

'Five years ago, in 1903, I first met Aurobindo Ghose and Niralamba Swami. Their vision of a sovereign motherland inspired me deeply. A year later, in 1904, I began my career as a stenographer to support my young family. I might have stayed there, taking shorthand notes until old age, if not for a personal tragedy.'

'What happened?'

'In 1906, I lost my eldest son, Atindra, to cholera. He was only three. That loss changed everything. To cope with the grief,

I threw myself into the freedom struggle. Soon after, I met many more young men ready to bear arms for our sovereignty. And now...'

'Now what?'

'Now, I'm seeking young sharpshooters with steady hands and nerves—those who have the courage to take out high-ranking British officers. How old are you?'

Mukund sighed. 'I'm 43. I assume your wife supports you fully?'

Bagha Jatin smiled. 'Yes, my wife, Indubala, is my anchor. Your eyes and nerves are too old for my sharpshooter openings. But if you can fend off one of my best swordsmen for five minutes, I will give you an emissary's role. At times, you may have to go to neighbouring states to acquire weapons and firearms. Is that acceptable to you?'

Middle-aged Mukund could not believe his impetuosity as he blurted, 'Yes! Where do I take this test?'

'Next Sunday, meet me at the Sealdah railway station ticket counter at 9 a.m. I will take you to one of my hideouts.'

'All right, but can I bring a faithful companion who has been with me since my childhood?' asked Mukund. 'He can be my backup.'

Stepping closer and now only inches away, Bagha Jatin scrutinized Mukund's face for what seemed like an eternity. Mukund felt exposed, as if he were standing naked in a bitterly cold wind.

'Very well, then. I will see you both on Sunday. But you must not share what you do for me and my band, not even to your wife and children. Can you keep such a promise?'

'Yes.'

Bagha Jatin then asked, 'Do you read and appreciate Rabi Thakur's writings?'

'Yes, I do.'

'I do too. But...'

Mukund inquired, 'But what?'

'Though I love Rabi Thakur's poems and songs, I do not know

what to make of the poet's recent over-reliance on C.F. Andrews to edit and translate his masterful short stories into English.'

'Do you mean the teacher from St Stephen's College in Delhi?'

Bagha Jatin confirmed, 'Yes. Andrews is altering our poet's stories published in *Sadhana* to make them palatable to Western readers.'

'But Andrews is strongly supporting our call for freedom, is he not?'

'That he is… See you Sunday near the Sealdah station's ticket counter.'

~

Bagha Jatin led Mukund and Bonka to one of the underground militant units located behind a disused railway signal cabin in the sprawling Chitpur shunting yard. There, Mukund passed the physical agility test by the skin of his teeth.

Amused by the middle-aged volunteer's swordsmanship mediocrity but highly impressed by his perseverance, Bagha Jatin embraced Mukund warmly.

'My agility with the sword and the gun has waned in recent years.'

Bagha Jatin responded reassuringly, 'Never mind. Willpower and desire are what matter the most. Now, I have one more man to help us with the purchase and distribution of weapons and in the recruitment of sharpshooters.'

'Thank you. Is that all for today?'

Handing the landlord a dog-eared rifle-and revolver users' handbook, Bagha Jatin said softly, 'Yes. Exactly two weeks from today, meet me right here.' His eyes glistened with emotion as he continued, 'Irfan Khan is one of my most trusted revolutionary agents. As we speak, his younger sister is nursing his broken nose at his home in Kidderpore. I met him yesterday… I won't regret confiding in you so soon, will I?'

Mukund assured him, 'No, you will not be sorry. But I will be honest with you. I will not tell anyone about your activities, not even my wife. However, I will share your efforts with my son Aneek. He is already imbued with the same spirit as you. It will inspire him.'

Bagha Jatin smiled. 'Try to bring him next time you come. British Police Commissioner Charles Tegart of Lal Bazar is already trying to build a national "conspiracy" case against me. Do you recall passing a railroad crossing before you got here?'

'Yes.'

Bagha Jatin continued, 'Riding in black cars, Tegart's sleuths have been snooping around the crossing. They have been asking shopkeepers and paanwallahs about my whereabouts.' Wrapping a brown khadi shawl around his broad shoulders, Bagha Jatin groaned like a wounded lion, 'How much longer will we Indians behave like woodlice scurrying from a campfire? How long will my countrymen try to avoid the ever-chasing flame of segregation, subjugation and humiliation?'

~

As the sky deepened into shades of velvety pink and scarlet, Mukund made his way home. Walking for miles through knee-high grass along the rail tracks, new hopes of freedom filled his soul. Life irreversibly changed for Mukund after that meeting. Yet on this evening in 1908, he had no idea that in just seven years, young Bagha Jatin would lead a massive wave of armed militancy against the British Raj.

After 200 years of British rule, a range of fidelity and righteousness seemed to have seeped into the hearts of Indian cops and lawyers loyal to the British. Mukund's resolve was unwavering. The motherland had to be liberated, no matter the cost.

Chapter 27

The Defiant Son

IT WAS THE DAY ANEEK WAS SET TO RETURN TO HIS COLLEGE in Calcutta. After passing his matriculation, he had secured admission to City College, and the prospect of leaving home weighed heavily on both Mukund and Archana.

Earlier that morning, just after dawn, Aneek bicycled to a shrimp pond Mukund owned. Heeding Archana's urgings, he needed to oversee the repair of a wooden footbridge spanning a creek—the only access to the fishery. Perchance, Bonka's younger wife was passing in a two-horse cart with her newly married teenage daughter, Shukla, to the latter's in-laws' place.

As the cart slowly made its way along the creek, two masons working on a nearby government building began to harass Shukla with lewd remarks. The masons, known for their loose tongues, approached the cart with unwelcome advances. The stalking artisans did not realize that Aneek had noticed their unwelcome and lusty advances from a distance. When the unprovoked sexual innuendoes continued and Bonka's terrified wife cried out for help, Aneek pounced on them like a starving panther. With his bare hands, the 18-year-old pummelled them until they turned black and blue. It was only at Bonka's wife's urging that Aneek finally relented.

It was around 2 p.m. when Aneek surreptitiously returned home. Archana had not yet broken her ekadashi fast. Quickly concealing his bruised arm by changing into a full-sleeve shirt, the teen avoided divulging his violent scuffle. A bit under the weather, Mukund napped in the master bedroom. Archana seemed pleased to find her son and husband home at the same time—a rare phenomenon of late.

As Archana finished grinding a medley of tulsi leaves, *draksha, brihati,* pipul, *vasak,* honey and *jastimadhu* into a thick solution—her husband's favourite medication for lung ailments— Aneek relished his final moments of relaxation before returning to Calcutta. He had enjoyed a restful week in Madaripur, a mini-break from his college and secret nightlife with fellow activists in the vicinity. He seemed to have enjoyed the lull, in addition to his mother's pampering and Bonka kaka's indulgences.

The previous morning, Aneek had visited some of the impoverished villagers living in shanties with corrugated iron roofs near Mukund's compound. Over puffed rice, onions and green chillies, he had attempted to persuade them to return to Calcutta and join the freedom movement.

A few minutes later, Aneek found both his parents in their spacious, high-ceilinged bedroom. It was the moment the youth had been looking for since the conclusion of a reticent lunch session.

Aneek warily glanced at the three-blade ceiling fan whirling inadequately in the heavily humid afternoon. Arranged by Flanagan, Mukund's farmhands and an English electrician had recently installed fans in almost all the rooms. The European-made fan replaced the *tana pankha*—a hanging, large, rectangular canvas fan fixed to a wooden beam and suspended from the ceiling. Aneek had seen them as a child in Darbhanga and at his old home when his grandfather Keshav was still alive.

'Ma and Baba,' Aneek began, his eyes gleaming with an unusual sense of purpose. 'In a little while I will be returning to Calcutta. I wanted to say goodbye before your afternoon nap.'

He looked down at his mother's perfectly shaped feet and felt enormously pleased to see her wearing a special brand of bright red *alta* he had brought for her last time from the big city. The long-necked, sharp-featured and statuesque woman's simple bold-green *dhaniakhali* sari with a molten gold border belied her husband's renewed financial prosperity and underserved her residual beauty. The slender limbs, flawless teeth and lotus-like eyes had remained mostly unfazed despite the loss of one of her two sons and the vicious razing of a flourishing ancestral zamindari. Only her blazing complexion looked more tempered than what Aneek remembered it to be in his childhood and lines now creased her clear face when she smiled or frowned. Tiny beads of sweat had created a rim around her large sindoor bindi reigning amid her shapely forehead.

Looking anxious, Mukund pressed his cracked lips tight for a moment. 'Stay a bit longer. Why not take the morning train and spend the evening with your mother?' His heavily lined forehead, sizeable bags under his eyes and slightly sunken cheeks hinted at a far more afflicted life.

Aneek said, 'Next time, I will stay longer. I know Prachi thakuma is working on renovating the area surrounding the village's Ram temple. But where is Flanagan? I was hoping to say goodbye to him as well.'

Looking utterly miffed by her son's imminent departure, Archana answered, 'Flanagan has gone to a village near Baghia. Despite his age and poor health, he is trying to investigate a rundown school that has fallen into the hands of the wrong kind of people. Its nefarious principal has been funnelling money away from the school funds, which your father has been contributing heavily for years.'

Mukund gulped the remaining ayurvedic concoction Archana had handed him. 'Son, what is it you want to tell us?'

Aneek responded, 'Baba, I plan to resume studies at City College and not Scottish Church.'

Even before Mukund could blink, the weary mother probed the 18-year-old, 'Why not? What is wrong with Scottish Church?'

Aneek appeared resolute. 'Do not worry. I have already filled out the necessary forms and the transfer has been approved by both colleges.'

Archana's voice rose. 'What insolence! You did not even bother to seek our permission before making such a big move! The location of your present college probably does not suit your underground meetings, bomb-making, etc. Is that right?'

Mukund sighed. 'Yes. It must be at the behest of one of those inexorable summonses from one of your freedom fighter friends...'

Aneek did not reply.

Archana's frustration boiled over as she clutched the mahogany bed's mosquito net poles. She tried to dismiss the proposal like a wounded but resolute tigress. 'I have already lost little Avirup to the worst of maladies. Is it not enough that in this home there is one man, my husband, who is already assigned to a life-risking cause?'

The mother's pathos-filled plea evoked no response from the steadfast son. Head bowed, Aneek stood quietly as Archana nearly screamed at her husband, 'Do you not envision the immediate future? I can almost see our son soon standing with the hangman near the scaffolds of Alipore Jail, his legs shackled in iron.'

Mukund addressed his agitated wife. 'Yes, Archana, I do not disagree with you that along with nationalistic ventures, Aneek should finish his BA from a fine college. But how do we ensure that our 18-year-old towering son will heed our advice any longer?'

Aneek stared impassively at a grand old wall clock his grandfather had bought from Calcutta, which had survived the dreadful arson.

Archana urged her husband, 'Why do you not try again to convince him while he is still standing here? You know what happened to Jimut's grandson? The Lal Bazar daroga and his two constables killed him and dumped his body in a ditch in Moulali, just for coming out of a samiti meeting late at night.'

Setting his hookah pot aside and repositioning himself in the armchair, Mukund turned towards his tall progeny whose head nearly touched the curtain rod. 'Son, your First Arts results were slightly less than expected due to the obvious distractions in the Calcutta mess where you now live. Why do you not complete the first year of your bachelor's degree in Scottish Church before doing anything drastic?'

Aneek defied his father for the first time. 'I will finish my BA, but not from the institution you have in mind. I will study at City College, near my operational units.'

Archana's eyes widened. 'Do you mean the freedom movement cells?'

Turning towards his son, Mukund knew times had changed. There was no point in an explosive confrontation.

Aneek pressed further. 'Ma, our family cook, Khushee, told me that a few days before I got home you and the mothers of many incarcerated young men from neighbouring villages travelled unarmed to Dhaka. As a band of 60 grown women, you performed candlelight vigil day and night outside the main prison. Why did you do such an unprecedented thing?'

'These women are my good friends. What else could we do? Falsely charged with sedition, many of their sons, young men like you, are being unduly held there for months. Somebody had to at least speak up...'

'Ma, if your heart compels you to fight for other people's sons, why will you not let me do a bit more?'

'But son, they were involved in peaceful protests while your efforts are mostly violent...are they not?'

The youth did not answer his mother's query. Archana stood there, feeling like a boatwoman stranded far from home.

Mukund, clearly frustrated, spoke with strained patience. 'Why not try to maximize learning the sound knowledge the Scottish brothers are offering? Will it not help in your nationalism as well?'

Aneek replied firmly, 'I will leave that decision to my unit mentors in Calcutta. The college location must allow me to stay close to the activist cells.'

'Can you at least tell us the name and particulars of a contact person should we not hear from you?'

Like thousands of other women in India, Archana too faced the insoluble dilemma between protecting her son's life and well-being, and furthering the nation's freedom. Only some parents understood where exactly to draw the line.

Archana knew about Aneek's affection for Damini, a passionate activist. While she secretly admired Damini's dedication, she was deeply fearful of the dangerous path Aneek was on, especially with someone as radical as Damini.

In vain, Aneek tried to hug his mother, but Archana, overwhelmed and desperate, stepped back. 'Having almost died while giving birth to you, I do expect a bit of compliance from you for a little longer, maybe another year or so. Maybe that will give us time to keep you safe.'

Archana rarely put her foot down with her son or her husband. When she did, no one dared to flout her command. The distraught mother's determination to keep her son out of serious harm had taken root a few months earlier after an anxiety-packed two days during which Aneek had disappeared from his Calcutta flat for the umpteenth time. The difference was, this time, Aneek had nearly died, caught in the crossfire between two rival thug gangs fighting for territorial supremacy.

From Aneek's childhood, Archana had pampered him endlessly. The maximum punishment Aneek had ever received from her was not speaking to him for a week. She invariably terminated the penalty after the passage of a few hours. Due to the turbulent times, whenever Aneek absconded for a variety of reasons, she curled up in her canopied bed and wept endlessly. She fasted as well. On several occasions, the search party for the youth, comprising Mukund and his friends, blitzed around Madaripur resembling a pack of chicks with their heads cut off. Once, they cruised along the Arial Khan and Palang rivers for three days at a stretch, looking for river bandits who reportedly might have kidnapped the carefree lad.

Aneek took out a revolver and a long knife from his innocuous-looking shoulder bag. Brandishing them over his head, he spoke with assurance, 'Ma, they have to work overtime before they can dump my dead body in the Hooghly River.'

Distraught but trying to maintain control, Mukund restrained his rare but sharp temper. Siding with his wife, he said, 'Son, put your gun and dagger away; do not scare your mother. She has good reasons to be concerned about you.'

'Baba, several of us...freedom fighters...we move together and cover for each other. All right, Ma, can I get a hug now?'

Archana grudgingly agreed and even managed a faint smile as her son enveloped her in a tight embrace. Mukund observed the scene with a quiet love that softened the lines of his face.

Mukund stood up and leaned over his Burma teak desk. A few minutes later, he handed three signed and filled-out cheques to his son. Bearing the imperial stamp, the Bank of Bengal note looked surreal.

Aneek stood near the window, drumming his fingers on the sill. He briefly looked outside where about 25 of the poorest villagers had gathered under a banyan tree to solicit funds for a new high-grade community *charkha*. In line with the Swadeshi Movement, they preferred home-spun clothes and to save their precious earnings for food. In vain, a baton-carrying constable loyal to the British Raj tried hard to chase them away. Aneek smiled. Yet he couldn't ignore the many more battles that lay ahead across the sprawling subcontinent.

Mukund remarked, 'Son, the flamboyant days of your grandfather are gone, especially after the arson and the reconstruction. Last week you were helping our gomosta with the farm income ledgers. Were you not?'

Aneek anxiously twirled a pencil he had just picked up from his father's desk. 'Yes. So, what are you saying?'

Archana raised her eyebrows. 'You know our financial situation. So, spend this money more carefully than before.' Her teeth, stained from the paan and zarda she used to cope with the stress, showed briefly as she spoke. She toyed with a set of silver forks and spoons lying on the sidetable no one had ever used in the household.

Aneek took only one of the cash envelopes and returned the other two. 'I will not need much of this money.'

Hugging her son, Archana nearly choked on her emotions. 'And why not? Keep some for emergencies...'

Aneek explained, 'Our samiti's unit head lets us keep most of the money we earn from making and selling indigenous soaps and oils.'

The most painful hour in Archana's household had arrived. Her son was leaving home for Calcutta. Like every time, she did not know if he would come back. He hardly divulged what exactly he was up to.

Prostrating before his parents and touching their feet with his fingertips, Aneek paid the customary respect and stepped out for Calcutta. Folding her hands, Archana shut her eyes tightly and prayed fervently for her only child's safety.

It was time for her to lock herself in the bathroom and let her tears flow. She did not want her husband, the cook or even Bonka's endearing wives to see her pangs of desolation. Sometimes she wondered if she would be overcome by a fatal heartache sitting on the bathroom floor. The printing press chores could wait for an hour.

As she gripped the veranda grille, for the first time the zamindar's wife felt a yearning for a sip of the 20-year-old bottle of sherry Mukund never touched. In the privacy of the bathroom, she thought of trying it as soon as her son left for Calcutta. Long ago, Mr Hall had brought it for a panic-stricken Anglo-Indian patient affected by a painful muscle sprain.

Archana fondly called out to her son, 'No more smoking... do you hear me?'

Aneek looked back from the gate and nodded. In a jiffy, the horse carriage took off and got lost behind a swarm of swaying betel nut, neem and mango trees.

Chapter 28

A Mother's Dilemma

IN DEFERENCE TO HIS MOTHER'S WISHES, ANEEK HELD OFF ON more overtly revolutionary activities, such as bomb-making, for a month after arriving in Calcutta. He instead joined a nest of spies supporting armed militants based as far as Punjab. However, in the spring of 1909, trouble tailed him doggedly. Sleuths from police stations in Faridpur and Calcutta hounded him almost with the accuracy of swallows looking for a winter home.

Tension between Archana and her son resurfaced over the extent of violence he should involve himself in. Their familial bond became strained when Aneek was wrongfully arrested following a jewellery store robbery in Calcutta. Although the sub-inspectors at Cossipore police station quickly identified the mistake and released him, the near-silent tiff between him and his mother raged for several more months. Archana was deeply troubled by the potential stain on the family's reputation and the prospect of her son being implicated in violence.

A year earlier, in 1908, young revolutionaries Khudiram Bose and Prafulla Chaki had failed in their attempt to assassinate Judge Kingsford, the chief presidency magistrate in Calcutta branded for his ruthless and prejudiced verdicts against Indians. The bomb intended for Kingsford landed and exploded in the carriage of two English ladies, causing fatalities. Aurobindo Ghose, suspected of masterminding the attack, was arrested and remanded at the Lal Bazar police station as an undertrial prisoner. His underground hideout at Maniktala was also searched by the police. Aurobindo and his brother Barindra had often advocated militant methods for India's liberation.

During this time, Aneek worked as a part-time bomb maker for various covert freedom-fighting organizations. Archana harboured the firm belief that her only son frequented the Maniktala and Grey Street hideouts in Calcutta. Meanwhile, a London-trained barrister and freedom seeker, Chittaranjan Das, successfully defended Aurobindo Ghose and secured his release. In addition, Bipin Pal's refusal to testify against his colleague led to his imprisonment. Though Aurobindo was acquitted, Archana wondered if Aneek would be that fortunate.

Hours of her day were spent in front of a surprise birthday gift she had received a few years ago—a noisy music player Mukund and the Irishman had collaborated on acquiring. Hunched on the carpeted floor of her music room, she sometimes listened to noise-injected German classical renditions. The magic sounds came from a gramophone made by Deutsche Grammophon Gesellschaft, which had been founded barely 10 years earlier, in 1898, by German-born US citizen Emile Berliner. Archana also cherished a tapered-shaft nickel-based pedestal telephone that Flanagan had bought for Aneek, though it was still nonfunctional in the villages.

One evening when a light-fingered thief nearly got away after stealing one of her chandrahaars, Archana chased him with a large mutton cleaver. Struck by her warring, intrepid determination to recover her gilded jewelled necklace, the thief dropped his loot and ran for his life along a narrow, less-trodden trail. That evening, when Mukund came home after handcrafting an escape-proof pen for his game hens, he could not have been treated to a more thrilling encounter.

Sometimes, Archana watched Mukund as he coped with his empty nest and nationhood disillusionments by playing football with the neighbourhood urchins, despite sore knees, back pain or stomach aches. She often felt her shawl singed by the hot iron while distractedly watching the handful of teenagers Aneek used to play with until recently. Surprise visits from Aunt Prachi were always a welcome change, as was the amusement she found in ranting incredibly tall tales to the cook's gullible, crass nephew. The little brat sometimes tirelessly spat streams of water in the air like a juvenile whale.

The copper plaque from Aneek's headmaster, awarded for securing first place in the eighth-grade final examination, had been long removed from the living room wall. His academic heroics had incurred a quick death thereafter. Archana tried hard to focus only on the positives unfolding in recent times.

At least her husband's hard work had helped them regain their ancestral farmland, rebuild the mansion and restaff the groves and fisheries, to unprecedented levels of revenue. Accompanying the village headman, Archana investigated bizarre incidents such as a horde of squirrels causing the toppling of a telegraph pole and an unexplained outbreak that devastated a tanner's village. She also inquired about the rising cost of morala fish in the colony of dye-makers and marvelled at how Mr Hall managed to balance his duties as a physician and a horse doctor.

Chapter 29

An Adopted Daughter's Solace

I<small>T WAS BREATHTAKING, THE WAY OLD MR HALL TOOK CARE OF</small> Madhuri, a 12-year-old girl he had newly adopted. Tall, fair and beautiful with very sharp features, she was the daughter of a poor village priest. Providentially, she resembled her adoptive father in many ways.

The ill-fated girl became a widow a year after being married at the age of 11 and without consummating the marriage. Her in-laws disowned her, accusing her of causing their son's untimely death when he died trying to save a drowning child from the Meghna River.

The young widow was allowed by her physically and emotionally abusive in-laws to return to her father's home only after he was about to die of kala-azar. Fortuitously, Mr Hall happened to be her father's doctor and was by his bedside on the day of his death. After learning the full details of Madhuri's suffering directly from her, Mukund and Mr Hall devised a plan to rescue her.

They threatened her in-laws with the cancellation of a recent loan waiver offer issued by the local government, and Mr Hall immediately sought permission from the local district magistrate and the judge to adopt Madhuri. During the formalization of the adoption in the district office, instead of giving her a new Anglo identity, Mr Hall asked Archana to pick a traditional Indian name for the preteen.

Madhuri soon became the solace of Mr Hall's later years. The once-inexhaustible talker handled her father's loss with increasing reticence. Hiding her grief with striking grace, she now became the apple of the eye of her adoptive father. Her prowess in quickly learning the basics of life sciences allowed her to play the nurse's role in Mr Hall's medical examination room and dispensary.

Flanagan, meanwhile, suspected that Mr Hall was using a portion of his recent inheritance from a baroness spinster aunt to fund his increasing acts of generosity. The medic was no longer accepting payment from poorer patients, and Flanagan noticed how he still managed to afford spotless white gloves, as well as distribute mouth organs, tincture of iodine and quinine pills to impoverished urchins. Mr Hall was now systematically targeting the needy families teeming in the rustic, waterlogged farmlands of Bengal to be the beneficiaries of his oblivious yet profound benevolence.

In the meantime, Archana's apprehension knew no bounds as she read reports in the *Dhaka Gazetteer* about the recent forays made by young and educated yet unemployed men. For the first time, a group had forcibly entered the collector's office, demanding jobs. Their concerted effort to find work ended unceremoniously with their immediate arrest. What the reports did not include was the brutal torture they endured at the hands of native darogas, who burned their arms with lit cigarettes and jabbed pins into their skin. From Aneek's letters from Calcutta, Archana came to know about a cunning British move in eastern Bengal, one that involved the titular nawab of Dhaka, Khwaja Salimullah. His family had supported the British during the Sepoy Mutiny, and now they helped the Raj. Salimullah, facing declining popularity due to family feuds and financial woes, saw his debts cleared by the British in exchange for political loyalty. In a clever scheme, the British helped him bypass the Bengal Tenancy Act of 1885, allowing him to buy intermediate tenures and *raiyati* rights with family surplus and settle them as *khas*. Under this arrangement, the khwajas became their tenants, preserving the estate for a few more decades. By providing a large portion of the land tax revenue and additional perks to the Raj, such petty kings, Hindus and Muslims alike, ensured the patronage of their British rulers. At the same time, they exacted complete control over thousands of hapless, non-tenured farmers forever ploughing the aristocrat-owned lands.

As time passed, whenever Aneek came home for special occasions and vacations, he meticulously avoided his mother. He felt like an intruder in his own home. Mukund, when present, would react by pacing up and down the veranda with his hands clasped behind his back.

Archana no longer raced to the front door when the wrought-iron gate squeaked its familiar sound upon Aneek's arrival. Instead, she harboured deep anxiety about his growing involvement in revolutionary activities. She secretly probed through his shoulder bag, alarmed to find essays railing against monopolism, neocapitalism and colonialism. Hidden within his mattress, she discovered books on the French Revolution, the American War of Independence, and the Mexican struggle for freedom. Most disturbing were the lingering scents of sulphur and saltpetre on Aneek's clothes, suggesting his involvement in bomb-making exercises.

In painfully honest moments of pondering with her local female friends, who came by her mansion for an afternoon's catch-up or chat, Archana voiced her frustration, 'Throughout history, why must children and women suffer at the hands of men constantly warring for control and supremacy?'

None of her visitors and acquaintances had answers that offered solace. Archana remained clueless about how to deal with the growing revolutionary fervour in her son, a painful paradox for a mother who despised violence but nurtured a child now driven by it.

In the privacy of her thoughts, Archana hoped for her motherland's freedom to be somehow miraculously realized without the shedding of any blood whatsoever. She would then scoff at her naivety, recognizing that self-preservation was the undyingly predominant face of the world order.

Despite her loving husband's presence, Archana's sense of loneliness and anxiety deepened each time Aneek left for the increasingly volatile city of Calcutta. Fearing for his safety, she became a light sleeper, tormented by hallucinations of a headless horseman galloping through the night. Her fears were amplified after she witnessed a horrific scene—a pile of bodies near an abandoned well—eight corpses heaped upon a green mound. No one dared ask who had committed the killings or why. The frenetic howling of inimitably doomed strangers she had never known shook her chest uncontrollably.

Archana began to read banned underground flyers detailing how aspiring freedom fighters were being tortured in the jails. The stories described how young men, initially fearful of pain, quickly lost their fear after the first blow was delivered by brown-skinned prison guards—natives loyal to the British. These prison employees, eager to prove their loyalty to the crown, bludgeoned their fellow countrymen to death, sometimes disembowelling them with a bhojali. Vivid accounts emerged of how the young men held hands and improvised nationalist slogans before accepting their brutal deaths.

These were the times when the British Raj was trying to steer a course between the shoals of high unemployment and rising inflation by putting more Indian rupees into circulation. Their goal was to stabilize the economy and silence the growing demands from men within the INC, who were persistently growling for self-government. But the once prized jewel of the British Empire now seemed too sickly and unmanageable, like a rebellious boar no longer responding to its master's commands.

Amidst this tumultuous backdrop, Archana found a sliver of hope in the rise of indigenous enterprises like Bengal

Chemicals & Pharmaceutical Works Ltd (BCPW). Founded by P.C. Ray in 1901 with a modest investment of Rs 700, BCPW quickly gained a reputation for producing affordable chemicals, drugs, and pharmaceuticals. It even expanded its product line to include consumer goods like fire extinguishers, toothpaste, soap, and hospital equipment. Eminent nationalist physicians such as R.G. Kar, N.R. Sarkar and Amulya Charan Bose supported the company, furthering its cause. Archana was heartened by the fact that these products, made in a humble factory in Maniktala, could be afforded by thousands of ordinary Indians.

Meanwhile, in Calcutta's market squares and suburbs, the once-happy-go-lucky throng of youths roared in unison and uttered only one word to the Raj: 'Leave!' The city's unemployed graduates, their pride wounded by the lack of opportunities, gathered in Dalhousie Square, waving sandals in frustration and demanding that someone, anyone, listen to their grievances.

Archana's unease grew as she watched the shifting political landscape around her, especially with the emergence of figures like Fazlul Huq. Though he had started as an apprentice to Ashutosh Mukherjee, the vice chancellor of Calcutta University, Huq's role in establishing the All-India Muslim League in Dhaka three years earlier left Archana feeling uncertain. At times when her husband was around, in vain Archana mused repeatedly, 'Should politics and religion mix? If so, is there a limit?' Mukund and Archana debated for hours and finally reckoned that for the complex and enigmatic India to some day become a sovereign nation, politics and religion would need to intertwine to some extent.

To fill the empty nest left by her sole progeny, Archana took up chores she had always delegated to others. To steal a few moments of peace, she sought distraction from small things, like sewing the slightly torn curtain that separated her back porch and barnyard. She also called Bonka's older wife to share her tall tales. In return, the zamindar's wife taught her mischievous tricks to keep Bonka in check. For Archana, the attractive and well-spoken woman's husky, raunchy laugh was reward enough.

To further occupy her time, she involved herself with the children on the estate, teaching them tongue twisters and games like tic-tac-toe on her portable chalkboard. One of her servant's sons even acquired a furry cat to rid the barn of rats. But the feline beauty often ended up napping on her owner's fanciest divan.

During the times both her son and husband were away, Archana found offbeat ways to combat loneliness. She invited Flanagan, who was also an amateur magician. On such occasions, he came for the entire weekend, accompanied by his wife and children, along with his trunk filled with magic kits. A carriage brought all the essentials such as caged doves, bunnies, playing cards and handkerchiefs. The paved yard at the back of the mansion provided the perfect venue for his performances. Bonka and his boys dragged a raised wooden platform usually stored inside a barn. It was a treat watching the Irishman moving swiftly from one end of the improvised stage to the other. Casting his dhoti and kurta aside, he wore a dark sporty jacket with sleeves invariably rolled up. Flanagan's attire was never complete without a magician-themed tie. All servants in the household and members of the estate's staff, including every farmer, fisherman and artisan, were invited. They roared with awe and laughter every time Flanagan struck a perfect chord with a new trick, clapping and cheering even for classics such as tearing one-rupee notes, or making a handkerchief or a bunny vanish from the unlikeliest of places.

Hours later, as the chilled night deepened and everyone had left, Archana would lead the Irishman and his wife to one of several guest bedrooms. Despite plenty of space, Prachi's young children liked to sleep with Archana. Making sure that they were deep in dreamland for the night, the zamindar's wife would sometimes tiptoe back to the guest bedroom to eavesdrop on the unquenchable whispers exchanged between the lovers, occasionally catching a grunt or a moan from their gentle romps on the creaky bed. Memories of her own early married years in Pabna would resurface, when, long ago, she and Mukund had talked in hushed tones or made love ever so quietly just to avoid being overheard by her brothers' nosy wives.

~

Archana no longer travelled the road that passed by Moi's home. She not only detested her erstwhile employee but the grassy fields nearby also reminded her of her son. It was there that Aneek used to play kabaddi. During the rainy months, Archana's carriage carried various essential supplies to the Bagdi villages. Living in huts with thatched roofs, these tribals were often the worst victims of the flood-prone monsoon. Bonka, and sometimes Flanagan, showed up to help with her relief work.

Archana often remembered her father-in-law's haunting tales of the Sepoy Mutiny, where British soldiers had publicly displayed the mutilated bodies of rebel sepoys as a grim warning. She couldn't help but fear for Aneek's safety. Gripped by utter distress, she remembered Aneek once reading about black powder explosives in an old worn-out copy of *The New York Times* supplied by a Calcutta classmate. The sparkle in Aneek's eyes had terrified her. The next day, her heart snapped into two when she walked into her son's private den and found bags of saltpetre, charcoal and sulphur stashed in a closeted, iron trunk.

By the summer of 1909, the life Archana had known for long seemed to be changing more rapidly than she had ever imagined. Though Prachi and the Irishman still visited her home often, a growing weariness gnawed at her. She suffered yet another heart-wrenching miscarriage but remained more than hospitable.

Yet, her mind would sometimes forget the details that once came so naturally—like offering Flanagan his favourite chocolate sherbet. Even the once-cherished mahjong games she played with Mukund during warm, humid evenings were now forgotten, their pieces gathering dust.

Chapter 30

Love in the Times of Rebellion

BY OCTOBER 1909, ANEEK'S LOVE FOR FELLOW ACTIVIST DAMINI had become an unshakeable part of his life. He had to be with her daily or at least see her every day. If not, he felt incomplete. Damini, a striking young woman, worked alongside him in the same North Calcutta samiti. Their shared passion for sovereign India and each other grew along with silent yet sublime steps. Through long summer nights, in hidden underground spaces lit dimly and fraught with danger, Damini taught Aneek soap manufacturing, modern weaving techniques, and crafting home furnishings and miscellaneous leather goods. A gleam of joy and interest shot through her eyes every time work brought them together.

Besides her beauty, Damini electrified Aneek with her overflowing ardour for India's struggle for nationhood and independence. She hailed from Kalipara, a village near Dhaka, and though she had never been married, she always wore a plain white sari like widows of the time, her dark hair tightly cloistered in a bun, and her movements as quiet as a cat's.

Aneek and Damini exemplified how romance can prosper without verbal acknowledgements. On rare days when they had no college or samiti work, they and a few other members would perform plays, often reenacting the story of the queen of Jhansi, who had led a tough but losing armed struggle to free the land from British control half a century earlier. As Damini played the part of the ill-fated widowed queen with deft precision, Aneek would watch her with a quiet euphoria, his heart swelling with every minute.

During samiti meetings, while organizing activities to unsettle the masterful colonizers, the olive-complexioned girl's eyes would glimmer with the fierceness of a tigress. Yet, the moment Aneek happened to be near, her expression would soften. Her lips curved into a bold cupid's bow, the subtlest of smiles and a flushed face communicating all the emotions they could not express openly.

Often, Aneek and Damini worked with a large group of fellow volunteers and rarely found themselves alone. When they did, Aneek coaxed her to play the 25-string *sarod* for him, and she happily obliged. He took care of the instrument as if it were a rare jewel retrieved from the Taj Mahal. Sometimes while she read the old classics of Homer, he endlessly polished the sarod's brass bell and the fretless steel fingerboard. Steadily pinching and scraping from his scholastic stipend but never asking his parents for money, one day, Aneek bought Damini a gold ring bearing a delicately carved crest. His ecstasy knew no bounds when she said nothing but started wearing the gift.

Aneek and Damini's mutual attraction and intense passion gradually translated into physical intimacy. One night in a samiti's underground storehouse, they made love again and again. And thereafter, they became ardent lovers—whether it was late afternoon or late night, it did not matter. For privacy, they sneaked in and out of the storehouse at the oddest hours and whenever they could. Whenever they made love, it seemed they both felt they might not live to see the next day. Their love symbolized and conjoined with their adherence to the greater cause of nationalism.

One early autumn morning, Aneek, Damini and two other samiti members boarded a tram from Kidderpore to Esplanade. Sombre rain clouds drooped over the metropolis. By noon, armed with placards, they began to demonstrate in front of Whiteaway, Laidlaw & Co., a popular British department store established in 1882 to cater to the city's wealthy European elite.

Two modest-looking native stores also stood nearby. The first store had a façade of an ayurvedic store but covertly sold ganja to the public. The other store's secret purpose was to recruit native sailors for commercial ships cruising weekly to Europe to protect Britain on various European fronts.

These stores, licensed by the British government, represented everything Aneek and his samiti despised: a betrayal of their nation's future and a reminder of the colonial grip tightening around their homeland.

The chants of the samiti members grew louder, their passion reverberating through the streets as they urged fellow Indians to boycott British goods. In the midst of the demonstration, another group of activists lit a fire and began tossing British-made cosmetics, shoes, clothes and appliances into the flames.

The bespectacled, slightly balding British owner of Whiteaway looked up from his ledger.

Through the shop's large glass windows, he glared at the growing number of demonstrators outside, some freely brandishing their swords and pistols. Matching Aneek's towering strides, Damini's tall and slender frame came into view. Her self-assured, immaculate face brimmed with vigour. A lack of hope had finally given way to an indescribable dream in the hearts of the natives. Angrily, the Whiteaway store owner threw his pencil on the floor. He dreaded what lay ahead. This firebrand throng of fearless youths seemed a far cry from the compliant, diffident babus he had come across in his two-decade stay in Calcutta.

Growing increasingly anxious about the potential loss of business, he pushed his pet rabbit aside and hastily dialled the telephone operator, requesting the intervention of the Calcutta Police.

At the time, British officers still led every cluster of native cops assigned to control political and nationalistic protests. A horse-mounted Bristol-born police inspector and a dozen policemen from the Lal Bazar Police Station quickly arrived on the scene. For a few moments, the lawmen watched in disbelief as Damini and Nilambari, another female samiti volunteer, vociferously described the domestic, alternative products their underground shop offered. Women had just begun taking to the streets to take up the long-protracted cause of freedom.

Raising his baton, one of the constables lashed out at the loudest demonstrator, narrowly missing. Groundnut hawkers and amulet traders, who had been plying their trades nearby, hastily sought shelter from the unfolding melee.

Suddenly, a native policeman engaged in a needless scuffle with a young protester. Seconds later, another officer leered at Nilambari, making derogatory remarks about her looks and curly hair, while his buddy added a crude sexual innuendo.

Aneek was about to retaliate when Damini hurled a stone at the leering cop. The diminutive policeman ducked, and the stone missed its intended target, striking the eye of the white inspector's horse instead. The ivory-coloured horse reared up on its hind legs and, without warning, collapsed, throwing the inspector onto the road. The enraged and out-of-balance inspector fired his revolver twice. One of the bullets struck Damini in the forehead. Poised at the threshold of a newly blooming life, she lay lifeless over a manhole by the time the inspector regained his foothold at the kerbside. Cursing profusely, he got to his feet, brushing dirt from his sparkling white uniform.

Standing in front of a confectioner's shop known for its ginger pudding with custard, the Englishman roared at the mob, 'Pull back, all of you, or I'll make a sieve out of you. Maybe roast you alive.'

One of the agitators pulled out a machete from under his kurta and menacingly slashed the air. Having limbered out of a tea house moments earlier, a group of old and retired men stood frozen at the edge of the footpath. They had been discussing the recent news of the British capital moving to Delhi, a tidbit they had heard from a younger relative working in the Writers' Building.

The inspector's henchman unleashed tear gas at the masses. Many onlookers and activists quickly dispersed. Unsure of what to make of the melee in the street, a terrified Anglo-Indian woman began ringing a bell on her long and narrow second-storey veranda. Meanwhile, a police officer struck an elderly, unyielding dissenter—a retired railway ticket collector—so forcefully that a tooth was knocked out of his pale, wrinkled mouth.

In the past, amid the gruelling and long hours devoted to the Anushilan Samiti work, Aneek had often felt alone. But all that changed after he met Damini, who had been a surreal anchor for him, a steadfast presence in a turbulent sea. Now, seeing her fall right in front of his own eyes, he felt an overwhelming sense of helplessness.

Consumed by grief and anger, Aneek snatched a baton from one of the cops and hurled it at the inspector, who seemed utterly unmoved by the fact that he had just killed an unarmed woman. The baton hit the Englishman between the eyes, and his forehead started oozing blood. Aneek grabbed his well-hidden C96 Mauser pistol from his waist and fired at Damini's assailant. Two bullets pierced the cop's heart, killing him instantly.

Desperate to save Damini, Aneek threw himself down onto the dusty street, trying in vain to stem Damini's gushing outflow of blood. Moments later, realizing that she was dead, he managed to retrieve and hide a pouch containing a planning sheet with vital samiti secrets. Overcome with a profound sense of finality, he gently closed her eyes, as her long hair now lay spread in the road's dust, dishevelled and matted with blood. The smell of her blood filled the air. Just two days earlier, her father, a schoolteacher, had sent her a bottle of medicine from the Kalipara dispensary to treat her mild bronchitis. Breathing heavily and snivelling, Aneek checked her purse and found the phial, with a dosage marker strip glued on its reverse side. He clutched it tightly, the last and unintended memento from Damini.

Almost immediately, three brawny cops viciously pounced upon Aneek. In seconds, they thrashed him into a hunched lump of black and blue. A more composed British police officer quickly intervened and stopped the violence. Tethering his horse to a lamp post, he quickly handcuffed and arrested Aneek as well as several samiti colleagues.

On his way to his master's grocery store, an impoverished coolie paused, tears streaming down his face as he watched the unfolding drama. Balancing two large aluminium cans of mustard oil on the ends of a bamboo pole, he jostled with a pushcart pedlar for a better view.

For the next two weeks, Aneek remained in custody in a dingy holding cell. Thereafter, since the jails in Bengal were overflowing with prisoners, Lal Bazar authorities transferred him by train to Bankipore Central Jail in Patna, Bihar. Devoid of any paperwork describing the charges against him he was moved again to Naini Jail in Uttar Pradesh, where he began to serve a seemingly indefinite sentence.

Aneek's eyes quickly opened to the harsh realities of prison life. Only a few select, utterly conforming inmates could sleep on corn-hay mattresses. The punishments for not following the warden's strict commands included handcuffs for a week, fetters for six months and solitary confinement. When inmates defied orders openly sometimes their nails and teeth were pulled out. The drinking water seemed muddier than a monsoon's rain puddle. In his section, eight latrines existed for 500 prisoners, with some of the superannuated prisoners routinely defecating near the drains. In the cold winter, four prisoners huddled under one blanket. Although there was no shortage of water, the jailer sanctioned only half a bucket of water per week per person for washing and bathing. Overcrowding had led to widespread skin diseases. Within the remote cells, whenever the opportunity arose, some older long-term convicts sodomized younger inmates.

Aneek quickly discovered that many of his jailmates had not had a visitor for years. Their rural relatives were often too impoverished to afford the transportation expenses to visit their kith and kin. Besides, those who braved the long bullock-cart ride were often made to wait for hours at the jail's gate while the gatekeeper extracted bribes.

The jail's senior officers unofficially employed orphan boys between the ages of 10 and 18. Colluding with the prison staff, local policemen routinely picked them up from the streets. These boys cooked, washed utensils, cleaned rooms, and fetched water for the staff and a few special inmates identified by the jailer. As vicious as fire-breathing dragons, the warden and his core cronies woke them up at dawn to prepare morning tea for everyone and kept them working late into the night, scrubbing pots and pans.

Despite being paid a decent monthly salary to do their job, the jail staff employed these ill-fated urchins as 'helpers' only to misuse their abundant puerile energy to the hilt. The ward where the boys slept was poorly maintained, with no sanitary facilities, but was kept brightly lit all night to ensure the warden could monitor all inmates. When the number of prisoners increased, the warden would ask the police to make false arrests and bring in more boys to help with the chores.

Meanwhile, Archana, terrified by the prospect of her son's indefinite incarceration, fell ill. She was plagued by insomnia and lay in bed, crossing her arms and glaring at her husband for not doing enough to secure their son's release. She knew that without the intervention of a powerful government officer, her son could languish in the dark and sinister shadows of British Indian jails for years. Bedridden and reduced to a frail, weeping figure, her persistent tears eventually bore fruit.

With a lump of lead in his throat, Mukund dispatched a telegram to Hubert Weatherilt, the deputy director of the Indian Museum in Calcutta and son of Robert and Cynthia Weatherilt, Mukund's old friends.

Fortunately for Aneek, the metropolitan magistrate overseeing cases in Calcutta owed a huge favour to Robert. Years earlier, Robert had helped the Chief Metropolitan Magistrate's nephew to crack the ICS interview and secure a high rank.

Hubert wired back immediately: 'Uncle Mukund, though I have had a slight tiff with Calcutta's metropolitan magistrate recently, since my father and the magistrate are longtime classmates, we should seek his assistance to maximize the chances of Aneek's release. Let's meet in Calcutta next Monday at the government guest house near Chowringhee. Together, we will visit my dad. Hubert.'

A few days later, Mukund and Hubert met with Robert in Calcutta. Robert had returned from England two years earlier and was living a solitary life in an austere Lansdowne Road apartment. Having deserted his wife Cynthia earlier, it was his fateful turn to be jilted by his much younger lover.

In recent months, Hubert had maintained contact with his 48-year-old father through letters, though he had not yet visited him at the new house. Mukund had briefly met Robert after Cynthia's death. Mostly clad in a kurta and trousers, Robert's lifestyle now represented the perfect amalgam of British and Indian predilections. Warmly embracing his son as well as Mukund, an utterly surprised Robert guided both men to an old and familiar sofa. With a pale but pleased smile, he perused his grown progeny and the best friend of his deceased wife. For a moment, he even quickly assessed his son's khakis and crew-neck pastel sweater. Then his bearings resumed the resemblance of a sage after a long penance.

Though the erstwhile property manager of the maharaja of Darbhanga could still afford a lavish lifestyle, he now lived more simply than ever. The painful break-up with his London-based much younger girlfriend, Helen, had sent him into a downward spiral. For six months, he had slept with a dozen women to regain his shattered self-confidence. Cynthia's death had left him adrift, and the financial losses from his time in England had not helped his spirits either.

Hubert slowly looked all around and scrutinized his father's new home. White-lace antimacassars still covered the headrests and armrests of the settee Robert and Cynthia had purchased soon after returning from their honeymoon in Ooty and the Nilgiris. The sand-coloured walls of the two-room apartment badly needed a fresh coat of paint, and the worn curtains draping the glass windows added to the sense of neglect. A thin layer of white dust covered most of the furniture and the delicate chinaware Cynthia used to entertain guests no longer gleamed or glowed from the wooden cabinet. The warm, soft light of obsolete spirit lamps cast oblong shadows on the kitchen overlooking the living room and the walls of the corridor leading to the bathroom were lined with paintings Cynthia had made when Hubert was still in elementary school. An oil-stained rag Cynthia used while making puffed mutton pastries lay on the counter.

Though Robert still owned a house in Alipore, he preferred to live in this rented flat. His landlady, a partially paralysed 73-year-old widowed Englishwoman perpetually wrapped in a dressing gown and wearing slippers, had hosted several lodgers before, but no one cared for her like Robert. Shuffling through the pages of Cynthia's scrapbook, he often listened to his landlady's sob stories while she knitted. To supplement his income, Robert worked as a translator of important documents from Bengali to English and moonlighted as a general store manager in Cornwallis Street. Every Wednesday night, he and his landlady shared a glass of bourbon and played rummy. Having sold off his car after his return to the subcontinent, Robert relied on a hand-drawn rickshaw for his twice-weekly trips to Park Street, where he dined at the same Chinese eatery almost every time. After all, the Mandarin owner offered him a sizeable discount for his loyalty.

Glancing at the dark rings under his father's eyes, Hubert said, 'We have come to seek your help.'

Robert wiped his cracked and blistered lips. 'Sure,' he replied, his voice tinged with bitterness. 'Who needs assistance from a lost man like me—you or Mukund?' He stood behind a Victorian painting of a kitten in a bucket—the only one in the room not painted by his late wife.

His voice lacked its former strength, and his eyes were slightly swollen, a far cry from the robust man Mukund first met nine years ago. Nervously, Robert peered through the front door peephole to make sure no one was lurking outside.

'Father...Uncle Mukund and I have brought bad news about his son.'

Shuffling forward, Robert turned instantly to fully face his more-than-welcome guests. He fondly recalled the best days of his life that he once frittered away in the hunt for cheap thrills. 'Are you talking about my little friend Aneek?'

Hubert nodded. 'Yes.'

It was as if something had jolted Robert back to life—a spark that reminded him of the boy who used to eagerly cheer him on during their Sunday chess games. The erstwhile property manager stood like a prehistoric stalactite with one single drip of water keeping him alive.

A flood of memories washed over him—the rain-flooded Kosi River rushing towards the banks of Darbhanga as he and his wife strolled along the swollen stream, watching the knee-high, moving walls of water crashing upon the banks. Flying their kites, Hubert and Aneek often tagged along during these riverine walks. The gushing waves would sweep away the tide-soaked clothes left behind by the rookie son of a jolly washerman. Robert's mind also went back to that first blissful year with Cynthia in the palace's plush quarters—lavish Sunday afternoon meals in the dense thicket of the residence's backyard, when servants, a fastidious butler and a caring wife ensured every lamb chop and almond candy met his exacting taste. Of course, all of this happened before Robert started drinking heavily.

Hubert's voice brought him back. 'Yes. I am talking about Aneek…my dearest friend and childhood playmate.'

Chapter 31

A Philanderer's Redemption

'TELL ME EVERYTHING ABOUT HIS TROUBLES,' SAID ROBERT.

'Aneek was arrested during a recent agitation here in Calcutta. They have sent him to a jail in Bihar and then to UP, and all bail pleas have been rejected. If recent trends for young adults hold, he is likely to be held there indefinitely.'

Robert burrowed his head briefly into a divan pillow, the weight of genuine anguish pressing on him. Oozing paternal concern, he reached forward and grabbed his son's arm.

But Hubert quickly wrenched his arm free. 'We need your help to secure his release by persuading one of your old classmates.'

Robert's eyes momentarily sagged from Hubert's coldness. 'Which one?' he asked.

'The all-powerful metropolitan magistrate of Calcutta.'

Robert sighed. 'Do you think he will still listen to me? Heed the plea of a stained man like me?' His face looked as pale and frayed as wind-whipped snow.

'Yes, I do.' Hubert looked out through one of the open windows. In the distance, little white boys in rugby uniforms trotted towards a giant field, while a burly, high-cheekboned Anglo-Indian man slowly rolled open the shutters of his whisky-and-soda and golf ball shop.

Robert sat there like the only lonesome 70-million-year-old survivor of the sea monster species that once caused havoc under the ocean's surface. Though immensely happy to see his son and his old friend Mukund, Robert felt stung by Hubert's detached demeanour. His bitterness, though long dormant, resurfaced momentarily. 'What makes you think I can succeed in such an anti-British mission?'

Hubert bristled. 'Wait a minute; I am as British as you are. There is nothing anti-British in my request. Aneek merely participated in a protest against the overwhelming amount of imported goods forced upon Indians. Aneek shot the British cop as an outburst of retribution after the same cop fatally wounded his beloved girlfriend, Damini. Both you and I were born on this continent.'

Robert sprang to his feet. 'Son, pray that I do not let you and your deceased mother down this time. I wronged her so badly.' He spent his surge of self-pity by slamming shut the kitchen door.

Hubert smirked. 'Again! Must you bring her up?'

Robert interrupted desperately. 'Please, allow me. Whenever my mind dwells on Cynthia, deep remorse scalds me in every waking hour. How I hurt the sensitive woman…and utterly ignored her artistic soul in the years before her death!'

Hubert shot back, cutting his father off, 'That is enough. I do not want to hear another word about her from you.'

Mukund intervened firmly. 'Let your father speak. No matter what…remember, long ago, it was his tireless efforts that made you who you are today.'

Hubert bristled, 'But he…'

Mukund's eyes steeled with resolve. 'No buts from you. Let the Almighty dispense his dues…good and bad. You are forever his child. It was your father who rushed you to the hospital and gave you blood when you were a boy. Do you not recall how you crashed through the attic skylight?'

Hubert, chastened by the gentle rebuke from his lifelong well-wisher, nodded silently.

Mukund almost glared at him. 'Do you remember how, on the spur of the moment, your father travelled all the way to Burdwan just to bring your mother's favourite grapes?'

After a long pause, Hubert nodded again, slowly but surely.

Mukund continued, 'You might have been too young to remember, but your father posed for hours while your mother painted him.'

'I remember that too.'

'And when you spat blood as a child,' Mukund pressed on, 'your father travelled through the night to take you to the best specialist who happened to be in Patna.'

Hubert sighed deeply.

'It is time to forgive your father for his sins.'

Stunned by the unexpected recall of his life's sweetest memories, Robert nodded gratefully at Mukund. For the first time in years, the forsaken Englishman seemed to find a shred of peace.

'How miserably I miss the sheer joy of your mother's laugh,' Robert whispered, staring at Hubert. 'Son, you do not have to put me in my place. Without her, I am already in a living hell. We were each other's first love. Please…forgive my trespasses.'

Hubert clasped his father's outstretched hands.

'Sorry I interrupted you… Go on, son…go on.'

Hubert resumed, 'Yes. As I was saying…one would think that you, of all people, would sympathize such gross inequity—between the rights of an imperial colonizer and its long-subjugated yet resilient subjects in this peninsula.'

'Of course I do,' Robert responded softly.

Hubert stood up. 'Then go and meet the city magistrate at the earliest…and help Aneek get out of jail.'

'Son, I will call on him tomorrow. However, there is stark irony in this situation.'

Hubert frowned. 'What do you mean?'

Raking a hand through his thinning hair, Robert sighed. 'It is bizarre that despite your ICS stature, your influence will not be enough to sway my classmate and get Aneek out of prison.'

Hubert groaned with deep-rooted frustration. 'I have been trying to mend my ties with the big powerbrokers, the men with far-reaching connections, but no luck yet. Life's alleys are full of people we pass by...' he trailed off.

'What about them?'

'You never know who will step forward when you need them the most...or who will let you cash in the chips for a worthy cause.'

Weather-beaten and weary, Robert Weatherilt quietly gazed at Mukund. 'Mukund, I am glad you came to see me. There is no hesitation in sharing certain feelings in front of my grown son.' Far from the post-bourbon tough talk he was once known for, Robert came across as an embodiment of modesty. 'I am indeed grateful to you for being with Cynthia when she breathed her last,' he said.

Struggling to hold back tears, Robert continued, 'Son, for once, let me voice my sins before you. Like a heartless leech, I left your beautiful mother for a younger woman. I wasn't even there to offer her a sip of water in her final moments. There is much more that I must atone for.'

Visibly anguished by his mother's painful past, Hubert groaned. 'Father, can we talk about something else?'

The once-compulsive gambler replied, 'Yes. In your last letter, you mentioned you were planning to marry soon... You have found a girl from Calcutta's elite circles...?'

Hubert nodded. 'Yes. I had a London-raised girlfriend—the daughter of an adviser in the British Indian government. But recently, she called off the engagement. She reckoned I was too much of an "India lover".'

A long silence ensued. Mukund stared hard at the ICS officer who had chosen to serve as the deputy director of the Indian Museum rather than a lawmaker.

Finally, a wave of reconciliation swept through Hubert's being. 'Father, I heard that you amassed a large debt during your time in

England. Would you want me to help you pay it off?'

Robert lowered his head and salvaged a sliver of pride. 'No, I will manage. After all, I have a second job now.'

Hubert left the room momentarily and headed towards the bathroom.

Mukund said gently, 'I have some of your wife's paintings... Cynthia compiled them in the last six months of her life. She insisted I keep them. Would you like to take them?'

Reaching forward, Robert suddenly clasped Mukund tightly. 'No, I do not deserve them. Besides, starting from the time you were my deputy in the Darbhanga estate, why do you always kill me with kindness?'

'What is done is done. But there is one thing that can soothe your deceased wife's soul.'

'And what would that be?'

'Take good care of your son and grandchildren.'

'Yes, of course...if they will let me.'

'Leave that to me.'

'But first, I must do all I can do to get Aneek out of prison. Do you remember, sometimes I tried scaring the lad by suggesting the possibility of vicious monsters lurking under his bed?'

Mukund smiled faintly. 'Sometimes you managed to scare Archana more than Aneek.'

~

An hour passed.

For the first time since their Darbhanga days, the three men sat down for a meal together. Afterwards, Robert brewed Darjeeling tea. As they sipped, they reminisced about Archana and Cynthia, and how the two women would turn wild whenever it rained, staying outdoors as long as the downpour lasted. Robert recounted how, in the nick of time, his wife had saved the princely estate's gardener from hanging himself from a neem tree in the dense, sprawling compound.

Just before leaving, Mukund turned around from the threshold and looked Robert squarely in the eye. 'So, can I count on your help in freeing Aneek?'

Hubert snapped, 'Father, you know how much Aneek means to me. Don't let me down.'

Robert, salvaging a glimmer of confidence typical of his early life, replied, 'Yes, yes. Go home now, both of you.'

Mukund added, 'Archana is far more confident than I am that you will not disappoint us.'

'Reckon I also disappointed Archana enough to last a lifetime when I left my wife and rushed off to England. How can I repay her kindness every time I dropped by your home and she cooked me my favourite curd-fish?'

Hubert retorted briskly, 'You surely can do that by arranging for her son's release.'

Mukund intervened, 'Hubert, there are people who have done things far worse than your father. There is no one truer than a reformed sinner. If your mother's life stood for anything, it was compassion. How can you turn your back on that?'

Before Hubert could reply, Mukund firmly pressed on. 'Stop arguing with me. I spent enough time with Cynthia, even after we left Darbhanga. A lot happened while you were away in boarding school and college. There was a time when she loved your father deeply. I am more than a witness to such tender moments.'

Hubert relented somewhat. Carefully taking out an old picture from the inner pocket of his stylish coat, he handed it to his father. Robert had been requesting this picture for months—a final photo of him with Cynthia before their marriage fell apart.

Holding the picture, Robert's expression wavered between sadness and gratitude. He pushed the curtain aside as Hubert and

Mukund stepped past the threshold. His voice, filled with sincere caution, came straight from the heart, 'My son, not everyone has to get married in this world. But if you do, do not mess around thereafter. Learn from your father's mistakes.'

'Yes, Father. I have learnt that lesson well. I will visit you again in the first week of next month.'

'Next time, come and stay longer.'

Hubert smiled faintly. 'Yes, I will.'

'Son, I hope you have arranged for Mukund's return to Madaripur. Archana must be worried.'

'Yes, Father. I brought two cars from my office.'

'Tell both drivers to go slow. The clouds have been louring all day.'

Hubert had arranged for an additional car to take Mukund back to Madaripur while he returned home to Hiranpur.

Mukund's face glowed with relief and joy as he and Hubert hurried down the winding, metal stairs to the porch.

Mukund was about to step into the car when Robert's voice rang out from the upper-storey balcony, cutting through the darkness like a reassuring echo. 'Tell Archana not to worry any more. I am going to get Aneek out of jail, by hook or by crook.'

Mukund smiled up at him. 'I know you will.'

A few weeks later, in the administrative offices of Dalhousie Square, a rare development came about. The metropolitan magistrate of Calcutta at the time was a British ICS officer like Hubert, though at least 20 years his senior. No one knew exactly why he decided to use all the power and influence of his high position to get Aneek, an Indian youth jailed indefinitely, released. Aneek's killing of the British cop was now recapped as self-defence. The metropolitan magistrate seemed aware that Aneek's misdemeanour stemmed from his burning desire to end British rule and trade monopoly in India. But why did the magistrate, a man of such high rank, intervene to free his friend's native colleague's son? Was it the deep bond he shared with Robert? Or had Robert, over time, influenced him to see the situation through the eyes of a land yearning for freedom? No one could say for sure.

However, after the event, the magistrate's native orderly claimed that he had seen Robert hold a gun to his master's head before the latter wilted and hurriedly issued a written order to ensure Aneek's acquittal and release from Naini jail.

In either case, aided by the metropolitan magistrate's voluntary or involuntary help, Mukund and Hubert were able to set Aneek free. However, the tragic death of Damini had aged Aneek by years. Aneek, who had contracted pneumonia during his imprisonment, took two months to recover. Almost immediately, at his father Mukund's insistence, he transferred his credits from the Calcutta institution and enrolled in Dhaka University.

Yet after only a few months, Aneek found himself restless. He felt stifled, longing for the pulse of Calcutta, the epicentre of the nation's struggle for independence. Damini's memory haunted him. He saw his first love's spectre beckoning him back—not only to the city but to the fight for freedom more intensely. Without asking his father's permission, Aneek transferred again, returning to study at Scottish Church College.

This time Mukund could not muster the grit to oppose his son.

Chapter 32

Rebels and Loyalists
Spread Nationwide

By NOVEMBER 1910 ANEEK, NOW IN HIS FINAL YEAR OF COLLEGE in Calcutta, had become entirely his own man. His fairly long torture-inflicted stay in jail of eight months had changed him forever. His trips back home to Madaripur had dwindled, replaced by frequent attendance at clandestine meetings of underground units organized by Niralamba Swami. The constant travel and the city's oppressive humidity took their toll on him. Surviving on steamed rice, lentils, boiled eggs and stewed vegetables, Aneek suffered from frequent bouts of waterborne infections.

Meanwhile, Mukund narrowly escaped death one evening when local police, tipped off by a mole, raided his location. It was Mukund's responsibility to report on the daily activities of senior British officers stationed in Dhaka and the most imminent legislation issues. Mukund and Joggeshwar attended various events in the district, frequently changing their appearance to avoid detection. They would sometimes enter busy buildings dressed as students and leave the premises wearing a Hindu monk's saffron garb.

Joggeshwar's distant uncle, Bhoba, was not on good terms with his family. Although his friends and neighbours knew him as a jute contractor working for the government, he was actually a detective in Dhaka's police force. He soon emerged as the mole who had trailed and sometimes innocuously mixed with Joggeshwar and Mukund's group.

One evening, when Joggeshwar and Mukund were returning home from a meeting, Bhoba followed them past a graveyard where a middle-aged woman in a green hijab was praying near a loved one's tomb. As Joggeshwar readied to cross the river, Bhoba struck. Slashing his nephew's throat, the detective threw Joggeshwar's body into the moat. By chance, slightly ahead of his cousin, Mukund managed to dive into the cold river and swim to safety. In the darkness, the detective shot at him repeatedly, but his aim was off each time.

Joggeshwar's death left Mukund devastated. His cousin's murder at the hands of a relative loyal to the British deepened his rage. Soon, Mukund began plotting revenge.

A week later, Bhoba threw another freedom fighter into a deep ditch, his confidence in suppressing the native uprisings growing with each passing day. He began to be openly accompanied by British sub-inspectors, ready to protect him and his efforts. A month later, following a tip from his allies, Mukund shot his traitor uncle to death in Khijirpur, about nine miles from Dhaka. Mukund did not feel one bit of remorse.

Meanwhile, now in her late 30s, Archana was aware of her husband's increasingly militant ways in dealing with equally violent British cops. Pregnant after three miscarriages, she knew this could be her last chance for childbirth. Driven by a mix of unprecedented passion coupled with a hunger strike, she implored Mukund to abandon his risk-ridden, freedom-seeking vagabond life. Unable to ignore her plea, Mukund took a brief respite from his militant activities, though his heart remained committed to Bharat's liberation.

Mukund's hopes for Aneek were twofold—he wanted him to further his education while also immersing himself in the freedom movement. Their discussions often turned into heated debates about how India's freedom would be achieved. Eventually, Aneek decided to seek admission into a law college in Calcutta.

By 1910, the Swadeshi Movement and the general passive

resistance, which arose during the anti-partition agitation in 1905, had gained momentum. The most prominent traders of Calcutta—the Marwaris—led a price battle against British manufacturers, causing a decline in the sale of Manchester-made cloth. Middle-class Indians, young and old, drastically reduced their purchase of British-made goods. Before long, Aneek and his college mates joined the fray.

Inspired by the nationalist publication *Dawn*, the Dawn Society's magazine, edited by Satish Chandra Mukherjee, Aneek became more deeply involved in the movement. Following his mother's example, Aneek and his friends began producing and selling soaps, oil, shoes and porcelain products to counteract British imports. After his classes, Aneek frequented the samiti and made time for physical training, social work, arbitration in rural areas and implementation of various forms of resistance to the British rule.

During the same year, after a false alarm of miscarriage, Archana gave birth to their youngest child—a daughter. Unfortunately, Archana's health began to steadily falter thereafter. While Mukund often spent time in Calcutta, fundraising for militant movements, it was Bonka who ensured that the family's needs were met back in Madaripur.

Between 1910 and 1913, the youth of Chandernagore became adept at producing home-made bombs at a rapid pace, and they also trained others across the nation. In 1911, the partition of Bengal was revoked, and the British government annulled it officially on 1 April 1912.

During this period, there were numerous attempts to kill Englishmen such as the then-Viceroy Lord Charles Hardinge in Delhi, military diplomat William Evans-Gordon in Lahore and British police officer Denham in Dalhousie Square, Calcutta. Two quiet revolutionaries of the French enclave of Chandernagore, Motilal Roy and Shirish Chandra Ghosh, inspired many men, including the nation's most daring duo of Jatin Das and Bhagat Singh. Around 1915, Mukund began printing banned pamphlets in the basement of his home in Madaripur. These included instruction guides on making small arms and bombs.

Aneek, meanwhile, worked part-time at a shop that made paddle boxes for steamboats and deposited 70 per cent of his earnings to a fund meant for explosives. There was no time left to watch the peaceful lapping of the Ganga River from the vantage points of Strand Road or the Outram Ghat. Effigies of past and present viceroys were being burned every other day. Violent demonstrations came alive among the freedom seekers who had thus far worked from the underground. With winks, nods, small talk, drinking and dining, some tried in vain to curry favour with the native police officers loyal to the British Raj.

The young revolutionaries, including Aneek, lived a rough life in Calcutta. They spent months away from home, sleeping in cramped rooms and on overused bedrolls. Burying long-standing differences, certain youthful adversaries worked together for their cause. In their rare moments of rest, the more educated revolutionaries helped their less literate peers write love letters. They spent their nights in makeshift shelters, some of which were barely concealed from the authorities. When despair driven by a lack of any major success hit them hard, they played chess with one another.

Driven to the point of paranoia, the British authorities intensified their efforts to suppress the movement. The construction of the new capital in New Delhi accelerated as a response to the growing unrest.

Before long, like his father, Mukund's toes bulged with painful gout. Aneek, deeply concerned, came home more often and remained at home during the day to help his mother care for his much younger newborn sister, Sayantini.

One night, seized by a renewed sense of urgency, Aneek attempted to refine the easy use of small handheld explosives. He secretly secured a copy of the procedure and slipped into his estate's rice barn. The arsenal manufacturing guides were meant for various revolutionary groups of northeast India, not just Bengal. However, to protect the freedom fighters' lives, the names of the involved men making the guides or receiving the explosives were never listed in the documents. Aneek tried to mix the explosive chemicals in miniature quantities. When his workbench, filled with various chemicals and two table-top lanterns, tumbled accidentally, the effort ended in a blast that gravely injured the youth in his ribs. The storage shed was well out of earshot of the mansion; hence, Archana never came to know about the disaster and the wound in his chest.

Mukund quickly transported his son to a friend's home. At Flanagan's behest, Prachi immediately rushed to the government dak bungalow to nurse her grand-nephew until he had recovered enough to return home. It took nearly five weeks for Aneek to recover enough to return home and hide his injury from his mother.

Meanwhile, starting around the end of 1909, several months after the Alipore Bomb Case, Swami Niralamba's (aka Jatindra Banerjee) team, including Bagha Jatin, succeeded in eliminating several Indians opposing the revolution by working for the British. The loyalists who were assassinated included Sub-Inspector Nandalal Banerjee, who had arrested Prafulla Chaki; Ashutosh Biswas, the government lawyer who tried and convicted Chaki; and Shamsul Alam, the tyrannical deputy superintendent of the British Indian police.

Although Bagha Jatin was arrested and tried, he was later released from prison, only to lose his government job and return to his ancestral home in Jessore in eastern Bengal. Coincidentally, around the same time, Mukund returned to Madaripur from Channa

Village in the Burdwan district, having met with the remnants of Jatindra Banerjee's once 30-member revolutionary team. He had delivered 250 hand-held explosives, secretly manufactured by Aneek in a highly concealed barn. To transport the explosives, Mukund borrowed and cleverly disguised one of the oldest coal-hauling lorries in Bengal, owned by his brother-in-law, Kanak.

Between 1909 and 1914 Mukund, Bonka, Aneek, and sometimes Flanagan cooperated secretly and regularly on many a militant plot with members of the Bagha Jatin team. Bonka volunteered his service in conducting a bomb blast near the residence of the British district magistrate of Dhaka. When a secondary explosive he was carrying exploded prematurely, Bonka found himself trapped in a trench under a huge boulder. In an attempt to rescue Bonka, Mukund exchanged gunfire with the magistrate's guards. He sustained a bullet wound in his foot, leaving him unable to walk normally for nearly a month.

Mukund's dual life, which began in 1910, continued until his death some years later. In June 1910, when a few members of Mukund and Aneek's underground band were arrested and jailed, he miraculously survived the night-time raid by the loyalists among the ruins of Jinjira.

Alongside working underground, Mukund dabbled in various private and government jobs. He joined the Survey of India, a British-operated public agency Archana resented this job since it kept Mukund away from home for long periods; with Aneek being fully out of the nest by now, she took up playing cards with the neighbourhood housewives to alleviate her recurring anxiety.

Despite Mukund and Archana's infrequent physical intimacies in recent years, the latter secretly wished that the rare times they did make love, her husband's passion would be long and sweet, just like old times. At times, late at night, Mukund would hug her sleeping frame tight and whisper sweet nothings into her ears—

especially the endearing names he had assigned her from the long-gone honeymoon years.

Archana never questioned him about his frequent trips to Cynthia's home or his role in her final months. She had once found a torn page from the Englishwoman's diary in Mukund's pocket after the latter's return from Cynthia's last rites. It read: 'I have been trying to get you to love me as much as you love Archana. But I seem to be getting nowhere. No idea how this will all end!' Archana never enquired about that note either.

Mukund perceived the Survey of India's activities as benefiting the motherland. For the first time, they churned out accurate maps of the vast peninsula, capturing the intricate details of its remote jungles, rivers, and lakes. His first assignment in Narayanganj, a major river port near Dhaka, involved surveying the area and overseeing a district bungalow used by British employees. Simultaneously, Mukund completed a covert assignment for the Calcutta underground freedom cell, retrieving a cache of weapons with Flanagan's help and shipping them to a secret location in the southern tip of 24 Parganas.

Chapter 33

Home Under Attack

MUKUND HAD PAINSTAKINGLY RESTORED MUCH OF THE zamindari that had been razed by arson, though it was far from the glory it once held during his father's time. Barely 30 years earlier, Keshav had had 108 sentinels to guard the expansive estate, while Mukund could now only afford 30 armed guards to protect their farms, orchards, fisheries and mansion. Despite their diminished resources, Mukund and his family primarily lived in the resurrected Madaripur mansion, only occasionally staying at their Calcutta home.

Mukund had long ago identified Nobin and Moi as the culprits behind the arson. Nobin had since become a far more successful wholesale grain trader in the area than he was at the time of the fire. When Mukund encountered either Nobin or Moi in the village, he never frowned at them or looked for ways to retaliate anymore. An air of forgiveness from Mukund's end seemed plausible since he had never even tried to lodge any criminal case against these men. Yet, a cold war raged on both sides. For example, during the panchayat elections, when Nobin tried to become the next village headman, Mukund had no choice but to support the undoubtedly upright, learned and retired headmaster of the only primary school in the village.

In October 1911, Sayantini died of typhoid. Archana remained inconsolable for months. Her depression steadily worsened with both her son and husband being away from home most of the time. Sundays became particularly unbearable. She no longer fussed about preparing the mutton curry the way Aneek liked it—the goat meat slightly overcooked, the pieces small, soft and succulent and mired in thick and spicy potato gravy made with sautéed onions, green chillies, garam masala, potato halves, cinnamon sticks and whole black pepper. On new moon nights, Archana would often be found wandering in the dark patio or playing the esraj or the sarangi alone in the music room, while the servants listened to her melancholic melodies from behind the curtains. She longed for the days when Aneek concocted innocent fibs to rush off to Calcutta to meet Damini. The moments when both father and son were home, Archana looked forward to settling the minor squabbles between them. She now believed in young hearts running free with their dreams and how such dreams ought to be realized—even when it came to the matter of seeking freedom for one's motherland!

Starting from his early years as a press owner, Mukund occasionally received surprise gifts from satisfied customers or friends. As one of the last vestiges of that practice, a few weeks before the Christmas of 1912, he received one such gift—a book. Seemingly so rare at the time, he prized the book and kept it with him all the time for as long as he lived. A publisher from Allahabad had sent him a copy of the seven-volume Sanskrit–German dictionary compiled by Otto von Böhtlingk. At the time, despite India's complete subjugation, there were ample Europeans who genuinely and deeply loved the country and its cultural and mystic heritage. Otto von Böhtlingk was one such German-Russian linguist and lexicographer and the dictionary, one of the most comprehensive dictionaries to be ever compiled, was his magnum opus.

One morning, having bathed and completed her mystic salutations just before dawn, Archana looked as fresh as a springtime daisy. She readied to bid goodbye to her Calcutta-bound son.

Archana gently urged, 'Let us have some breakfast.'

After serving her son an elaborate early morning breakfast consisting of kochuri stuffed with green peas and beguni, Archana led him into her painting room. She knew the recent changes in her favourite chamber of the eight-room house would make him happy.

Aneek scanned the room, his eyes lingering on a side table where one of Archana's latest artistic endeavours rested. Lately, she had drifted from her usual portraits and landscapes, and at her husband's behest had been creating hordes of 'BUY ONLY INDIAN GOODS' banners in English and various Indian languages. Made from canvas, jute, silk and cotton, Mukund planned to ship these banners to various revolutionaries in Bombay and Baroda by the month's end. Fuelled by figures such as Bal Gangadhar Tilak, Lala Lajpat Rai and Bipin Chandra Pal, the Swadeshi Movement was in full swing. A scholar as well as a poet, Veer Savarkar launched the might of his pen into the fray and kindled many youths' dreams. From Kashmir to Kanyakumari and from Bombay to Calcutta, thousands of young men and women resonated for a sovereign nation.

Aneek felt chatty with his mother. He picked up and approvingly gazed at the only landscape of a Bengal village she had created of late.

'Ma, who is this painting for?'

'It is for Mr Hall. He is growing older and ailing more often these days. I go to see him from time to time. This one is to cheer him up. I know how much he likes landscapes such as this.'

'Wonderful idea! I will drop by and see him as well.'

'Please do. Many of his teeth are wobbly now, so instead of mutton, I make him hot khichuri and omelettes. He likes that.'

'Where is Baba right now? He must be up and about already.'

'Of course, he is smoking his cigar in the study room. He declined breakfast and is already glued to the Sanskrit–German dictionary.'

As the youth peered out of the window, he saw his father was now outside, standing at the edge of a long and wide patio, helping Bonka fix a dinghy's scull. Mukund was also subjecting his long-time sidekick to an orally administered test of the Sanskrit language. Fixing boats and sculls came easily to the tribal. Though versed in the basics of English and Bengali, when it came to Sanskrit, fear crept into his eyes each time Mukund probed his understanding of the ancient language.

Archana hurried to the kitchen and returned with a tiffin carrier filled with sweets.

Taking the shiny brass cylindrical box from his mother's hand, Aneek asked, 'What is in it?'

'Give these *chandrapuli* to Hubert. Knowing how much he likes these coconut-stuffed sweets, I made these especially for him.'

As they stood side by side, mother and son looked out of the open window. The rustic trail disappeared inside a dense thicket of ashok trees, their evergreen leaves watching worldly proceedings with timeless patience. Chanting nationalist slogans and carrying placards, a small group of dhoti-kurta-clad students seemed to be heading to a meeting of the INC; other than the newly formed Muslim League, it was the only Indian entity officially allowed by the Raj to assemble and rally.

After the activists disappeared from view, Archana rushed back to the kitchen once again. This time, she returned with a cup of hot tea for her son.

Her lips stained red with the juice of a freshly chewed betel leaf, Archana suddenly said, 'How tragic! Two freedom-seeking Indian patriots, G.K. Gokhale and Tilak, fought like dogs over the bone of liberty. Their egos got in the way. Again and again, they tried to seize the bone, did they not? We need a mix of both approaches, do we not? Look at America; they had to fight a pitched battle to get their freedom, did they not?'

Though she spoke with sympathy, Aneek, a quiet Tilak supporter, pretended not to understand the implications of her statement. 'What do you mean?'

'The two wings of the party fought each other instead of rising together for a common cause. Which of the two men do you support?'

Aneek smiled but did not answer his mother.

Wiping away a tear that had begun to well up in her eyes, Archana said softly, 'Your father has been trying to hide the news of your latest arrest from me. But I know all of your activities in Calcutta from a sleuth of mine.'

'It must be good old Bonka.'

'Your actions speak loud enough about which camp you belong to. All I can do is pray every day for my sanity and for you to come back alive.'

Just then, the estate's new accounts clerk stuck his head inside the room through the slightly open door. He seemed to want an audience with Archana. So did the cook, sneaking in from the kitchen to seek help with a new hot and deep-fried snack. She held a wooden spoon covered with a gooey batter of gram flour.

Sensing the interruption, Aneek placed the tiffin carrier in his leather bag and bent down to touch his mother's feet. He was ready to depart.

Archana called out after him. 'Son, I know you are in a hurry to go to Dhaka and catch a train for Calcutta. But don't forget that my spy in the big city is as good as the ones who help revolutionaries like you.'

At that very moment, the sound of a single gunshot followed by multiple rounds shook the early morning air. Through the rustic trail, Nobin, Moi and three mercenaries charged towards the mansion's gate, their faces concealed by indigo-dyed tagelmusts. The hate and envy they had long held for Mukund still burned fiercely, despite the passage of years.

This time, the renewed vendetta was driven by Mukund's refusal to support Nobin in the village headman's election, causing him to lose. Nobin's growing economic and social clout had led him to believe that he could settle all disputes and possible hurdles in life with a sheer show of force and violence. After all, being busy with 'bigger' issues, the faujdars of the nearest police station of the British Raj rarely intervened.

Armed with rifles and pistols, Nobin and company planned to exploit a weakness: the recent delays in the shift change of Mukund's guards. Normally, the estate was protected by two guards who worked from 7 a.m. to 7 p.m., but lately, the morning shift had been starting a few minutes late, leaving a small window of vulnerability.

This morning was one such occasion. After Mukund had given permission for the night guards to leave before the morning staff arrived, Nobin, Moi, and their mercenaries seized the opportunity they had been waiting for. For those crucial 10 minutes, the estate lay unprotected, and the attackers were ready to force their way in. However, the attackers had overlooked a few important details.

Though Mukund was working outside in the front garden, he had momentarily gone into his study to fetch a worn-out ugly-looking flower-bed trowel that Jimut had given to him when he was a child. Like a precious but contraband game, he liked to hide the gardening tool from Archana, hiding it in his locked vault of miscellanies in the study room. When the day felt apt for a bit of digging and soil turning, he would use it early in the morning while his wife was usually busy organizing breakfast.

The attackers' overconfidence led them to make their first mistake. One of Nobin's mercenaries fired a single and premature shot into the air even before they entered the unguarded gate. What they also failed to notice was the household cook's eight-year-old son who happened to be playing with his marbles behind a dog access slit in the main gate. Moreover, the assailants had underestimated the time it would take them to reach the steps of the mansion from the main gate, which was at least 40 yards away. And what they hadn't factored in was that both Bonka and Aneek were proficient marksmen. Bonka had learnt sharpshooting from the maharaja's elite guards in Darbhanga, while Aneek had been groomed in the art of firearms by the underground freedom fighters of Calcutta.

At that very moment, old and emaciated Mr Hall, now in his 80s but still riding his bicycle daily, was passing by the mansion. Alarmed by the sound of the first shot, he reacted instinctively, rushing to block the hoodlums' access to the manor. He quickly tied the iron knobs of both the vehicular and pedestrian gates with the iron chain he carried with him to secure his cycle.

A blind corner caused by a thicket nearby helped Mr Hall create the obstruction and then hide behind a bush incognito. This action delayed the five men's arrival at the foot of the mansion's steps by a few precious seconds. A few life-saving moments passed. That was all the time Mukund needed to prepare for the shooting exchange. Having heard the warning shot, he had immediately gone to grab the three loaded rifles hanging in his study room. Ever since the arson, the zamindar of Madaripur always kept his weapons locked and loaded, periodically checking to ensure adherence to safety as well as readiness.

Like lightning, Mukund dashed into the painting room and threw one of the rifles to Aneek and, in a voice filled with urgency and terror, shouted, 'Let us all shoot from the living room windows.'

He threw the other rifle to Bonka, who had sprinted in.

Without wasting a moment, both Bonka and Aneek positioned their rifles on the windowsills. As the assailants struggled to untie the ropes that Mr Hall had secured at the gates, the three defenders aimed carefully and fired with precision.

Shots rang out, filling the morning air with a deadly symphony of gunfire. They did not stop until their magazines were emptied.

Perhaps due to destiny's intervention and the assailant's proximity, not a single shot missed its mark. Between the three of them, they had shot four of the five intruders down by the time the assailants could even make it halfway across the red-stone pathway leading to the mansion steps.

Archana, who had been watching in stunned silence from the rear, witnessed the moment her son's first shot struck Nobin in the heart, sending him crashing to the ground. Moi fell next, his head struck by two successive bullets fired by Mukund. Aneek fired again, this time at the hired thugs. As did Bonka.

When Aneek's rifle's rounds ran out, he pulled out a pistol strapped to his waist—a weapon Archana had never seen before. He emptied all its bullets into the fleeing mercenaries, while Bonka used his final rounds to ensure that only one of the three hired thugs could get away.

Mr Hall's frail heart gave up in the melee. Archana wept softly while holding his motionless head in her lap. Aneek rushed towards this venerable family friend whose body lay on the grimy ground near the gate.

A few moments later, like a man possessed, Mukund prostrated full length before a painting of Vishnu hanging on the wall and tearfully mumbled, 'Forgive me, Lord... Purely in our self-defence today, we have killed some men. You know more than all others that we had no other choice. They have hounded us for so many years.' Then he looked at Mr Hall's corpse and prayed again, 'Take Mr Hall to Vaikunth, my Lord. Take him home. Forever take him home.' Then he started to cry bitterly like an utterly broken man.

Less than an hour later, the village morol and his men arrived to collect the bodies of the dead hoodlums. Due to the self-evident nature of the violence, no charges were filed. The one surviving assailant was never seen again in Madaripur. Everyone speculated that it was Bhabesh, but no one was sure. Aneek postponed his departure by a day.

The day after the gun battle, the first rays of dawn found Archana and Mukund fondly gazing at Aneek as he hurried out to catch a horse-drawn carriage heading for the railway station.

Not long after Aneek's departure, tragedy struck the family again. Kanak was caught by forces loyal to the British Raj—Police Inspector Basanta Chatterjee—and hanged in Alipore Central Jail for his active participation in a plot to assassinate Lord Minto, the former viceroy. Grieving for her devoted brother's demise, Archana wept for days on end.

By this time, owing to the efforts of British governor generals such as Lord Bentinck and Lord Bethune, Indian education was undergoing a significant transformation. By the late 19th century, institutions like the Bengal Academy of Literature had taken root, flourishing with the support of prominent figures such as Rabindranath Tagore, Satyendranath Tagore, Jyotirindranath Tagore, Narendranath Mitra, Ramendrasundar Trivedi, Rajanikanta Gupta and others.

Inspired by this zeal for spreading education, Aneek and Hubert opened a night school for visually impaired children. With the help of Hubert's friends in the Calcutta Police, they secured the necessary permission from the administrators in the Writers' Building. They also received much help from a Belgian Jesuit padre.

One winter evening, as Aneek wrapped up the last class of the day, robbers with no allegiance to the nation's freedom descended upon the building that housed the night school. The visually impaired children had spent the morning collecting medicines and clothing to donate to flood-stricken areas such as Majlispur and Nagarpur. However, the assailants, indifferent to the plight of the disabled, showed no mercy. Aneek tried to reason with them, pleading on behalf of the children, but his words fell on deaf ears.

In desperation, Aneek grabbed a large black slate and hurled it at the chief assailant. Sensing trouble, Aneek ran to the main road. One of the hardened criminals sprinted after him hitting him with a thick bamboo cudgel, sending him sprawling into a nearby drain filled with bacteria-infested water. The hoodlums fled with the measly Rs 100 Hubert and Aneek had collected to purchase additional books, carbon filament lights and study chairs for the two classrooms of their night school.

The aftermath for Aneek was grim. Falling into the contaminated drain had left him severely ill, and he soon became bedridden with a debilitating case of stomach flu, forcing him to remain indoors for almost a month and live on a diet of sliced plantains, barley and bread. With no other choice, he transferred the operational responsibilities of the special school to an old college classmate.

Chapter 34

Lifelong Friendship

By 1911, MUKUND AND ANEEK WERE PRINTING REVOLUTIONARY flyers at breakneck speed. These leaflets, aimed at inspiring the nation's youth, focused on bomb-making techniques, physical fitness and the rich history of India. Mukund and Aneek were constantly on the move, travelling like nomads to deliver these pamphlets to more than 500 centres of the Anushilan Samiti, a revolutionary group that openly endorsed violence as a means to overthrow British rule.

That same year, Mukund met a 16-year-old revolutionary named Basanta Kumar Biswas. Inspired by Rash Behari Bose, this teenager from Nadia had already become an expert handbomb-maker. Mukund took a train to Lahore and stayed there with the young revolutionary for a week, hugely gratified when Basanta Kumar Biswas helped him rewrite and improve his bomb-making flyers.

One year later, on 20 December 1912, Basanta Kumar Biswas travelled to Delhi. He knew that on 23 December, Viceroy Hardinge would parade atop an elephant to celebrate the transfer of British India's capital from Calcutta to Delhi. Aiming to assassinate the viceroy, Basanta and three others came quite close to the procession when Lord Hardinge was passing through Chandni Chowk. With deadly precision, Basanta hurled a bomb he had made at home at the howdah of the viceroy's elephant. Hardinge escaped with injuries, but his mahout was killed in the attack.

Six months later, Basanta was implicated in the bombing at Lawrence Garden, Lahore, in May 1913. By February 1914, Basanta and his comrades were caught, and a year later, they were sentenced to hang. At Mukund's urgings, Hubert offered to send an Anglo-Indian defence lawyer to the Lahore court to defend Basanta, but the intrepid youth declined. Basanta was only 20 years old when he went to the gallows with a proud smile.

Aneek played a direct role in the attempt to slay anti-freedom activist Abdar Rahaman at Midnapur. When the plan to use bombs was confirmed, Aneek toiled overnight and prepared four hand-held bombs. Then he took the train to Midnapur to personally deliver the bombs to the handful of activists planning to kill Abdar Rahaman. He rued for days when Abdar Rahaman escaped.

Meanwhile, after Mr Hall's death, Mukund had asked Mr Hall's adopted daughter, Madhuri, to move into his mansion. Now a teenager, Madhuri began to help Archana in every aspect of the household affairs. In Archana, she found a mother figure as well. By now, suffering from acute back pain, Mukund also welcomed the charming quiet maiden's presence in the mansion. The forgetful zamindar relished her gentle attention. Incessant stagecoach travel on rusty, bumpy roads plus the far-off travels as the Survey of India's representative had worsened the tissues and nerves around Mukund's spine. Even now, when many zamindars owned and travelled in cars, he still refused to purchase the 'lavish' transportation.

Like a silent yet nightlong drizzle, Madhuri's sheer goodness gradually besieged Aneek's lonely heart. Whenever home, Aneek watched her from every unlikely place—cowshed, kitchen and backyard—while Madhuri affectionately fed mendicants every week in the mansion veranda on Archana's behalf.

Six months later, Aneek married Madhuri. It was a joyous occasion wherein everyone Aneek and Madhuri knew was invited to the lavish wedding feast. Despite their advanced age, Flanagan, Prachi and Bonka took care of all the arrangements including the final dinner. Farmers and fishermen came from faraway villages to attend this gastronomical bonanza.

~

During one of Aneek's travels, he unexpectedly befriended Ted Hawkins, an employee in a British armoury in north India. Always interested in the latest events not just in Bengal, Aneek pined to know about the developments all around the world. Ted's correspondences provided him with the perfect insider's insight.

By 1914, Mukund quit the Survey of India job and distractedly dabbled with a limestone kiln venture. The effort failed due to the many ill-wishers he attracted from his nationalistic activism.

In February 1915, Mukund received devastating news. He had been aware of Bagha Jatin's and Rash Behari Bose's grand plans to incite a rebellion among the Indian troops of the British Indian government. However, the effort failed due to a treacherous act by one of their men.

In September 1915, Bagha Jatin and his four comrades were attempting to cross the Buribalam swamp on the Orissa coast when the British Indian police arrived at a critical moment and surrounded the entire area. A fierce gun battle broke out between the band of five revolutionaries and a large police force deployed by Deputy Police Commissioner Charles Tegart for the next few hours. In the end, Bagha Jatin and one other comrade were fatally wounded. The remaining three revolutionaries were captured and later hanged.

In a bid to lift his spirits, Aneek decided to visit his old friend Hubert in Hiranpur and sent him a telegram. Not receiving any reply, Aneek was left puzzled. Meanwhile, his wife Madhuri, who was expecting their first child, had gone to her best friend's house. Mukund, sensing his son's restlessness, suggested Aneek take a trip to Calcutta to handle an estate-related transaction and handed him a front-row ticket to a Russian circus that had been receiving rave reviews.

For the first time in his life, Aneek watched endless stunts by jovial elephants, bovine tigers and stunningly beautiful young men and women striding upon speeding rings before gracefully landing on galloping horses. The spectacle concluded with thundering applause and a standing ovation. Utterly charmed by the gymnastic ability of the performers and the acts of the well-trained animals, the audience slowly filed out of the bamboo-propped and canvas-covered pavilion as the golden hue of the setting sun cast a magical glow across the sky.

As Aneek walked through the bustling streets, a familiar voice suddenly called out his name. Aneek could not believe his ears. He had just finished buying toys for Bonka's grandsons from a street corner pedlar. The haul included a paper snake, a rubber ball and a small Taj Mahal cube carved from *shoal*.

Again, the all-too-endearing voice of Hubert rang out, 'Aneek, what on earth are you doing here?'

Aneek spun around in surprise. 'You are here! No wonder you did not reply to the telegram I sent you in Hiranpur.'

A cigarette dangling between his lips, Hubert asked, 'What telegram? Is everything alright with you and your parents?'

'Yes, of course. But Jimut's grandson Aritro is fighting on Europe's Western Front. Having already lost one son to the war, his mother is desperate for him to come home...'

'What is Aritro doing there? Is he an infantryman?'

'He was, but now he is an ambulance driver on the front lines. That is equally dangerous.'

'Oh yes. I will see what I can do for Aritro when I get back to work.' Hubert paused for a moment before asking, 'Hey, Aneek... Have you heard Mohandas Karamchand Gandhi? The recently returned lawyer from South Africa... The one who is organizing protests by peasants, farmers and urban labourers?'

'Oh yes...the one concerned about excessive land tax and discrimination.'

'He seems pretty dogged, does he not?'

Aneek's eyes lit up. 'After almost 150 years of despotic British rule in India…it is about time; is it not?'

'Perhaps.'

The news of Aritro's situation weighed heavily on Hubert, who, despite his best efforts, couldn't secure a furlough for the infantryman. The reality of the ongoing war seemed insurmountable, and Hubert could only hope and pray for Aritro's safety.

~

One day, Hubert sent a long telegram to Aneek: 'As you know, my house in Calcutta is located very close to the residence of the notorious Police Commissioner Charles Tegart. He has filed sedition charges against me for being a sympathizer to the Indian freedom movement. The real reason is that he thinks I am his hostile neighbour who masterminded the recent attack on his orchards.'

Aneek, though already fighting charges of illegal possession of firearms with intent to aid in the freedom movement, was determined to stand by Hubert. Upon receiving the telegram, Aneek and Madhuri rushed to Calcutta.

The next few days passed grimly and painfully. The night before Aneek and Madhuri were to take a train back to Madaripur wore on ominously. Robert had returned to Calcutta to find a lawyer to defend his son the previous day.

Dismissing the Englishman's cook for the day and taking help only from the round-the-clock manservant in the bungalow, Madhuri had cooked for the pale-looking, appetite-devoid Hubert.

'Hubert, I do not know what went wrong in the orchards that night, but as a character witness, I will testify on your behalf,' said Aneek.

Madhuri, who understood most of the conversation carried out in English, began to silently cry. Her mind was plagued with fears of the worst possible outcomes—of seeing Aneek and Hubert sent to a penal colony and their lives ruined.

Aneek continued, 'The big question that hangs over us is whether, influenced by Police Commissioner Tegart's high position, the judge will "see" any treasonous connection in our friendship.'

Hubert sighed deeply. 'God only knows. Yes, they might see me as anti-British as well, once they find out about your efforts with the Swadeshi Movement.'

Madhuri added, 'But Hubert, you have never helped him or any samiti members in making indigenous goods. All you have done is help avoid indefinite imprisonment. You two were playmates in Darbhanga for several years; does not one do that much for an old friend?'

'That is true. Hopefully, Father will find a good barrister to defend me.'

'I think Mr Broad will help you,' Madhuri said. 'You must revive your faith. Every time I have met you, I have heard you say that God is good. If God is indeed that good, He will prove your innocence.'

Hubert nodded, then, seeing his friend attentively reading a piece of paper, he asked curiously, 'What is that?'

Aneek replied, 'It is a letter from your Uncle Shawn. Believe it or not, he still stays in touch with me.'

'How is he doing lately?'

'All right. Forsaking the plush Writers' Building job, he has started a restaurant in Calcutta.'

'I know.'

Aneek continued, 'In his eatery, he overheard a conversation involving a payroll officer from the Chittagong armoury. According to him, Winston Churchill is in the process of taking a huge gamble in the war with Germany.'

'What else did he hear?'

'Churchill is looking for ways to gain an advantage in the protracted war.'

Hubert said, 'One can only hope that for both India's and Britain's welfare, the British Navy ships' sudden switch from dependence on Welsh coal to imported petroleum will work.'

Two months pregnant with her first child, Madhuri gently redirected the conversation, 'Many of the women in our village, including my mother-in-law, are still praying every night for Aritro's safe return.'

Hubert replied in Bengali, 'I have already written petitions on his behalf. My sub-divisional officer has mailed and wired them to the War Secretary and the Minister of Munitions.'

Soon after, Madhuri summoned everyone to dinner. It was the quietest and shortest dinner they had shared together.

The next morning, once on the train to Dhaka, Madhuri asked, 'You look so worried. What are you thinking about?'

Aneek frowned. 'We must help Hubert overcome this groundless lawsuit. Then I will worry about my case.'

The train began to gallop. Jaws dropping, Aneek leaned forward from his seat and blinked. 'How do you suggest one makes Calcutta's extremely busy chief metropolitan magistrate defend Hubert?'

Madhuri smiled and leaned into her husband's shoulder. 'First, you must write to Shawn to chase the big lawman.'

Travelling in a two-berth cabin, Aneek looked around. In the complete privacy of their cabin, he held her in his arms and kissed her eager lips. 'I will do that, my darling.'

A few months passed.

Shawn shuttled between Chittagong and Calcutta to convince the metropolitan magistrate to defend his nephew. To everyone's surprise, the magistrate finally agreed. Several British colleagues and neighbours came forward to provide testimony about Hubert's character. The magistrate also underplayed Hubert's friendship with the freedom fighter Aneek.

A few days later, the magistrate electrified the Calcutta High Court with brilliant arguments, proving that Hubert's gun had been planted during the deadly attack on Tegart's orchards. The next day, Tegart's wife fell ill and was hospitalized. Three days later, Tegart withdrew all charges of sedition and trespassing against Hubert.

By November 1916, the Royal Military Police arranged for Aritro's permanent return. Although Aritro had suffered a fractured leg from enemy gunfire, he had managed to kill the enemy parachutist before being hit. With help from his colleagues, Hubert managed to get a pension approved for the injured soldier.

Chapter 35

Romance Reigns amid Revolution's Turmoil

DESPITE HIS INVOLVEMENT IN MILITANT ACTIVITIES DURING the freedom struggle, by 1917, Aneek managed to burn enough of the midnight oil to earn his master's degree in law from Calcutta University.

By this time, his wife Madhuri's exceptional beauty shone more than ever. She not only resembled her adoptive father, Mr Hall, in appearance but also in spirit. Like the late Englishman, Madhuri liked to see harmony and the spread of universal love in the world. Kindness and a knack for matchmaking seemed to come naturally to both father and daughter.

Madhuri's secret plan to romantically bring together Hubert and Claire began to unfold slowly. Madhuri introduced Claire, the Anglo-Indian granddaughter of their neighbour Girindra, to Hubert. The rich landowner's daughter Koli had married her British private tutor. In the beginning, the still-grieving Hubert hardly accepted the banquet lunches Madhuri offered in her Madaripur mansion. But time has its way of healing all wounds, and by early 1917, Hubert began to notice the slender, brunette Claire, who frequently fussed over the exquisite dishes served by her family friend.

As the matchmaking process reached its final stages, Archana, Aneek's mother, joined forces with her daughter-in-law, Madhuri. After a particularly delightful lunch, Archana smiled impishly at her aged neighbour and queried, 'My dear Girindra Kaka and I can endlessly sing praises of his charming granddaughter, but Hubert, have you made up your mind?'

Hubert blushed and nodded in agreement.

Archana pressed on, 'Then what is a good wedding date for you?'

'Mashi, it can be any day you and Girindra babu decide on.'

Elated with the developments, Madhuri clapped with joy and went to the kitchen to prepare tea for everyone.

When it was time to leave, Archana nodded approvingly as Hubert bent down to touch her feet before heading for the front door.

'Stay safe, Hubert, and send me a letter once in a while.'

Hubert nodded and waved just before his white Morris Motors car disappeared along the curved garden road.

Within two months, Hubert and Claire were married at Girindra's mansion in Madaripur, following both Hindu and Christian traditions. Even the cooks and guards from Aneek's mansion were warmly invited.

Chapter 36

Settling of an Old Score

ONE MAY RECALL SEVERAL YEARS EARLIER, AFTER THE DEATH of his cronies Moi and Nobin and his defeat in a gun battle against Mukund and his men, Bhabesh had fled from Madaripur. After his remaining goons spread a false rumour that Bhabesh had escaped to the Himalayan Mountains, he assumed a new identity and rented a small cottage in Rangoon. Bhabesh's mother was of Burmese origin—a heritage he had hidden from society, much like his bisexual inclinations. Being of Burmese descent, he feared, was akin to being marked with a pariah's disease in the eyes of his peers.

Living in self-imposed exile in Burma, Bhabesh took in a prostitute as his live-in mistress. He dared not return to his opulent mansion in Madaripur, as the police warrant issued against him for the attempted murder of Mukund still stood. No longer young or wealthy, Bhabesh found himself incapable of luring or coercing young beauties or charming boys as he once did in his Madaripur heyday. The ageing, incorrigible philanderer, now suffering from Parkinson's disease, could barely control the shaking in his hands, jaw, and head. His only motivation for a brief return to Madaripur was revenge—specifically, to exact vengeance on Aneek, the grandson of Keshav, the zamindar he had never been able to outmanoeuvre.

Bhabesh meticulously planned Aneek's murder. With Aneek back in Madaripur, Bhabesh knew this was his ultimate opportunity. One late evening, Aneek was walking through a dense thicket, returning home after collecting a rare medicinal herb. Bhabesh followed him, driving a worn-out horse-drawn cart along a narrow, tree-lined road. His plan was simple but brutal: get close enough and smash Aneek's head with a heavy cudgel from behind.

But fate intervened. Just as Bhabesh prepared to strike, he suffered a massive heart attack. Crying out in agony, he lost control of the cart. His horse panicked and reared, causing the cart's front wheel and wooden axle to snap. The horse broke free, and the cart veered sharply to the left, crashing into the thick trunk of a massive tree. Bhabesh's head struck the tree first, followed by his body. The old, vengeful man died instantly, without even time to scream.

Twenty yards ahead, Aneek, unaware of his would-be assassin, heard the crash and turned around to find Bhabesh lifeless, slumped against the wrecked cart. Stunned, he stood silently, absorbing the scene that had unfolded before him—a man consumed by hatred, felled by what seemed like divine retribution. A farmer's bullock cart eventually broke the stillness, snapping Aneek out of his trance.

Everyone who later came to know the details of the accident deemed it a supernatural phenomenon, while others saw it as long-overdue justice. Aneek, however, chose never to speak of it again.

Chapter 37

The Legacy of Ultimate Sacrifice

MUKUND BEGAN TO SPEND PART OF THE YEAR IN HIS CALCUTTA home with the septuagenarian yet ever-energetic Chris Flanagan. Even now, the Irishman spent much time preparing and printing wide-ranging inspirational and tactical booklets for circulation among the underground freedom movement cells. At other times, he was busy trying to keep Mukund's well-armed activist son Aneek out of jail.

In the summer of 1924, the Calcutta Police arrested the white-haired Flanagan for teaching young freedom-seeking men how to make hand-held bombs in the storeroom of a Kidderpore eatery. The officials let Mukund and Aneek go due to a lack of evidence.

In the next few weeks, Mukund began mobilizing funds from his savings, press and estate earnings and from his friends to help Flanagan. Due to reasons known only to him, he decided not to lean on Hubert Weatherilt. Mukund felt compelled to hire a noted Calcutta lawyer and to secure Flanagan's bail.

Thus, one sun-scorched noon in May 1924, hoping he had collected enough money to arrange for the ageing Irishman's bail or an equivalent miracle, Mukund arrived in front of the Lal Bazar jail. Just then, a chaotic gunfight erupted between the police forces and an armed, growingly violent band of demonstrators. At the same moment, the freshly released Flanagan happened to be coming down the steps of the jail. Overwhelmed with joy, Mukund rushed forward to embrace the Irishman when he spotted a young freedom fighter aiming his gun at Flanagan from behind a tree. The revolutionary, mistaking Flanagan for the British jail superintendent who had wrongfully imprisoned many of his peers, was preparing to fire.

Mukund threw himself in front of Flanagan to shield him. Unfortunately, his protective dive came too late. A bullet intended for the supposed jailer struck Mukund in the chest. The 57-year-old zamindar of Madaripur fell instantly, dying on the spot.

By late afternoon, Flanagan and Aneek hurried back to Madaripur with Mukund's lifeless body. After preparing the body for cremation, they brought it to the murky riverside. Countless farmers and fishermen gathered to mourn the loss as a priest chanted the Vedic mantras for the final rites.

A fellow activist from Calcutta asked Aneek, 'In the last four hours, I noticed that at some point or an other, all the women here have cried or at least wiped their moist eyes. Except...'

'Except whom?' Aneek's lips turned pale and his eyes watery.

Nearby, a 12-year-old girl, the daughter of a newcomer to the village, asked Afzal's eldest son, 'Do you know why the deceased Dadathakur's wife has not yet shed a single drop of tear?'

Having overheard the little girl's query, Aneek felt relieved that his mother stood far away from their earshot. Squeezing through the crowd, Archana had drifted away from the pyre and was standing under a babla tree, acknowledging the well-wishers' polite and heartfelt bows with innate grace. Leaning on the tree, Prachi quietly stood close to Archana, having already dealt with the grim task of cleaning the dried blood from Mukund's wound and body before the cremation.

Before the aged shell-shocked farmer could reply, Bonka intervened, defending his beloved master's wife. 'I will tell you why our Thakurani has not cried. It is because she is the proud widow of the most extraordinary zamindar named Mukund. She stands by all he believed in and aspired for. She did not cry because she could not have hoped for a nobler end for her husband—a martyr's death in the cause of freedom. Dadathakur died trying to release Flanagan sahib, the most compassionate man I have ever known.'

Bonka's composure shattered. His prematurely aged and shrunken frame seemed to be overtaken by a deep-seated madness and a private raving for a liberated nation—a quiet but indomitable frenzy that was kindled a long time ago by his onetime playmate and later revered master.

Walking slowly, Archana returned close to where Aneek stood poised to light his father's pyre. Her face had lost its colour, drained by the shock of her husband's death. She listened in silence to Bonka's uncharacteristic outburst without the outward display of grief.

Her words came across as a soft whisper of the farthest star from a distant planet. 'Bonka is right. Flanagan is an eternal knight guarding the worthy essence of all humankind. My husband did not die in vain... He died trying to save a man among men.'

A few minutes passed. No one spoke for a long time as the smoke from the pyre rose higher and higher into the steadily darkening sky. By now, Prachi's trembling voice resonated with the priests. Inside her heart, she moaned inconsolably. Her one and only nephew had sacrificed his life to save her husband. Many others followed her lead, mumbling the Vedic mantras beseeching divinity to grant the zamindar peace and liberation from life and death.

~

Overwhelmed by the loss of his younger protégé, Flanagan often sat alone in the rice fields and by the silted rivulets of Madaripur, seeking solace in nature while recalling gilded memories. After all, it was Flanagan who had taught Mukund how to fire a gun, polish and use a sword, ride a horse, operate the printing press, ride and repair a bicycle, fly a kite, fix a doorknob or a tube well, repair musical instruments, and so much more. He had also imparted the wisdom Mukund needed to uphold his fort with honour.

By the time Mukund was shot and killed in Calcutta, the already ageing Keshav was a broken man. His once-sharp eyesight had dimmed and his physical agility had waned, but Mukund's sudden death drained the last spark of life from him. One day despite the objections of his daughter-in-law, Archana, Keshav mounted his 16-year-old horse to oversee the restoration of his beloved, though decaying, lotus lake. On the way, his horse, failing to clear a makeshift wooden fence, stumbled. Keshav's forehead struck a heavy log that lay across an orchard he owned. The erstwhile zamindar of Madaripur died instantly.

After his passing, besides Madhuri and Aneek, Prachi and Flanagan kept a vigilant eye on Archana for as long as they lived. Even while visiting their sons in Rangoon and Madras, the Irishman never stayed away from Madaripur for more than a few weeks. At his daughter-in-law's insistence, Robert Weatherilt moved into his son's Calcutta home. However, he did not give up his role as a Sunday English teacher at a school for the disabled in Calcutta. At least once a month, he, too, took the steamer to Madaripur and called on Archana, Aneek and Madhuri.

Chapter 38

Dream of a Sovereign Nation Is Realized

ANEEK EVENTUALLY BECAME THE PRINCIPAL OF A COLLEGE IN Faridpur, a rapidly growing suburb, located only 70 miles from the bustling city of Dhaka. He still remained deeply involved in the struggle for India's independence, opening an underground nursing home in Madhyamgram to help revolutionary youths. In their militancy to shake up the British Raj offices in Dhaka, Calcutta, Chittagong and other areas, they were getting injured in various armed, violent encounters, successful or not. Once every fortnight, Madhuri travelled to Madhyamgram and worked as a nurse at the facility.

Aneek and his comrades in the Anushilan Samiti mostly tried in vain to sabotage the British police trucks heading to Calcutta port and British ships taking arrested Indian freedom fighters from overcrowded jails to the Andaman Islands for indefinite incarceration. Occasionally, if Aneek and his mates were lucky enough to free a gravely injured or tortured revolutionary, Madhuri housed them in their Madhyamgram nursing home.

For those with critical wounds, she arranged for treatment at a disused bungalow once owned by her deceased adoptive father, Mr Hall. Despite the emotional toll of witnessing such human cruelty, Madhuri worked tirelessly to heal the battered faces, fractured shoulders, whipped backs and shattered bones of the freedom fighters.

In addition to her nursing work, Madhuri fulfilled her inner calling by establishing a new high school for girls in Madaripur. She honoured Mr Hall and of Aneek's grandfather, Keshav, by placing their framed portraits near the school entrance. Her deep sense of gratitude for Mr Hall's benevolence, which had provided her with a new home, identity and a second chance at life, never left her. Humility was an attribute she never deserted, even in the best of times. During the 1920s and 1930s, Madhuri became increasingly active in the Indian freedom movement. With their ample salaries, zamindari incomes, orchard profits and Mukund's savings, Aneek and Madhuri generously funded the Anushilan Samiti of Dhaka and Calcutta.

Shawn, the long-kidnapped biological son of Mr Hall, sold his profitable eatery in Calcutta and resigned from his government position to oversee a large orphanage in Uttar Pradesh. His wife, Linda, steadfastly remained by his side and supported his altruistic life.

Madhuri was well aware of her husband's first love and revolutionary peer, Damini, who had died at the hands of the British cops. She provided financial support to Damini's widowed mother until her death. Madhuri also sent money orders to hundreds of young freedom activists imprisoned in Calcutta, who had no money to hire lawyers to defend themselves. She sold the gold necklaces and bangles she had inherited from her in-laws, Archana and Sheela, and auctioned prize saris and the last elephant of their zamindari to raise funds for various Indian revolutionaries.

In 1918, as the Spanish flu swept through India, thousands of Indian soldiers returning from Europe after the First World War succumbed to the virus aboard British Navy ships. Their dead bodies clogged the numerous rivers across India due to the dearth of firewood needed for cremation. To respectfully bury at least those corpses floating to the surface of the nearby Arial Khan River, Aneek and Madhuri's farmers collected as much straw, twigs and deadwood from their farms and orchards as they could.

One day, to his great sorrow, Aneek found that one of the corpses that had floated up the river was his own cousin he had met only a few times in his entire life. The deceased youth was the son of Kanak Mama.

In 1929, Madhuri secretly sent money to the revolutionary Durgavati Devi and her associates from the Naujawan Bharat Sabha, a militant group striving for India's independence. After the 1928 assassination of British official J.P. Saunders in Lahore, Durgavati Devi had helped revolutionaries Bhagat Singh and Rajguru to escape the wrath of the British cops via train.

When Bhagat Singh was hanged and Durgavati Devi was jailed for her failed attempt to assassinate Lord Hailey, Madhuri was devastated. She mourned for days, retreating to the shade of a white teak tree in her backyard, lamenting the missed chances to further the cause of freedom. At times, she felt as though the blood of her country's revolutionaries was seeping into the earth, evaporating before true liberation could be realized.

In the increasingly tribulating years that followed, Madhuri bought and sent spinning wheels to women freedom fighters incarcerated in various jails across India. She bought nationalist books and sent them to the young boys and girls in the orphanage run by her brother Shawn and his wife Linda. Shawn had left his government job and shut his eatery in Calcutta, shifting to Uttar Pradesh and opening an orphanage there. Every year, Shawn and Madhuri remembered their lion-hearted father on his birthday, by meeting up in Benaras for two weeks along with their respective spouses.

Meanwhile, for the first time in his life, Robert was living with his son Hubert and his wife Claire in their south Calcutta home. Struggling with guilt over his past philandering, Robert's mental health began to deteriorate, leading Hubert to place him in the Indian Mental Hospital in Ranchi. There, Robert was cared for by a compassionate Vaishnava nurse and a skilled psychiatrist, who helped him recover over two years. The nurse sang hymns and devotional songs to Robert, translating their messages into English for him.

Claire, with her mixed Anglo-Hindu heritage, prayed fervently for Robert's recovery. She attended both church and Hindu rituals, fasting on sacred ekadashi days and worshipping at the altar of Goddess Durga in her home. Even Claire's widower grandfather and Aneek's neighbour Girindra travelled to Benaras and offered prayers to Lord Shiva at the Kashi Vishwanath temple for Robert's well-being.

Thereafter, defeating the rarest of odds, the erstwhile racecourse gambler recovered his sanity gradually. After Hubert brought his father back home, Robert immersed himself in the study of Sanskrit and the Bhagavad Gita. He cherished the memories of his late wife, Cynthia, often gazing lovingly at the scrapbook she had kept throughout her life, which Hubert had carefully restored. Surrounded by her paintings, now framed and hung in Hubert and Claire's elegant home on Belvedere Road, Robert spent many hours in quiet reflection, remembering the woman whose beauty and talent he had taken for granted during his reckless past. On hot summer nights, he would retreat to the terrace, where, under the cool evening sky, no longer pouring fire on everything below, he sought out his first love amid the many constellations. Around 1926, Robert passed away due to unknown causes, with Cynthia's name on his lips and a copy of the Bhagavad Gita resting on his chest.

Hubert and Aneek maintained their close friendship throughout their lives. After earning his law degree, Hubert devoted his career to defending the impoverished in Calcutta, embodying the principles of justice and compassion that defined their family's legacy. Aneek assisted Hubert in investigating crimes and locating impoverished inmates who had been wrongly accused. Together, they worked to set these prisoners free through court trials, providing them with a chance for justice.

In his later years, Girindra underwent a transformation. He sold off his luxurious possessions, like large diamonds, emeralds, gold bullions, unused Italian furniture, granite water fountains and the fanciest unused marbles. He donated generously to the Indian Independence League (IIL), and when the IIL morphed into the INA (Indian National Army), Girindra sold his American and European cars, entrusting the money to Aneek and Madhuri to be transferred to Anushilan Samiti and to the legal defence funds being secretly collected in Calcutta for the jailed freedom fighters.

After suffering severe injuries during the First World War, Aritro lived for a while on a meagre pension. However, his life took a transformative turn when he joined Netaji Subhash Chandra Bose's INA in 1942. During his time with the INA, Aritro nurtured a habit of writing letters to Aneek. The latter felt immensely proud of how the once timid, stammering little boy had bloomed into a courageous soldier. From Aritro's letters, Aneek came to know how the British Raj tried to force Aritro's 18-year-old cousin to join the British Army. When the teenager refused, they tortured him by breaking many of his teeth and pulling out his nails, ultimately jailing him in the infamous jails of the Andaman Islands.

Aneek learnt, almost in real time, of the INA's movements from Aritro. By January 1944, the INA's First Division was redirected from Malaysia to support the Japanese assault on Manipur. Back in Bengal, the situation was dire. The British Raj, determined to feed the Allied forces in Europe, had imposed devastating taxes on Bengal's farmers during the Second World War. British soldiers ransacked villages and confiscated vital food supplies, leading to the Bengal Famine of 1943, which claimed millions of lives. Yet, amidst this devastation, due to the heroics of their loyal and diehard farmers, Aneek and Flanagan's agricultural endeavours persisted.

Through stringent cost-cutting and tapping into reserves, they ensured their farmers did not perish due to starvation.

From Aritro's letters, Aneek also gleaned the harrowing conditions faced by the INA soldiers. Armed with subpar weapons provided by the Japanese, they endured the harsh monsoon and tropical maladies of Burma. By March 1945, the INA was entrenched along the Irrawaddy River, their morale waning as some began to surrender while Japanese forces retreated.

However, history's pendulum was swinging. Not just Calcutta, Dhaka or Chittagong, but many more parts of India, including Punjab, Maharashtra and other areas had become violent cauldrons of fire for the British police, administrators and viceroys. Britain's hollow victory in the Second World War, coupled with the audacious mutiny of the Royal Indian Navy in 1946 in Bombay and the sacrifices of countless Indians, incited a fevered apprehension among British administrators. Their iron grip loosened, and in 1947, India finally broke free, albeit amid the sorrow of partition and the bloodshed of a divided nation.

Epilogue

Shortly before Indian Independence and soon afterwards, the close-knit circle of Keshav's progeny began to dwindle into the inevitable passage of time.

A brave wanderer at heart, Bonka departed from earth one majestic spring in Madaripur. By then, he was no longer a drifter from one job or place to another. His childhood tuberculosis relapsed after many years, and he yearned for the tender care of Keshav and Sheela, whose love had once nursed him back to health. Bonka died peacefully, surrounded by his family.

Remembering Bonka's life-saving contributions to his family, Aneek and Madhuri mourned Bonka's passing for weeks.

Even in his 90s, Chris Flanagan still walked without a stick, his head held high. An epitome of affability and charm, Flanagan continued to interact with local farmers, share stories and maintain his physical vitality well into his later years. Fluent in Bengali, he became a pillar of the community, running a thrift shop to support the poor. Even in his advanced age, he could repair bullock carts, operate farm tools, and share the joy of harvests with his workers.

The Irishman, who had come to India as a teenager after being jilted by his young lover, died in his own bed after a bout of typhoid. The aged Prachi, all this while, nursed her husband round the clock until his death. Following his last wish, his body was cremated on the banks of the Arial Khan River in Madaripur, a place he held dear.

Prachi, too, lived a long and healthy life. Without a single hint of disease, she breathed her last. Leaning against the temple column, she passed quietly, her spirit moving on to the next world with the same grace and devotion that had marked her life.

The sudden passing of Archana, Aneek's mother, was a devastating blow. While teaching her grandchild how to swim in one of the family ponds, her heart gave up, causing her abrupt demise.

Several hours later, standing close to Archana's funeral pyre, her estate employees, farmers and well-wishers wept silently. Without taking the help of priests and clad in a single piece of white cloth, Aneek decided to perform the last rites himself, with the help of Madhuri. Archana's deceased body was anointed with ghee, sandalwood paste and holy ash, surrounded by flowers and camphor. Her cremation took place with the dignity and love that she had always shown to others. A Muslim shipbuilder, Suhail, whom Archana had reformed in her final months, was also invited to partake in the last rites. Suhail offered a lotus at her feet before Aneek lit the pyre, honouring her selfless soul.

As Aneek circumambulated the dry wood pyre upon which his mother's corpse lay, he recited one last hymn and placed sesame seeds in her mouth.

Weeks later, Aneek travelled to Haridwar to scatter her ashes in the sacred Ganga River.

Archana's legacy was preserved through the stories she told her family about the valiant Bonka, Mr Hall, Mr Flanagan and Prachi, her in-laws Keshav and Sheela, and her beloved husband Mukund.

The lives of these extraordinary individuals became integral parts of India's history, their personal struggles and triumphs reflecting the country's fight for freedom. United by love, moulded by hardship and guided by destiny, they navigated through a time that demanded courage and resilience. The land they cherished— the banana, mango and jackfruit orchards; the coconut and guava groves; the ponds and rivers—stood as silent witnesses to their journeys, where joy and sorrow intertwined. As their journeys concluded, their legacy became entwined with the timeless rhythm of a land where the simplest lives carry the deepest truths, and resilience endures through generations.

Glossary

Akhara	A wrestling arena
Alta	Red dye applied to hands and feet of women
Bajra	Large boat
Beels	Depressions in the land
Beguni	Fried eggplant dabbed in turmeric
Bhojali	Dagger
Bigha	A measure of land area
Chandrahaar	Gold necklace with five chains of golden beads
Charkha	Spinning wheel
Chatuspathi/tol	Hindu school
Daroga	Cop
Dhobi	Washerman
Didima	Grandmother
Diwani	Civil court
Farman	Charter
Fatua	Sleeveless white kurta
Faujdar	Police
Gomosta	Estate clerk
Gur	Jaggery
Haat	Open market
Hara chana	Chickpeas
Jarigan	Pathos-filled indigenous music
Kachari	A law court
Kala-azar	Tropical fever
Kasundi	Mustard sauce
Kheer	Rice pudding
Khichuri	A healthy dish with rice and lentils
Kobiraj	Physician

Kos	Unit of measurement; one kos is approximately three kilometres
Mahjong	A matching tiles board game
Majlis	Entertainment
Malmal and *reshmi*	Soft and silky
Malpua	A traditional Indian sweet
Morol	Village head
Nagra	A type of footwear
Naib	Deputy
Nirjala	Complete fasting
Pargana	Subdivision
Pasari	Equal to eight seers, a weight unit
Pitha	A traditional sweet dish
Raiyati	Right to hold land for the purpose of cultivating it
Sadars, mahakumas	Administrative subdivisions
Sarson ka saag	Mustard greens
Shoal	Thermocol
Sindoo	Red or vermilion powder worn by married women in India
Suji	Raisin-garnished cream of wheat
Tanga	Small carriage
Upadhyays	Vedic scholars
Yajnas	Ritual performed in front of a sacred fire, often accompanied by mantras

Acknowledgements

I am grateful to my parents for instilling in me a deep love for my motherland, India, and a sense of nationalistic pride. An Indian Railways officer, my father often quoted the ancient pandit Chanakya—'One who lacks Rashtrabodh has nothing at all!'

The seeds and the inspiration for writing this historical fiction come from my two late grandmothers—Sarat Kumari Chatterjee and Kamala Ganguly. When I was barely nine and living in Patna, both my grandmothers took turns teaching me the Vedas, the Puranas, the Mahabharata and the Ramayana. My paternal grandmother, an inveterate vegetarian Vaishnav, also ardently taught me the Bhagavad Gita. Their ancestral stories spanning 37 generations from the time our ancestors migrated to Bengal from Kannauj in northern India mesmerized my mind from my early teenage.

I owe my expanse of the English language to my Jesuit American schoolteachers in St Xavier's Patna and St Michael's Patna, especially to Father Zubricky and Father Cleary. I am indebted to my school principal, Father Gordon Murphy, and rector, Father James Cox, for encouraging me to dream big and persevere relentlessly. They taught me to believe that nothing is impossible and to recognize that even a US-based aerospace engineer can eke out time to write poetry and stories, long or short.

In recent years, I am hugely indebted to my son Abiral and daughter Anurupa, who have constantly encouraged me to keep writing even during the roughest of patches in my personal life.

Finally, I express my gratitude for the wealth of historical artefacts I avidly read during my visits to the Indian National Library Archives in Kolkata. The passionate voices hidden among the many history books I bought in New Delhi, Kanpur and College

Street, Kolkata, were no less powerful in collectively spurring me to write this fact-based novel, *The Zamindar, the Rebel and the Revolutionary: A Saga of Madaripur.*